Dusk Mountain Blues

Dusk Orbit Blues | Book 1

Deston J. Munden

Text copyright © 2020 Deston J. Munden

This is a work of fiction. Names, characters, places and incidents either are products of the author's imagination or are used fictitiously. Any resemblance to actual events or locales or persons, living or dead, is entirely coincidental.

All rights reserved. No part of this publication may be reproduced, distributed, or transmitted in any form or by any means, including photocopying, recording, or other electronic or mechanical methods, without the prior written permission of the publisher, except in the case of brief quotations embodied in critical reviews and certain other noncommercial uses permitted by copyright law.

www.djmunden.com

Dusk Mountain Blues: First Printing

Cover art by Matthew Ward

Editing by Nicole Ball

To friends and family. To supporters and fans. To my editor cover artist, and my formatter. And to you who has taken the time to read stories like mine.

CONTENTS

Chapter 1: Drifter: Bluesky Swindling

Chapter 2: Appetite: Catfish and Biscuits

Chapter 3: Kindle: Red Fires to Keep Warm

Chapter 4: Appetite: The Workings of a Patient Man

Chapter 5: Drifter: A Somewhat Quiet Kinda Hoedown

Chapter 6: Kindle: Crocodile Walk

Chapter 7: Appetite: Shadows in the Well

Chapter 8: Drifter: Sensible Brooding

Chapter 9: Appetite: Simple Gathering

Chapter 10: Drifter: Brimstone

Chapter 11: Kindle: Moth Wings

Chapter 12: Appetite: Humility//Hubris

Chapter 13: Drifter: Red Touched Dreams

Chapter 14: Kindle: Vanilla and Cloves

Chapter 15: Appetite: Gluttony Incarnate

Chapter 16: Drifter: Torchlight Trigger

Chapter 17: Appetite: Shadows, Fire; Separation, Love

Chapter 18: Kindle: Breaks and Cracks and All Things Bad

Chapter 19: Appetite: Starlight Exodus

Epilogue

Dusk Mountain Blues

Chapter 1

Bluesky Swindling
Drifter

"In my dreams, the world is mine. Awake, only half of it is." -
Luke "Drifter" Caldwell

Luke Caldwell - Drifter by his folks - thought himself a smart man for one without much schooling. He had to be. Not many fellas made it here to his ripe old age of seventy-four outta being stupid. His brothers had doubted him in the past, but they should've known by now not to doubt what old Drifter could do. Their little sting operations here and there had made them quite the successful "entrepreneurs".

Was it terribly legal? Nah, not in the slightest; but it got food on the table and, later, respect in their names. Who could ask for more?

Drifter always asked for more.

Drifter investigated the rearview mirror of his old, beat-up, white-and-blue truck, checking on the cargo of his recent pickup. Salvage for the most part for today; parts of old crashed ships, ancient technology from the Old Planets, and a few canisters of ship fuel that Drifter permanently borrowed from a few of those fancy

Bluecoats - all stuff that was more Thunder's or Doc's type of thing. His brothers were good with their hands and head both - like the tech-savvy young'uns these days, always tinkering with one new thing or another. Drifter weren't that type of fella. Give him a good old-fashioned gun and brew him a nice strong drink, and he was set. But, eh, everyone had their hobbies.

Drifter tugged his mesh red cap over his long white hair, checking the cargo and staring deeper into the smudged mirror. Blue and red lights swirled in the distance. He snorted and grabbed his flask from the cupholder, turning up his radio to better hear bluegrass over the rushing wind. He downed a long draught and pressed the pedal.

The Bluecoats knew better than to meet him on the road. Or on foot. Or anywhere, really. They might've assumed that he was Big Thunder this time around, not that that was any better - nobody touched his kin. There was something particularly silly about trying to catch him on these dirt roads cutting through *his* mountains. Drifter sped through the winding path, cutting through the trees, little truck sailing through the air. The sirens went on behind him, whistling against the howling wind. Drifter yanked the steering wheel and turned through a thick thatch of tall, black- barked trees and thick muddy soil. He grinned as he sped faster through the banks of the valley, the world becoming a green blur around him.

He howled and slapped his knee as the thrill of the chase coursed through him. They wouldn't chase him over some ship fuel alone, would they? Drifter shrugged. It didn't matter. Whatever he had; it was his now.

Shouldn't leave yer stuff lying around, then. The young fancy coats couldn't seem to grasp the idea: if you left it, Drifter and his boys were gonna take it. That was the law of the world. The Caldwells were the driving force on this planet, even if the Bluecoats thought otherwise.

Gonna have to teach these young ones some lessons. By the heavens, they were trying their hardest too. The very thought of it gave him a buzz better than the contents of his flask could.

They chased him through Rippling Creek down another dirt road, bumpier than the last. Tall trees surrounded them on all sides, reaching out with their dark green leaves into blue above, and patches of red grass with giant brown bulbs grew tall around them. A long freshwater creek snaked through the land, cutting through the field of red, brown, and green with clean rushing water. Rusted machines left over from the Old World - like Drifter's truck was before he restored it - lay abandoned on the side of the road along with newer technological beasts from the Bluecoats, fresher than the abandoned hunks of metal, but all the more stripped to the bones.

Drifter looked out the window this time. *Still following, are ya?* Drifter put down his flask momentarily, rummaging through the glove compartment with his free hand. He found his pistol, a simple revolver. It was always loaded. Always.

Tossing his hat to the passenger's seat to leave his white hair fluttering in the wind, Drifter leaned out of the window, one arm on the steering wheel, A good day. Smelled of fresh water, fragrant flora, and exhaust. He leveled his revolver, watching the small black and blue shuttle come down a hill.

He shot three shots.

The bullets shattered through the windshield, each shot landing precisely where he wanted. The little shuttle spun, the driver splashing into the creek. Whether the driver was dead or not, Drifter found that he didn't care that much.

Another one came rolling around the corner; the first shuttle was never the only one when they tried to catch the Caldwells. They often brought out the big things for them - today was no different. The beast came out next, stomping over the horizon. The laughter in Drifter's chest died. *Had to bring out the 7-A's.*

He drove in silence, turning down the radio, a man's voice lowering to a whisper against a faint banjo. The 7-A's were standard-issue mechanical behemoths controlled by a single pilot. This one wasn't the biggest he had seen. They came in different sizes - from full battle models equipped with missiles and lasers, to standard capture models meant for detainment of enemies of the Viscount Corporations. This one was equipped with two machine cannons and a large dreamwater tank strapped to its back for the eventual subduing of the prisoner.

Drifter eyed the small reactors on the sides of the 7-A. *Can't shoot through that. Don't want to blow 'em up.* Not because he cared about the person inside, but his boy and his granddaughter fished in that creek sometimes. *I don't want their space crap in my water.*

The biggest fear Drifter had when he saw the massive beast stomping through the red grass was for his truck, not his life. The Bluecoats had already ruined one truck he'd intended to give to one of his sons, daughter, or granddaughter. Drifter slipped back into the truck, placing the revolver beside him. Though he was having a good time, he wasn't going to risk the idea of losing all his cargo for this nonsense. The smile fell off of his face as he pulled over to the side of the road near the shoulder of the creek's bank, the smell of a freshly-pulled trigger and whiskey in the air. Going from small amusement to anger within a second, he yanked the keys from the ignition and tossed them into the passenger's seat. Drifter stepped out of the car, boots crushing the dust and red grass underfoot.

Drifter rolled his shoulders and watched the 7-A with harsh grey-blue eyes. The beardless pilot looked in horror through the glass of the cockpit as he and his monster froze in place. Drifter licked his yellow teeth, a savage hunger rushing through him. They hadn't expected it to be him, or they would've brought a bigger mech. He smiled as he kicked off his boots and took off his shirt. They were his nicer clothes; the wife wouldn't like it much if he ruined them.

He roared. Pain and power ripped through him as his body bent and twisted. His muscles grew, a black chitin tearing through his pale skin. His sight, a little faded from age, became clear, clearer than even when he was young. He hunched over; the rain of bullets came a bit too late. They ricocheted off his skull, off his chest, off his legs and arms; all the while he grew to the size, dwarfing even the mechanical beast. Detainment model 7-A's didn't have a strong enough stopping power to breach his skeleton. The world trembled with every step beneath his feet, green liquid dripping from his massive maw. That taste was something he could never get used to; like warm drink mixed with battery acid. Four-legged, he approached the Bluecoat, long tongue dragging against the grass.

Drifter walked up, bullets still ricocheting from his insect-like armor. With a big meaty claw, Drifter tapped against the glass of the cockpit. The young man inside gulped and pulled a lever. The cockpit opened, slowly sliding back to reveal the stench of a man who'd just relieved himself on his own leg like a dog. *Don't mess up that fancy uniform on my account.*

"'Noon, officer," Drifter began, grinning with thousands of teeth, his voice deep and guttural. "Whachya pulled me over for?"

The Bluecoat gulped. He didn't have a detainment field big enough for this, Drifter reckoned.

"C'mon, speak up, boy. Don't have all day."

"T-that…that's not yours," the beardless boy said weakly. He reminded Drifter of a few of his nephews, down to the trembling jowl and lost wide-eyed looks that only young men can pull off.

"Oh?" Drifter eyed the cargo safe at his truck. "That? Consider it tax."

"Tax."

"You're on my land, buddy. Caldwell land."

"You weren't when you--"

Drifter blinked an eye the size of the boy's entire body. "Don't matter. It's on it now."

The Bluecoat shook in his plush leather seat, throat closing with every second. Drifter plucked the long grey seat belt with a claw, snapping it within a second. He picked the young boy up by his waist with his long tongue; it took some carefulness not to melt the boy into a puddle of meat or break his spine. He placed him on the ground.

"Come to think of it, this is mine too. Got something to say about that, little Blue? Speak up now, boy; or do I need to crunch some bones to make my point?"

The boy found his cowardice once again, judging by the smell.

"I'm gonna need you to leave your weapons, leave this here beauty, and drive off in your partner's shuttle. I hope he ain't dead. Gonna have a hard time explaining that to your *people*."

Drifter looked at the boy for a while, still thinking about biting him in half. *Not tasty, though.* He had tried it before when he was young man; he didn't quite have the taste for it like his son did. He would if he had to, though. A man would do anything if he gotta.

Luckily, this time he didn't. The little Bluecoat scrambled away, crawling on his hands and knees, trying to get away from the giant mutant. Never once did he look back.

Good man. Drifter laughed at the desperation, huffing and puffing with amusement. The Bluecoat got to the car, tore his partner from the driver seat, and drove off without a second thought.

Mutants frightened kids. There were a-plenty in the Dusk Orbits, both humans and animals, after years and years of evolution and genetic tinkering from people higher than them. They came in all shapes and sizes, as unassuming as a young woman on the streets, or a bearded old man in the the mountains. He hadn't known the power he had for a very long time, the immense strength he possessed. It took time. He was a slow learner, but he learned.

The young were often short-sighted, and with age came ambition. His grandkids wouldn't have to know hunger or pain or struggle. That was his dream here; a dream that he was gonna give to every member of his kin. This was his planet now. His and his's. No one else's.

Drifter let himself relax, his body returning to the thin, old man with much-too-long white hair. He grabbed his boots, shirt, and cap from the outside of the truck and entered the car in his birthday suit, reclining in his seat. After a moment of rest, Drifter leaned over the seat and found his spare pair of jeans and undergarments.

"Ruining my darn clothes. Bluecoats and their dang kids. Greener than a dang bell pepper." He wanted to curse, but the wife had gotten on him for that; not a good example for the grandkids, so he had to curb the habit.

He couldn't quite take himself seriously naked as a baby bird. He dressed and grabbed his keys and tossed them back into his pocket.

Exiting the truck again, he went to check the rest of his cargo. Everything was there. He frowned, turning towards the now-empty mech. *My, she's a beauty.* Not a combat type, but the pieces...well, Doc was working on something nice for the kids. Nobody was gonna come this far into his lands to retrieve it. Drifter stuffed his hands into the pockets of his spare jeans, finding a small figurine once belonging to his granddaughter with a smile.

"Now, how am I gonna get you home, big boy?" Last time, he had torn the arms off, and Doc and the kids lost their dang minds. "Guess that's gonna be his problem figuring out."

He shrugged. The least he could do was to take some of the batteries with him. Drifter walked around the 7-A and found some small climbing studs on its back. Machines weren't too difficult to figure out after a while; though not as technologically savvy as some of kin, he knew the workings well enough. With a heave, a turn, and hiss of steam, Drifter pulled out the small blue glowing battery on the back, shouldered it hot against his neck, and climbed back down. Once firmly on the ground, he grabbed the battery by the handle and walked to the bed of his truck, frowning. He didn't have enough space for everything to fit and be safe too. *Ain't a young man anymore, can't be doing like I used to.* He shook off the thought.

"Guess you're riding shotgun today." He tapped the battery core for good measure, feeling the residual heat against his skin.

Drifter entered his truck again, put the battery in the passenger seat, and locked the battery and himself in with the seatbelts. It didn't matter if you could become a fourteen-foot monster that could crunch a man's bones and spew highly acidic liquid - a man gotta put his seatbelt on. He hadn't before, forgotten in his brief span of youthful thrill. Drifter touched the figurine in his pocket once again, a silly little soldier in Old World camouflage they had found, cleaned, and repainted. Kindle was fond of it, gave it to him as a lucky charm when she realized she didn't play with it anymore. A feeling of pride filled his chest. Excitement was well and good; he hungered for it from time to time. But there was nothing like home. Nothing. He started the car and went on his way, the familiar sounds of his favorite songs blaring through open windows.

Ø

Drifter returned to the Dusk Mountains with all his spoils intact—most of it, anyway. One piece of salvage, part of a wing, was determined to free itself from its bungie and sail back into the sky. Ain't much Drifter could do about that. He considered it good sign more than anything. If part of a wing wanted to head to the sky once again, who was he stop it? So he drove on without it, up the winding stony roads of the snow-topped mountain ranges where the Caldwells settled.

At first it was just him, this mountain, and his brothers when they escaped the mines of another world. Now their kin reached from the mountains, to the valleys, to the creeks, to the grasslands, and the plains besides. They were a force of nature on the planet C'dar. The Bluecoats forgot that before they got here, the Caldwells thrived. Only a few others predated his kin on this planet and they had reached an agreement to leave each other's lawns alone. No way no galaxy corporation was gonna step up to him, not after all the time it took for them to get away from those money men. Drifter lowered his shoulders, trying not to get tense thinking about it. They had picked a beautiful place to have their family. It wasn't paradise all the time, but he supposed nowhere was - this was the closest that he was gonna get.

As he drove up and up, he began seeing more and more of their own influences on the land. He came upon Doc's Scrapyard first. Mounds and mounds of metal from ships, cars, shuttles, and mechs lined the small cave. Donald "Doc" Caldwell was out in his yard, short, barrel-chested, with a strong, muscled gut. He pulled off his red goggles, revealing thin white lines on his dark skin where they once settled on his meaty face. He grinned like an absolute idiot when Drifter rolled up with a truck full of things for him.

Drifter cranked down the window. "'Ey! Got some things for you!"

"Oh thank heaven," he heard his shorter brother shout. "Thought you brought something for Pit, Thunder, or Moses. Like you've done for the last umpteenth times."

"'Thank'ya, Luke, for the ship fuel you found me. I appreciate you. You're a good older brother,'" Drifter said, mocking his brother's husky voice, sounding of smoke and metal.

"I don't, though." Doc grinned. "Pull around, can't have you hitting my fence like that one time."

"That was years ago."

"It was my fence; I get to forget it on my time."

Doc shuffled outta the way, waddling to the side. Drifter turned the truck around and backed in (perfectly, might he add) through the cave's entrance. That was when Doc saw it - the glowing battery sitting in front seat, all strapped in and safe - and almost tripped over the laces of his black combat boots, mouth salivating with the very thought of having a battery for his new project. "How'd you get that? It's barely used! They didn't have that lying around, did they?"

"Am I the good brother now?"

"Urgh." Doc all but tore off the passenger's side door. His fiery red eyes, the color of his forges, sparkled with delight. He picked up the battery with care remarkably close to when he held his children as newborns. "I guess I can forgive you for the fence."

Drifter rolled his eyes.

"Vermin!! Get this stuff outcha Uncle's truck before I snatch a knot in you."

Beau "Vermin" Caldwell, Doc's son, shuffled from the junkyard. Young, oil-covered, and blonde, thin as a whip and as small as his father, he wandered over with a piece of straw in yellow rotten teeth. He wiped a black rag over his brow and then against his loose-fitting blue coveralls. He boasted a beard longer than even his uncle's, with wisp of brownish-black hair on the top his head. Drifter wished he would've cut the top off already; the boy had been balding since he was fourteen. Vermin gave an ugly grin at the spoils too, very much his father's son. Not an appealing fella, but very few Caldwells could boast on their looks alone.

"'Ey, Uncle Luke," he said, his voice small but deep. "How's it going?"

"Seen my boy and girl?"

"Appetite and Kindle just got back from fishing. Brought back enough for everybody."

"Good, they're home now?"

"Yup."

"Boy, if you don't get to work," Doc shouted from the cave, "I'm gonna come over there and stick my boot up your--"

"Language, pa!" Vermin shouted back. "I gotcha Uncle Luke, let me unpack you."

Vermin got his family nickname (a family tradition of sorts) from his mutation, which gave him four arms and an adhesive goop that leaked from his palms. Came as quite the surprise for Doc and his wife. Drifter barely even noticed; it was a part of who he was. Each arm was functional, though the lower set was a bit less muscular than the upper one.

Drifter watched Vermin from the back as he took bit by bit from the truck bed with a strength impressive for a man so slender. He finished unloading the truck within fifteen minutes. The stickiness of his sweat made lifting jobs easy, allowing him to pluck heavy objects and kept them in his grasp with little to no resistance. After the young fella was done, he closed the bed of the truck, walked around to Drifter's side and slapped the side of his truck, earning Drifter a thick green slime handprint on his door.

"You rotten--" It was gonna take forever to get that off.

The young man cackled. "Thanks for the stuff, Unc. Don't be shy now! Drifter's leaving, pa! Say something!"

"Don't get killed by nothing!"

Vermin sighed. "We're trying to work on his manners."

"'ight, I'm gone. If I can't get this gunk off, I'm coming right back, so get the hose ready."

Drifter started his truck, turning the truck around (again, perfectly, might he add), and continued his way. He blared his horn at the scrap yard, feeling the lightness of an unloaded truck. Vermin waved for the sake of his now distracted father, the sparks of whatever he was working on lighting up the entrance of his cave.

Drifter couldn't fight off a grin. Doc was a tough nut to crack. He didn't like many people outside of his kin; it took a special something to get a smile out of the cranky old geezer. *Old geezer. I guess we all are now.* Drifter shook his head as he drove back up the mountain.

Doc was the only brother sharing his mountain. Moses, Pit, and Big Thunder each had a bigger family with enough children and grandchildren to fill an ark. Though the head of the Caldwells, Drifter's was smaller, with two sons, a daughter, and a grandchild.

He came upon the land of his middle son first, Evan "Loner" Caldwell. He had a small shack on a cliff carved out from rusted out old models they had salvaged. Loner was a quiet man, with great ideas like his uncle Doc, the foresight of his mother, and a temperament Drifter liked to think that he got from him. Passing by and honking his horn earned him a wave from his pepper-haired son leaning over the edge of his "porch" made of rusted metal. Loner sipped his rum over the edge, the ominous red glass of a dead machine's eye glowing behind him from the shadow of his home.

Driving a little further, he came upon his daughter's land. She was tucked into a sloped part of the mountain in a small wooden cabin, overlooking a plain of yellow flowers and a small ranch. Jo was a willowy woman with none of her father's features aside from those harsh green eyes. Her hair wasn't the clay red-brown of Drifter's youth, but gold like her mother's, in a sharp ponytail high on the back of her head. She waved at him as she glided through the field, looking every part lady and every part survivor. Drifter couldn't help but notice the sawed-off shotgun dangling from her leather holster. *That's my girl,* Drifter thought, giving a small salute with two fingers. To think that he worried about her for so long. She was her papa's daughter through and through. Bluecoats, raiders, animals, mutants - they all knew better than to mess with her.

Up and up he went until he reached the top. Up here was the Homestead, once the land for the Caldwell seniors. Fond memories of decades ago passed through this land, and through the ol' mind.

Long ago, when they were young men chasing dreams and women, the land was good; it was surprising at the time, before the atmosphere stabilized and became livable for anyone other than mutants. He remembered stepping out of that mangled mess of a ship they stole, bleeding and smiling all the same. The ship remained on their stake of the land of Dusk Mountain. Around the small ship (stripped of everything important) were two sizable houses made of wood and metal, a fenced-off area where the animals stayed, and a barn.

The last of his sons, the oldest, Woodrow Caldwell--or Appetite, as everyone called him - lived on the Homestead itself with his ma and pa and his daughter, Kindle. Drifter saw them pull up to the cabin, each shouldering racks and racks of fish. Appetite lived up to his name. He was much bigger than a normal man, made of pounds and pounds of pure hairy weight, and towered over almost everyone he came across.

Always has been big, Drifter remembered. Appetite's birth almost made his wife swear off pregnancy forever. He lumbered from place to place with a slow, deliberate movement, big arms placing things down with an obscene amount of care. Flecks of fish scales and blood (Drifter assumed it was *only* fish blood) stained his white tank top and Old World green-and-brown camo pants. At his side was his daughter, Kindle, with warm dark skin, kinky black hair, her father's and grandfather's eyes - and her pa's fashion sense.

Kindle hardly waited for the truck to stop to come running. "Grandpa!"

Drifter stepped out of the truck and into the arms of the teenage girl. *She's fifteen now, not a child no more.* Still, he picked her up all the same and swung her around like she was five. But she wasn't anymore. She wasn't the young girl who begged him to take her fishing and hunting any chance they got. She was a young woman as stubborn as her grandmother, as quick tempered as her grandfather, and as a sly as her father. *Have mercy on our souls.*

"Where have you been?" she asked once her feet were on the ground.

"Yeah, where've ya been, Pa?" Appetite grinned. He knew exactly where his pa had been.

"Out and about," Drifter said, shrugging.

"You went to steal some stuff, didn't ya? You can just say that, y'know. I ain't a little girl. I know what we do."

Drifter gave an honest and awkward laugh. "Yeah, I know you know by now. Ain't much a secret 'round these parts."

"That's what the Bluecoats said too."

Appetite frowned. "They've been gettin' kinda close, Pa. Bold even. They shoulda known better by now."

"Bill and Jose says that they got a new commander on planet." Kindle's eyes brightened with the reckless excitement for trouble found in all Caldwells. "Gettin' kind of handsy with other planets. Ours is next, they said."

Drifter sighed. *Another one.* "No need to worry 'bout that, Kindle." *Not right now.* "Get those fish inside before they jump back into the river you found 'em in."

Kindle nodded and took the fish racks from her pa. Appetite smiled as he watched his daughter run into their cabin.

"She's right, you know," the big man said after a while. His speech was slow; he planned his words like he planned his meals. His chunky build and sluggish speech made him an underestimated member of the family, but he was strong. Drifter had seen his son crunch a man in half. Crunched into the fellow soon after. His strength was matched only by his smarts. He knew his stuff. Not technical things like his uncles or trigger skills like himself;

Appetite was more of a planner, a *strategist*. "They're gettin' mighty close, Pa. Ain't long before they cross our borders."

"We don't got no borders. This is our planet."

"Okay, Pa, I get that, but they aren't aware. New guy on the scene. Captain Xan. S'posed to come down to finally clean up the mess that is us."

"Captain Xan." The name sounded familiar. Drifter assumed it was the fella's last name, but he couldn't be sure; Bluecoats didn't work with no sense after all. The name tugged at an old thread in his head but he couldn't quite remember where. "Ain't the first to come here and expected the land to be theirs, son."

"Didn't say it was, Pa. But you were the one that told me, don't underestimate no one. Don't care if it's a fish, a dog, a raider, a man or a woman, family or Bluecoat. You gotta be careful, always."

He's right, Drifter thought. *I taught 'im that.*

Chapter 2

Catfish and Biscuits
Appetite

"A bigger man's naturally hungrier than a smaller man. It ain't gluttony if ya need it." – Woodrow "Appetite" Caldwell

Any good meal started with one thing: patience. This mentality was what he lived by, what shaped him throughout his childhood and into who he was. Never settle for anything you don't want and work slowly to make it work for you. That meant playing the long game, learning how to satisfy the hunger for more and more. Some might call him greedy - and they would've been right. He would do anything for his family, take anything, hoard a mountain of things to make sure his baby girl had a good life.

She deserves the best. Better than the best. Appetite rubbed Kindle's head, earning an annoyed pout from his teenage daughter. "You aren't gonna get too old for that, I hope you know that."

Kindle sighed. "I know." She tried to wrap her arm around her father's back, not getting even a quarter a way around his waist. "Shame we had to stop fishing early today."

"It's better that we don't start fights."

"I can handle myself, Pa."

"Did I say that you couldn't?" Appetite gave a deep and slow laugh, wiping the sweat from his brow. "Don't wanna risk it as all. Ain't a problem being safe, is it?

"Guess not," she said with another exaggerated sigh. "I wanted a fight."

"There's a time and place for that."

Appetite wasn't like the rest of the family. He was so massive that he couldn't fit into most cars or shuttles and he spoke with a thoughtful care. This came with a reputation of being a slow giant - or a coward, given that he rarely went out aside from the occasional hunting or fishing trip. Even his cousins, nephews, and nieces thought him to be a gluttonous idiot; but anyone with half a brain knew that Appetite was none of those things. He knew to never jump into things without knowing what he was getting into. Whether that made him the brunt of jokes or invited general judgment from other family members, it didn't matter. He would choose protecting his girl and his family over fighting the Bluecoats at the lake. *There's no rush. There's never a rush.*

After tossing the racks of beheaded fishes on the nearby table, Appetite sunk into the comforts of his big plush chair. He rubbed his jaw, feeling the smoothness of his clay-red beard. Kindle wasn't wrong; the Bluecoats were getting close. This new Captain Xan knew his stuff.

It had been a while since they'd had a legitimate threat. It was easy to get comfortable - he would know. *Respect 'em; don't worry, respect.* They were getting bold to even get close to the Four Water Lake or cross the line to the Rippling Creek. Appetite groaned. "Kindle. Do you blame me for not killing those guys on our land?"

"I--"

"Be honest with me, Cassie."

Cassie. He never used her name like that. "The cousins say we're getting weak."

Appetite laughed, brushing the fish scales off his belly. "What? 'cause we aren't slaughtering them in the streets like we used to? Or that we have a home on the mountains?"

"No…"

"That's exactly why. I've been there, Kindle. My generation thought the same."

"Salvaging, the ship fuel, the pillaging. It's not…"

"Exciting?"

Kindle went quiet as she tossed the catfish into a bed of flour and then into the fryer. The bubbling oil popped.

She paced back and forth, watching the fish rise to the surface one by one. She then walked to the oven on the other side of the room and pulled a fresh pan of biscuits from the oven.

Appetite's stomach roared something mighty fierce. That was half the reason he got his nickname among the family - he was always hungry, for food or otherwise.

After Kindle plopped six fish and six biscuits down on a plate, she spoke again in a soft voice. "I want stories of my own. Like yours and Grandpa's. Is that silly?" She put the plate down. Appetite smiled at her. The food was great, but she was better.

"Nope. I get that," he said, grabbing the nearest fish and eating it bones, fins, and meat all the same. He only felt a mild discomfort as the spikey bits jabbed his throat. Not a good feeling altogether, he reckoned, but he never had to worry about choking. He licked the hot grease from his lips. "Don't ever be satisfied. It takes time. You'll find your story soon. Perhaps sooner than you think. Don't be impatient." Appetite took a biscuit from his plate, tearing the flaky crust with ease. "Your cousins been giving you trouble 'bout your big slow pa, have they? Which ones?"

Kindle froze and said nothing. Appetite leaned back in his chair, chewing with a practiced care. "Which ones?" he repeated, softer this time. "I ain't gonna hurt them; I'm curious." To be fair, he was more amused than anything. He had a good idea of which ones already - probably some of the Hounds. But if they were gonna give his little girl some problems, he wanted their names. Whether Kindle wanted to give them up or not was on her. "Never mind," he said after a long silence, filled with the scraping of her deboning knife. "I gotcha. Forget I asked."

"I punched them."

"You did what?"

"I punched Zeke and Jeremiah. In the nose."

Appetite choked and swallowed, thankful for his mutated throat and stomach. Without it, he might've found an early and stupid grave. *Guess there's a first time for everything.* He hacked out a few meaty coughs, beating his broad chest with his fist and reaching for a beer by the foot of his chair. He fumbled with the small metal cap and downed the lukewarm drink in one long gulp. "What?"

"I punched 'em in the nose. Broke Zeke's. Only bloodied Jeremiah's."

Zeke and Jermiah were the oldest of the Eleen's sons. They were big fellas of muscle and height, who, already at sixteen, had the bodies of grown men. "They're twice your size."

"And I'm twice the better puncher than they are."

"Guess you don't need your pa fixin' all your problems."

Kindle smiled. "Thanks for offerin' though."

"I'm glad I have you 'round."

She finished making her food and sat down across from him in their chair. No matter how old she got, this wonder never truly left. Appetite remembered bringing her home, a small little girl that fit in the palm of his hand with a tuft of thick black hair on her head. To see her now often brought memories he thought lost in his head. She did remind him of *her;* he couldn't bring himself to even think of her name. It brought the soft kind of pain that brushed against the heart and lingered all day.

Sometimes, feels like it would've been easier if you were dead instead of gone. Then I'd have a reason why you're not here with your daughter. He knew he shouldn't have thought that. It was an awful thing to think - terrible. But he felt it all the same while also wishing she was here, twining her delicate fingers into his long auburn hair and kissing him on the cheek.

He shook off the thought. Kindle was here. Her gun was here. *She* wasn't that was how it was.

They sat and ate together. Appetite slowed his already sluggish eating pace to match his daughter's. They talked for a while about simple, more pleasant things, Doc's new project, the red cloud and acid rains to the north, news of the Fleets. In the solitude of the mountain, it was easy to forget there was a whole galaxy around them.

This was a game for them, a pastime. They talked about things, trying the catch the other off guard with information they didn't know. Little tells told them whether the other knew about the news given. This afternoon ended in a pleasing draw. *Thought I got her with the news of Vice Admiral Blitz.* She was getting better; kinda made him feel old.

"Got some chores to do, and you need to get outta the house for them," Kindle announced after she finished her food.

"Oh? I thought this was my house, missie."

"Then you're mistaken, Pa."

"What am I gonna do?"

"Do something manly like fix a truck or shoot a gun or drink a beer with the boys. I don't know, figure it out."

"Ain't that a little sexist?"

"Not if it's true."

"'Ight. 'ight. I'll figure out something to do. Heaven's name, kid." Appetite opened his mouth to stuff a whole fried fish and a biscuit inside, swallowing effortlessly. Kindle winced. "What, you wanted me out now?"

"You can take the plate with you…"

Appetite laughed, pulling up the sagging straps of his white tank top. He grabbed the halfway-done plate. "Guess I'll take my company somewhere else."

"Yup."

"Can you at least sound a bit hurt for your lonely old man?"

"Um. Dang. You will be missed for a whole couple of hours. Better? Now git."

When it came to keeping the house clean, she was the leading expert. He would only get in her way. Grabbing a few beers from the counter, slipping on some cheap plastic flip flops, and grabbing a hoodie in case the weather got cool, Appetite shouldered through the front door to the yard of the Homestead.

The sweet smell of grass and trees filled his lungs as he stepped onto the porch. His yard was a small plot of wild grass, budding vegetables, and thick reddish mud fenced off by barbed wire. Over the wire and a walk away was Drifter's cabin; the wood glowed a soft red in the setting sun. It wasn't much different than his - small, with a garage on the side for their vehicle.

The garage door was up, and the truck was on the dirt sidewalk. The familiar sound of the water hose sputtering listlessly against bluegrass music ran through his ears. Appetite wandered over, the sounds of his flip flops following his every step.

For a few long seconds, Appetite stood with his father as he washed his truck. The memories of doing this as a child filled his head. Jo and Evan were always there, playing in the wildgrass behind the house. Mom was there, sitting on the porch in her massive wooden rocking chair, knitting. He gave a rueful smile. Loner and the Rancher Queen had their own lives now. Mom preferred the warmth of their cabin, the company of her husband, and the lure of her dreams. That left them remarkably unchanged through the decades, only a little older and a little different.

"Pa," Appetite said, sitting down on the dirt road, plate and six-pack in hand.

"Eh? Oh, 'ey, what's going on?"

"Nothin' much. Need a drink?" Appetite raised the six pack of beer.

"Won't say no to one."

Everyone knew that it was almost impossible for either of them to get drunk or even buzzed, but not outta lack of trying. They had drank everything from their own brews to stolen alcohol from anyone that stepped foot on this planet. Not one thing did the trick. Still, it made a good trade for them to smuggle off planet.

Appetite opened a can with a satisfying hiss and spray of white foam. He handed it to his pops. "Working kinda hard. Need some help?"

"Nah, I'm getting it. Vermin's gunk's hard to get off."

"Urgh." Appetite opened another can in a satisfying hiss. "You might need this one for later."

Drifter laughed. There was a tinge of sadness in his voice, soft on his words. "You're still young, Appetite. But you're right."

"What am I right about?" Appetite stroked his chin. Wasn't much like his pa to admit that he was wrong about much of anything.

"We've been looking down on the Coats." Drifter rubbed his temples. "When will they come over to get rid of us? The refugees and mutants from the Civilization. Worse, when will Buck and his Hounds lose their patience with them? It's only gonna take one spark and we're gonna be in flames."

Appetite had no response to that. Pit and his branch of the Caldwells, known collectively as the Hounds, had tempers. They weren't the nicest or smartest fellas. They were bold, brash, dangerous, and violent. Given the chance, they would start a war with the Bluecoats over their Junkyard alone. "Uncle Moses is the only one that can stop that from happening."

"Moses doesn't like to fight, but he ain't nice either. You haven't seen him pushed over the brink."

"Reckon that's true."

Drifter wiped the door of his truck clean again before grabbing his beer. He downed the entire can within a second. "We're gonna keep doing what we're doing, but I got a bad feeling, sonny. Mary Lu has been getting more and more restless. I feel it in my gut."

"Yeah yeah, I getcha. What's the plan for tomorrow?"

"We got a few things to take off planet. Ain't nothing big, trading for a bit more ammo and batteries, maybe get rid of some of the stuff that I managed to, uh…"

"Procure?" Appetite offered.

"Yeah, procure. Shouldn't be a problem though."

"You're taking Buck?"

"I am."

"Should I come?"

"I can handle your uncle, if that's what you're askin'. Getting him and his kin out and about might cool their blood." Drifter paused, motioning for the other opened beer. Appetite handed it to him. "I'd honestly prefer you here with your mom in case things get outta hand."

Appetite nodded. "I getcha." He chewed on the rest of his food, downing everything on the plate in minutes. "This might be what we've been lookin' for. If they're right, Captain Xan's a big shot. A real player. With a real player comes the good stuff - *real* good stuff. Actual stuff we can use and survive on. Purifiers, ammo, guns, and crap that we can't create on our own. If they wanna fight, we can give it to 'em. We gonna have to play it smart though. Ain't no playing around with people like this, Pa."

"You ain't wrong, son. You ain't wrong. We have to play it smart. For now, we gotta see what they got. Have you gotten anything on this fella?"

"I can if I try." Appetite shrugged his big shoulders. He knew people that could get some info on the Bluecoats. Might need to leave the mountain for it, but they were nice people, so the trip would be well worth it. Besides, he hadn't seen them in a bit. Would be nice to catch up on some old times, maybe take Kindle if she was ready for it. *She's said no for the past few times, though.* Appetite wondered if she would ever be ready to see the other side of her family. "They'll know what's cookin' down there."

Drifter smiled. "I'd like that. Gotta know what's happening. Can't do much if we go in blind."

"Gotta agree with that." Appetite wiped the crumbs from his lap. He stood up, feeling the amplified energy of the food coursing through his body. "You missed a spot." Appetite wandered over, grabbing underneath the truck and lifting it up easily with one arm. He pointed to the green spot dripping underneath the truck. Drifter cursed underneath his breath, grabbing his bucket and muttering about ripping all four of Vermin's arms off their shoulders. He began cleaning with an old rag and a sweet-smelling soap used often for ships.

"I'm proud of you. I don't feel like I tell you, Jo, and Evan that enough."

"We've always known, Pa. Always."

"Y'know, I never expected to have kids."

"You didn't?"

"I didn't. Not 'cause I didn't want kids; I did. I thought I wouldn't be a good pa, y'know. There's a reason why we don't talk about your grandpa. He wasn't...a good man. I mean I ain't either." Drifter finished cleaning, wiping his hands dry. "You can put it down, now; you don't need to strain your back or anything."

"A strain? On a full stomach?"

Drifter gave him a stern look and Appetite knew what was going to be said next. "Full?"

"Relative term, Pa." Appetite groaned.

"Thought so. Thanks for the help though."

Appetite eased the truck down, muscles bulging for a second before deflating back to their normal flabby state. He rolled his shoulders and took in a deep breath. Doing something like that wouldn't put a scratch on the abnormal amount of energy he got from food. Habit made him wish that he had something else to snack on to replenish himself. Appetite rubbed his neck and relaxed for a moment.

"Heavens, you're strong. I forget how strong sometimes. I don't know how; I've seen you rip a man in half and then--"

Appetite shuddered. That was a little after Kindle's mom left him high and dry with a baby. He didn't talk about those few months sitting on a broken heart. He had taken every job the family needed with violent eagerness. The incident his pa talked about was an extraordinarily terrible day, ending with a man ripped in half, the man's muscle and sinew hanging from Appetite's lips. He learned how to pray that night. *I needed to be better for my baby girl.* "I wasn't in the best head space right then."

"Fair point."

Drifter took a long draught from his second beer, turning off the hose with his free hand. This time he took it slow like his son, savored the drink. He exhaled again, his long white hair a veil over his eyes. Again, he looked a little bit sad - but this time there was something else, something that Appetite hadn't seen often. The thoughts of a big pull brought something out of his old father. He hadn't even considered the thought of this working to their advantage. Still, there was a look in his eye that danced on the edge of worry. He hid it well enough. If not for the years of living with his father, it would've slipped passed Appetite as easily as oiled snake.

That ain't the whole story.. "Did Ma say something?"

"She had another dream."

"Oh?"

"It's better that you hear it from her. Come in."

After drying off the truck and gathering their things, father and son wandered into the Homestead's main cabin shoulder to shoulder. Appetite walked to the big brown door and felt a wave of nostalgia the moment his feet hit the porch. He came over often, but every time he wondered if he could ever stand in this house without thinking about the chubby little boy raised here. Every stone underfoot, every board and nail felt unmarred by the decades. He could make it to this door from the road blindfolded.

He remembered sitting outside, looking at the crashed remains of his father's escape spaceship, and thinking of traveling. Funny, when he got old enough and did get to traveling, he only thought of here. *Sometimes where you are is where you belong.*

Drifter opened the door to the cabin. They stepped into the warmth of the fireplace, wood crackling in the air. The living room always made the big man feel smaller. Appetite took off his flip flops out of habit, feeling the familiar slick wood and then the thick fur pelt from a giant beast that Appetite and Kindle hunted together.

The cabin was barely furnished. A small table was set in the corner, covered with that ol' red-and-black tablecloth, a few mugs, plates, and silverware. The soft, unsteady hum of the fridge inside and the hobbled generator was a sound he remembered. The smells of light cigar smoke, cedar-scented candles, and cheap beer also brought the memories on. His mother was sitting by the fire, knitting and rocking in yet another rocking chair.

Mary Lu Caldwell was a small woman, petite in her massive chair. Her white hair was tied tight into a bun atop her head. Her skin was paler than his father's, without any of the redness that came from the sun. She looked over her shoulder and smiled, the light in her bright aqua eyes shining as she put down whatever she was making and rose from her chair, grabbing for her cane.

Drifter rushed over to offer his skinny arm as leverage.

"Dear, you should know by now that I'm stubborn," she admonished him.

She was the Augur of Owls. No one spoke of it, not even the family. Drifter, Appetite, Kindle, Vermin, the Hounds - those were names they chose for their abilities and personalities. The Augur was a legend, a title; something brought over from a time long ago. Appetite felt his heart pound in his chest as his mother approached. She grabbed his hand, rubbing his hairy white knuckles with her old, cold hand.

"Sit down. I made some tea for the both us." This time she caved and rolled her eyes when Drifter offered his arm. "Fine, if you're gonna treat me like an old woman at least act like an old man, Luke. You're not a young stag anymore."

Drifter kissed her on the brow. "Everyone's gotta have a hobby."

"I suppose you're right." Mary Lu sat down at the the table. A small kettle whistled a high-pitched note. She poured the scalding water into cups painted with white and yellow flowers, along with a single stick of cinnamon. This was a rare occasion, so rare that Appetite had a hard time remembering when they'd last had that otherworldly tea. She stirred the drink with the cinnamon. "I've had dreams of black fur and fire."

"Black fur and...fire?" A sharp wooden crack struck Appetite on the side of the head, sending stars in his eyes. "Oww, Ma!"

"I wasn't done. Don't ask questions until the end."

Drifter laughed. He had been on the receiving end of that cane too many times.

"Fire and black fur. Rot and mud." She took a sip from the tea, relaxing her shoulders. "There's howls of pain, of rage, of death. There's a small fire among them, keeping them warm. There's a laughing man wrapped in shadow and a white mare riding on the distance. There's a young boy on a ship and a fire in the woods. There's a man swathed in sunlight, a sweet smell on his lips and coppery smell in the air. An old city and a broken spire.... It's..." His mother's voice stopped cold as though she'd slammed on the brakes of her own mind. "There's a lot. Too much even to speak. What you need to get out of this is simple: your daughter is going to be involved. She's important in all this."

Appetite shook, feeling cold and helpless. He drained a cup of tea and a can of beer in hopes to gain feeling back in his fingers. This was the first dream she had ever had involving Kindle, and it involved fire, rot, snow, and Heavens knew what else. Bad signs. Bad signs everywhere.

The Augur of Owls. The seer of bad omens. The Caldwells were always superstitious, believed in hunches and luck - both good and bad. Her visions weren't words to be taken lightly. They were truths, though they were vague and took some good ol' fashioned thinking. *What does any of that mean?*

"Whatcha mother's trying to say is that there's some hard times ahead. Tougher than anything we've faced in your lifetime."

Appetite shrugged. "Ain't nothing we can do about it."

"Is there much any of us can do when hard times creep on us?" Mary Lu gave a soft laugh, her voice low as though tiring from the very prospect of the dream. "You're smart, Wood, much like your father."

"Much smarter," Drifter corrected.

"Ain't true, but thanks, Pa." Appetite tried to gather his thoughts. "I'll think on it."

"Don't. That's my job. It was a heads-up. Your job - like my husband's, your father's - is to do what you do best. Protect our family and provide for them; that always comes first. That's all I needed to say. Do you have anything to add, sweetie?"

His father held his mother's hand and gave her another kiss on the brow. A million expressions flashed against Drifter's face; from love, to thoughtfulness, to something Appetite knew all too well.

People often wondered where he got that look from, that hungry-for-everything look; and though Appetite's hunger was considered more literal than anything, Drifter had been who he inherited it from. If dark times were going to come, they were going to take whoever brought it down with them. That was how they worked.

The Caldwells didn't back down from anything.

Ø

Appetite returned back home at night to a clean but empty house. He frowned as he walked through with heavy footsteps. Kindle was gone, not even a trace or a letter left behind.

Dusk Mountain Blues

In any other situation, he wouldn't have worried; she was a smart girl, resourceful, and a good shot to boot. Tonight, though, as the night grew cold and the dark turned black, he felt a sense of dread roll through his body.

He wandered their three-room house, heart thumping tight in his chest. Only his own footsteps echoed through their cold wooden halls. His throat tightened further. Kindle would've been back by now; she would never let him come home to a cold house. She never liked the cold. She must've left hours before. But where had she gone?

Despite her efforts, his mother's words had clung to him. She meant well, of course; perhaps that was why she told him. His father's family trusted the Augur's words warily. They knew it was true, yes; that's why they were wary of her. They didn't want to hear something that they didn't *need* to hear. They acted like Mary Lu had no control over what came out of her mouth, but she knew what to tell them. The fear for his daughter rolled in his stomach. She hadn't spoken of Kindle's death. Or did she? *Dangit, Ma.* Only she could do this to them.

He walked through the empty house to his bedroom, which was as clean as the rest of the house; his massive bed perfectly made, blankets folded back, four pillows stacked up. Appetite walked through room to his closet, hearing the crickets outside his window and thinking for a shockingly brief moment of his night clothes and the fixed bed. The very thought of his girl hurt rammed the tiredness out of his bones. A new energy rolled through his body, thick like curdled milk in a glass. He frowned and rushed to his closet, *the* closet. He opened the door to his armory.

It was nice to be able to keep the arms unlocked now that his girl was old enough to have her own. Shotguns were his favorite weapon. Something about them, the sound and the mess they made, satisfied that thrill. He owned other things: pistols, knives, rifles, swords, hatchets, composite bows. He found devices, energy weapons, and bombs in his travels as well. Instinct alone brought his hand on Ham Bone, a sawed-off shotgun from a gunsmith off planet. He remembered having it made in the deserts with–

Never mind that. He grabbed a knife, a pistol, and all the shells he could carry.

He laced up his nice boots and threw on some body armor – his body had some resilience of its own, but he needed to be careful. The energy of passion rose through him again. *Where would I go at her age?* He would want to go somewhere to prove himself, but she wasn't like him. Someone must've pushed her.

His mind rolled through the thoughts in his head. *Black fur, and a small fire to keep them warm.* She was with the Hounds.

He didn't know which ones; Pit's side of the family was numerous, to say the least. That meant figuring out where they were going to go.

The only place he could think of was back to Four Water Lake. There was a Bluecoat encampment near there – Kindle had seen it with their own eyes. She would know how to get back. The Hounds would need that; they were known for their ravenous impatience, inherited from their father and grandfather. Kindle got a little of that from her Uncle Pit too. They would want to try something.

Appetite growled, fastening the weapons to his waist. He hated this. He hated doing things without a plan. But it was what it was.

Armed to the teeth and stuffing some protein bars into his pockets, Appetite journeyed out into the dark for a late-night hunt.

Chapter 3

Red Fires to Keep Warm
Kindle

"She's tough, reliable, and dependable." —Appetite
"She's a nice girl, that Kindle." —Vermin
"Oh. I'm talking about the gun. Kindle's much more than those things. I ain't comparin' no gun to my baby girl." —Appetite

Kindle knew it was a stupid idea when the Hounds showed up to the cabin as the sun's light fell into crimson.

She had finished her chores for the day with every expectation to relax and enjoy a vid or a good nap. Granduncle Pit's Hounds showed up at her doorstep: Bulldog, Mastiff, and Dane. They were the children of Shepherd, the meanest of Uncle Pit's children, the only ones left on-planet. They had all inherited his large size, thick black hair, and cold red eyes, leaving nothing of their soft-spoken mother aside from her warm skin.

Dane approached first. When it came to it, she was the leader of this pack of Hounds. She was the tallest of the three with thick muscles, soft pink-red eyes, and hair shaved at one side. When Kindle was younger, she'd thought that Dane was the coolest thing on this side of the universe; now, a little older and with more awareness, Kindle saw that there was something deeper than cruelty in her cousin's eyes. She listened to Dane's intoxicating words of glory and fun all the same. She went with them despite every part of her body telling her otherwise.

She had gone, tied to the steep promise she knew the Hounds couldn't keep.

She sat in their beat-up truck frowning and hoping. The Hounds liked her well enough, but not enough to let her sit up front with Dane; she sat beside Mastiff in the backseat. He wasn't as tall as his sister, but he was well-muscled, and covered with cheap tattoos and poorly healed scars. The embers of his cigarette glowed in the dark as he stared off into the trees. They hadn't exchanged a word since she entered the jeep. Kindle tried; Mastiff was never the talker. Tonight though, the Hounds didn't speak at all. They rode in tangible silence through the bumps and turns of the road, not even the sound of a radio or a disc to fill the gap. Kindle opened her mouth, taking in a mouthful of ash and smoke. Her coughing earned her the smallest smile from Mastiff. *Might've imagined it; it's mighty dark out.*

They continued down the dirty road and through the forest. The Rippling Creek to the Four Water Lake was a well of interesting things. Even through the dark of the night, Kindle saw remnants of the Great Exit from the Old Planet. There were parts of their civilization littered all around them; cars, broken down buildings, up to a certain point where it all stopped. The Caldwells had long ago scraped those things of any value when Grandpa and his brothers landed, but it was still a wonder to see the remains of what was once a great civilization now gone and scattered amongst the planets. Only they remained, and even they were different, not even entirely human anymore. Anyone who had seen her grandfather transform or her father eat knew that. Things evolved, and the old things remained rusted and abandoned. That was life. That was all she ever knew.

"Ain'tcha gonna ask where I saw them?" Kindle said after a measured time on the road. "You don't know if you're going to the right way."

"You would've told us if we weren't," Dane said from the front seat, hands casually on the wheel.

"I guess that's true, but I can't be sure. Can't see as well in the dark as you guys."

"Gotta point there," Bulldog said, the shortest of the three Hounds. He grinned over the seat, his sharp teeth stark white against his smushed face. He kicked his feet up on the dashboard. Out of the three, he was the loudest. "But you gotta know where we at. You know the Four Water Lake better than the three of us combined."

Dusk Mountain Blues

"You guys aren't normally this quiet though."

"Ain't it the truth?" Bulldog said, laughing. *More like barking.* "You'll see why we're quiet in a sec though. Keep your voice down."

A few more miles of silence passed before Kindle heard the familiar rolling waves of the Four Water Lake. The smell hit her first, punching a hole through the cloud of cigarette smoke.

Kindle leaned out of the window to see the shore, bask in its glory. The yellow moonlight touched the surface of the water of reds, blues, greys, and soft silvery-whites. Each section of the late housed a color, divided by lines of black-barked trees and redgrass. There were even different fish in each part of the lake; from normal fish like the catfish in the white waters, to monstrous super fish in the red ones, which Kindle knew from her hundreds of visits. It had become a blessing of sorts to her father; it meant that he wouldn't overfish if he played his cards right. It was odd being here without him. This was their spot.

Kindle frowned, feeling a little guilty. *He wouldn't care, it's just a lake. ...our lake.* Her frown deepened.

That was when she saw them. Sprinkled on the edge of the shore glowed a line of campfires. Dane slowed the jeep, turned off the headlights. The Hounds exited their car, leaning low as though the people on the other side could see them. No, that wasn't right – they lowered their bodies like this was some hunt and on the other side was prey, living meat they could consume.

Kindle's eye caught a waving blue flag on the other side. She couldn't make out the symbol on its surface; a white….something. She hoped, prayed that it wasn't what she thought it was. "Guys, I think–"

She only earned three sets of red glares as response. Bulldog, at least, had the decency to shush her with his finger.

They loaded their guns. Mastiff brought out his familiar red-painted axe from the back trunk. Kindle remembered the first time seeing it cleave through a man when she was only eleven. She remembered the man's face, red spray leaking from his gawking mouth, eyes glazed. It came with the awful memory of a rancid smell and Bulldog's barking laughter. Only a year later, she'd killed her own first man, like her pa always said she would.

That memory she couldn't hold clearly. Kindle pushed it away; not that it bothered her. She'd made her peace with that. Tonight, she had to focus on the here and now.

Slipping Coal–her pistol–from its sling, she stalked after the hounds with a dryness caught in her throat. *In too deep now.* The Hounds needed her.

"Alright," she whispered in a low voice, assuming a more commanding tone, "since you dragged me along to this, I'm leading."

Dane arched an eyebrow. She opened her mouth to speak, but Bulldog stopped her.

Kindle squared her shoulders, unperturbed. "You heard me. And we leave when I say so. We ain't going to get ourselves killed 'cause you guys can't keep your fingers off triggers."

The three Hounds made a perfect "o" with their mouths as though they hadn't expected such authority. Kindle shouldered ahead to take point, her trusty pistol in her hand. Everything her grandpa and pa taught her flooded through her head. Her cousins were older than her, that was true – but that didn't mean they were wiser. Quite the opposite, really. Yeah, deep inside, she wanted a fight, but common sense overrode her urge to prove herself. This needed to be recon and nothing else. Judging by the amount of campfires on the other side, there were at least ten squads, much more than what they had seen on the lake today. The bad feeling clawed her stomach with every step forward.

She led them through the trees on the edges of Four Waters to a dirt road that cut through the winding maze of tall trees and grass. Small local wildlife scurried around them, accompanied by glowing green eyes or a rustle of leaves in the canopy. Small bipedal mammals with green and silver fur and a naked tail scurried into the branches. A massive *Abk* stomped past them, its black fur caught in the moonlight and hooves thumping. They snuck past, through the Souring River, and passed a small hill of old cars and abandoned buildings they had named the Old Grounds. She needed to keep that in mind in case things got bad.

After more than a few miles, they were on the other side of the lake. She hushed the Hounds as they stalked through the trees.

A buzz of conversation rose through the night air. Bluecoats unlike Kindle had ever seen walked through the black of night, large white lights dangling from their hands, flashing from one side to the next. They were taller and meaner, far better trained with weapons. From here, Kindle could see a massive tent erected on the other side, flanked by posts topped with glowing, translucent blue orbs.

On the shore walked two men, each with a Coat she didn't recognize. The first man caught her eye. His body was lean, his shoulders and arms wide. Though much shorter than the man with him, he held a scary, confident air; his walk was more casual in comparison to his partner. Every step he made came with the sound of metal hissing and a small puff of smoke from his knees. In the light of his white lantern, he looked normal, with his wide stubbled chin, cropped short black-and-grey hair, and pale, scarred white skin. What was different were his eyes made completely of metal, moving back and forth with a clearly audible hum like metal shutters opening. He was smiling towards the other man, who flinched as though prepared for a slug in the face.

The second man gritted his teeth, hand stuffed in his pocket of his finely-pressed blue uniform. He was much taller, made of harsh angles like he was wood-cut by a rickety saw. His bald head glistened with sweat against his light skin and the odd red scales on his cheek. His beady green eyes blinked. To Kindle, it looked like he was hoping that the first man said nothing – it was written all over his face in layers. She recognized this one, saw him once on a trip down the mountain into increasingly rare land that the Caldwells hadn't claimed. *Captain Owen Xan of the Sixth Battalion of the Bluecoats Fleet.* "I'm not saying I'm here to make you uncomfortable, Xan, *but* – I'm here to make you very uncomfortable." The shorter man had a familiar backwater planet twang to his voice, much like the Caldwells, though softer and emphasizing different letters. It had an almost charming quality to it. "Come on, talk with me, Owen."

Kindle's heart throbbed in her chest, so loud that it beat in her ears. Who was this other man that shook Xan so badly?

"Second Major Debenham," Xan started.

"You can call me Steve, I insist."

"*Second Major Debenham.*" The Captain squirmed. "I don't see why you're here on C'dar. It doesn't require your attention."

"*I* don't plan to do anything. I'm here to observe, is all." Major Debenham continued to stare with those chilling metal eyes, the lights within them blinking red for a brief second. He cocked his head. "Is there a problem, Owen?"

Captain Xan froze, silver-colored sweat dripping from his face. "We have everything under control."

"Do you, though?" Major Debenham squinted. "Even the mutant problems I've been hearing so much about? The ones in the mountains?"

"The Caldwells aren't–"

Major Debenham grinned. "Oh, they have a name? That's nice."

"The Caldwells aren't a problem, sir." Captain Xan forced out a nervous cough. "I'm handling it."

"Our definitions of *handling it* must be *very* different. Having a 7-A stripped and carted off doesn't quite seem to be...optimal for what we're trying to do here. Do you care to explain?"

"I–"

"Don't answer that." The Major put a metal hand up. "That was a rhetorical question. You need–"

Kindle felt herself being pulled away by the arm. She turned, Bulldog nudging her with his elbow. A mild irritation washed over her, being torn from the conversation like that – but Dane and Mastiff were gone. She clenched her teeth,–turning away in a wave of panic. They had left her to inspect the campsite further, or worse – try to take something. Kindle stifled a scream of frustration, knowing all too well the men on the other side of the trees would hear them. She centered herself, stepping back with careful steps, keeping herself aware of everything underfoot.

Kindle and Bulldog stepped away from the shore and a little back to the clearing. "Where did they go?" Kindle hissed. "I told them to follow me."

"And they did, until they saw something they liked." Bulldog shrugged.

Kindle wanted to punch him in his stupid squashed face. "There's a Captain and a Second Major of the Bluecoats. *Here*. We aren't the people to be making this call. We can put our whole family in—"

Gunshots.

Kindle wanted to strangle her cousins. Sirens began blaring around them, lights flashing. She raised Coal and slipped through the trees and shrubs. Another squad of Bluecoats rushed past a hair's breadth away. *How many are here?* Bulldog stepped forward, grinning with his weapon in hand. It took all her power to stop him from lunging at the men.

"There's a difference between being brave and being stupid," Kindle huffed. "That would've been stupid. What is wrong with you people? How are we related?" She pushed an annoying lock of hair from her face. "Alright, we're going to find your brother and sister before they get us killed. Then we're leaving, got it? Do I need to put it in writing or somethin'?"

"My brother and sister are out there."

"Didn't I just say – never mind. Follow me. They don't know we're here."

The sirens screamed louder, and so too did the gunshots. Kindle rushed through the lines of trees adjacent to the shore. The soldiers didn't notice anything, not yet; they were too focused on Dane and Mastiff.

Kindle knew better than to rush into a fight like this. There were too many factors. She scanned the Four Waters, seeing those massive mechanized monsters – 7-As – immobilized on the other side. Good. They didn't have to worry about that for now. What they did have to worry about was superior numbers and firepower. Whatever the Hounds saw in that camp, she hoped it was worth it.

Through the mist rolling off the lake, Kindle saw them. Two forms were running away from the campsite, arms full of what Kindle assumed were guns. She ran in their direction, heart and feet pounding. More squads were coming their way, and even Dane and Mastiff couldn't handle that number. It was now or never. Kindle took a deep breath, feeling the heat rising in her body. They needed to make it before the rest closed in. Deeper she pushed, the heat in her body pressing hard against her skin and muscles. The speed helped. She wasn't nearly as strong or durable as her father, but she was fast. They could make it.

Heat rolled off her, burning in waves as she ran. Too much, she'd overheat and faint. Too much and she might burn everything around her, but she had never gone that far. Still she pushed as much as her body would allow.

She came bursting through the shrubbery to the other side and rammed into a large man; the contact sent the man flying, the heat from her charge scorching him. She turned, landing three shots and downing three men before they had the chance to respond. She went to shoot another, but they came for her fast. A rain of white and black energy whistled behind them, lasers from their energy-cell weapons – a mistake. Her body knew heat.

She put up her arm, the heat beams tearing through the cloth of her sleeves and shoulders. Small holes opened up in her skin, breathing steam out like a vent. The men frowned in confusion for a brief second. That moment was enough for Mastiff to cut through them with his raider's axe. Dane was behind him, laying down cover fire with the familiar puttering of his rifle. They backed up together and formed up in the cover of the trees. Kindle protected them the best she could, using her body as a shield to absorb the energy from their weapons. She flicked from side to side, absorbing what she could and burning off the excess. *Keep moving. Keep moving.*

Kindle lead them away from the campsite, now noticing the sack on Dane's shoulder. She cursed again. *What was so dang important?* At the very least, the Bluecoats knew there were three of them now. They had to double back. If not, they were going to –

The conventional weapons came now. Bullets, good ol' fashioned bullets. Grandpa hated fancy technology for smuggling aside from batteries and cores; he'd much rather smuggle ammo, alcohol, and gas like a normal man. She'd inherited that. She liked the feel of the good ol' fashioned weapons in her hand. She didn't appreciate being shot at with them, though; those would hurt her, kill her if they had the chance. They had to keep moving, they *had* to.

Kindle looked over her shoulder to see that their pursers had curiously stopped once they hit the shrouds of shadows and leaves. She turned to see Captain Xan and Major Debenham standing before them, the stars on their long blue coats glistening in the moonlight. Kindle stopped. Fear gripped her tight the moment she saw them, and in that second, she knew they were unmatched.

She was the only one who realized it, though.

Mastiff charged at them.

Time felt slow for the moment in the moonlight. The smallest of smiles reached Major Dedenham's lips in a way Kindle hadn't ever seen on anyone but her grandpa before. Confident. Dominant. Like a god playing with a piece so below them that it wasn't worth the use of his finger joints. There was a kindness in his face, in the crow's feet against the corners of his eyes. Major Debenham pulled out what was left of a lollipop, spitting out the white stick and leaving small crystals of red candy speckling his perfect row of white teeth. He took one step forward. One, slow deliberate step forward and then...blood.

Only blood. Everywhere. On the trees. On the ground. In the air. Red on his metal robotic arm. Major Debenham hadn't moved, or at least it didn't look like it, yet Kindle only saw blood on his fist and a hole in Mastiff's chest where his heart had been.

Dane howled. She would've rushed in too if Kindle hadn't tackled her.

"I promised not to get involved, but," Major Dedenham laughed, "I couldn't keep myself. Look at your faces!" His laugh grew harder, to the point that he snorted. "Alright, alright, alright." He calmly centered himself. "That might've been traumatizing for the rest of you."

"We can't. You can't. He'll kill us!" Kindle shouted, trying to keep the thrashing Dane calm. *Where are you, Bulldog?*

"That one's smart. I like her. I would keep you alive if I could. Alas, that's not my word. Captain Xan; thoughts?"

"Not much to add, sir. I just want them gone. Let them be a message for the rest of the Caldwells."

Kindle felt her mind swimming. They were surrounded, no way back through the trees. Squads closed in on them on all sides. They were two women, trapped in a circle of men with weapons of all kinds. Captain Xan nodded to the men, their weapons raised.

They got me killed, Kindle couldn't help but think. *They got me killed. I should've never come.* She imagined the bullets mowing her down, each individual pain piercing through her skin. An anger filled her, hotter than anything she'd ever felt. The anger went through her in a wave as she heard the familiar clicks of fingers against metal weapons.

She stepped forward. "This is *our* planet. What do you want?" Kindle asked. "What right do you have to be here?"

"Every right," Captain Xan said. "It's your family that doesn't belong. You're backwater experiments, nothing more. Firing squad –"

An explosion of wood and splinters filled her ears as she saw him. Kindle gawked with wide eyes as her father's massive footsteps hammered into the ground, as he ran like an ape monster from one of the Old Planet vids. He roared, his impossible long tongue whipping through the air, insanely sharp, stained-red teeth.

Appetite leapt and crunched down the men as though they weren't even there. He shot one of his loaded bullets from Ham Bone, the pellets spraying in the commanding officer's direction. The projectiles bounced off an electric blue portable shield, put up by Xan. That was all he needed; killing them would've been nice, but it wasn't Woodrow Caldwell's way.

Seamlessly, he tossed Ham Bone to Kindle, sweeping both her and Dane into his arms instead. And then, just like that, they were off with one of his massive jumps, sailing into the night air.

He carried them through the air, jumping and landing in a rhythmic beat. Kindle fired off one cover round from Ham Bone. The recoil alone almost dislocated her arm. Ignoring the pain, she slung Ham Bone over her aching shoulder to switch to her lighter-weight Coal again, firing off another few shots in mid air. It wasn't about hitting targets, though given enough time, she could've. Coverfire was what they needed right now.

"Dane! Focus!" Kindle shouted.

"Matt's back there…he's…"

"He's dead! And it's—never mind. You have a better weapon on you for the job."

Appetite grunted in something that sounded like an approval.

Dane took a deep breath. That was her brother back there, dead on a forest floor with a hole in his chest. Kindle fought back tears herself. *Time and place. Time and place.* Dane seemed to realize this too. She fired off rounds from her rifle over Appetite's back, laying down coverfire in a rain of bullets until they made it back to the Old Grounds. Only a few squads of Bluecoats followed them, the two commanding officers oddly uninterested in the pursuit.

Appetite paused in an empty clearing, puffing from exhaustion.

"You can stop, Papa. You didn't eat enough today to keep this up."

Appetite gave another grunt underneath the occasional burst of bullets.

"You have to stop now!"

"We're…almost…there…" Appetite responded in his sluggish voice, taking off again.

They landed outside the Old Grounds near a collapsed multi-layered building. Bulldog sat in the front seat of the Hounds' jeep. Vermin sat nearby in a large truck of his own. Appetite slowed his speed, the red fur on his arms, legs, and face slowly regressing. He huffed and grunted, allowing his daughter and cousin off his back, wandering over with slow steps to Vermin's truck. Vermin handed him a box of protein bars, and Appetite ripped open cardboard and scarfed the contents, plastics and all.

He soon found his words and his breath. "What happened? Who was that?"

"Where's Mastiff?" Bulldog added.

"He's….dead," Kindle choked. "Major Debenham killed him…I–I couldn't do anything. I tried to tell them…"

"Not to go," Dane whispered. "She told us not to go. It wasn't her fault. We …dragged her along."

Appetite pulled Kindle into his arms and hugged her tight, kissed her on the head. In that small moment, she felt the hardened walls in her soul come crashing down. Emotions swelled in her stomach. Grief? Fear? Relief? She didn't know. All she knew was that she was happy to see her dad.

They held the embrace for a little longer and took a deep breath before breaking apart. Again, Kindle wanted to cry. She knew this wasn't the time. The Bluecoats were still on their heels; it was only a matter of time before they closed that considerable gap Appetite had made.

"This ain't like nothing I've seen before. Major Debenham and Captain Xan aren't the run-of-the-mill boys we've been dealing with." Kindle reloaded her weapon. "We have to get back to the Mountain. This isn't something we can handle here." She saw the shock on everyone's faces. "We gonna have to go."

"She's right," Appetite said after a small pause. "We gotta go now."

Chapter 4

The *Workings of a Patient Man*
Appetite

"They want us dead and that's unfortunate; whether for us or them, I can't say, I reckon" – Montgomery "Moses" Caldwell

This was the drop of nitroglycerin, ready to blow their little world to pieces.

They hadn't pursed them, hadn't even cared to pass the first bend on the main road. Whether they knew the Caldwells had their own defenses or not was irrelevant. They hadn't tried or bothered to find out. The Bluecoats knew where they lived, knew where they stayed. At any time, they could mount an offense on them. They had all the time in the world given their resources.

Appetite recognized the workings of a patient man. They would wait, and that alone left a bad taste in his mouth. *Don't look back. Gotta focus on what's going on ahead.* The only real regret he had was not getting Shepherd's kid's body back. *If that was Kindle, I would've wanted the same.* The very thought of her dead sent an indescribable anger shooting up his chest. *She's right beside you,* he had to remind himself. *She's right beside you.* He went to grab at her much smaller fingers, but she had grabbed his middle and index fingers instead. Appetite swallowed his tears and found he still didn't like the taste of them.

They sat in silence in the bed of Vermin's massive truck, staring up into the sky. Small threads of morning rose from over the horizon, the soft pink glow of the sun peeking over the belly of the world. Threads of stray light touched the horizon, bleaching the dark land in patches of pink and yellow here and there. Cool air breathed against Appetite's bare shoulders and his face as they drove down the back roads leading up the mountain. They took the long way around through the Copperhead Plain and close to the Dusk Mountain Valley. The raw smell of vegetation hit them the moment they punched through the grassy lands. They drove through a field of orange poppies on their way, their petals torn into the air by the tires and gently drifting up by the wind. Appetite tried to think of the positives, see the beauty in all this, but he couldn't find the effort. Not when his daughter struggled to even sleep.

Kindle thrashed in her sleep, kicking and shouting every so often. He watched her, frowning. He was there when she had colds, flus, and a rare virus known by the Breaux in the swamp as wild bloom. He remembered the last one clearly. That night was like this one, quiet and beautiful. Appetite had hated every second of it. That night had been the longest night of his life, watching her thrash out in pain, her thin broken breaths. He had brought her maternal grandfather up the mountain. It was one of the few times that tested his resolve to take things slow. There was nothing more tortuous than watching your child in pain. Physical pain or nightmares, it was the same.

He couldn't bear it any longer. He nudged her awake.

"Pa…"

"I'm here."

"I keep…" Kindle centered herself. Sometimes she didn't allow herself to be a fifteen-year-old girl. "I keep seeing him. Every time I close my eyes."

"Yeah…" Appetite frowned. His thoughts drifted to the people that he had lost, cousins, nephews, nieces and friends. Of course, his mind unwillingly went to *her*. She was living. She was only gone. To put *her* in the company of the dead…was both wrong and sickening.

He turned to his daughter, pressed his head on hers. "Don't think that ain't normal, buddy. You did good out there. Bulldog told me that without you, they might've died. And from what I saw, I agree. You kept your head there when no one else did. Ain't no better leader than that."

"I shouldn't have gone in the first place."

"Without you, though, they were dead."

Kindle rubbed her raw red eyes. "How do you think Shepherd's gonna take the news?"

"He's not gonna take it well. He's been wanting a war like this for years. He's never been okay with the pot shots, the heists and the smuggling. Nothing satisfies him. This might put him and his pa over the edge. But we can't fight the Bluecoats like they can fight us. There're more of them than us. Now with these bigwigs on planet, we're only in more trouble. We gotta play it smart." Appetite tried to ignore his creeping headache and heavy eyelids. "Right now, I just wanna go home. That's all I'm asking for." He leaned his heavy body against the back window of the truck, only to get a rather irritated knock from the inside of the truck. "Hey! You don't get to be annoyed, Vermin. I'm a big boy! Now shutya trap and keep your eyes on the road before we get in a dang wreck, ya dang fool." He reclined in the truck bed further, wrapping his arm around his daughter. "Go ahead, take a nap, champ. Enjoy the ride, as best you can with this man's terrible driving."

Kindle laughed a weak laugh. She rested her head on her father's chest and promptly fell asleep.

He was weak, too. His mutation left him tired beyond reason. For her safety, for her peace of mind, he would stay up all night if he had to. *You would do the same for me,* he thought with a smile. Appetite held her head and let his hero rest with the knowledge that her father would protect her. The cold air pressed his long, auburn hair against his neck and over his shoulders. The trees rolled by, the wind continued to blow, the moon shone as bright as it always did. He still felt wrong. The world felt wrong.

Ø

They stood over the remains of Matthew Caldwell the next cold morning.

Appetite had awoken in his recliner at his cabin, still clothed in the armor of yesterday's debacle. He hadn't bothered to clean himself up; he looked as grungy as he felt. His oily and sweaty hair clung to his forehead, stray beard on his lips. There was blood still on his armor, forcing him to change into whatever he had on hand. Wiggling out of his war clothes, he threw on his overalls and headed to his room for a few more z's when he saw the crowd outside on the Homestead.

He wandered out rather underdressed, bare feet slapping against the wood of his porch and his hairy arms raising with goosebumps. Everyone was here, a rare display of the entire family. Appetite wandered over, wiping sleep from his eyes and drool from his mouth. That was when he saw the body of the young man lying on flattened grass, arms crossed, and pale as the snow on the caps of their mountains. At the forefront of the chaos was Buck Caldwell and Spencer Caldwell, the boy's grandfather and father respectively. Anger boiled off the two men in thick waves, their eyes unwavering as they stared at the corpse as though hoping he would wake. An odd silence drifted between the core families, each huddled around a smoking bonfire. Appetite approached his pa in the crowd of kin, standing beside his sister Jo.

The Rancher Queen looked over her shoulder first and invited her brother into a hug. Appetite accepted it with grace.

"You look a mess, honey," she said gently. They couldn't have been more different. Though she almost matched his height, she was thin with a veil of golden hair, and much better-looking. She released her hug, turning back to the dead body of a boy forever lost in the prime of his life. "We've really messed up this time, haven't we?" Her voice was soft against the whistling wind. "I've never seen Pit and Shepherd like this. I'm worried that they might lose their cool." She tapped her boot against the dusty dirt road. "Pa and I was talking; if they do decide to go to war with the Bluecoats, we'll most definitely lose.

They haven't colonized hundreds of planets by givin' out birthday cards."

Drifter nodded in a solemn silence, tugging his mesh green cap over his head.

"But," Jo began again, "we can't sit by and do nothing either. If we are gonna do somethin', we're gonna have to play it smart and do what we do best."

Appetite cocked an eyebrow. "And what's that, Jo?"

"Be scoundrels." She smiled. "Think about it: what's got us to this point? We need to turn it up a bit. Reckon that we can pull that off."

"That we can do," Appetite agreed.

Drifter tapped his fingers against his lip, nodding. There was something chilly about how quiet he had been. Without a word, he walked in the direction of his brother.

Appetite and Jo tried their best to follow their father's stride. There was a certain purpose to his walk as they followed him. Drifter came upon his younger brother, dwarfed by Pit's size and mass. Pit's hair hadn't gone white with age; only his beard threatened the transition with its flecks of grey. Pit – or Buck, as his momma named him – towered over Drifter, beard to his navel and eyes the crimson color he passed down to all of his children. Beside him was his son Spencer "Shepherd" Caldwell, the father of the Hounds; tall and made of wiry muscle, his appearance looked to be forged from an underworld of some kind. There was a certain hate in both of their eyes when the branch of the senior Caldwell approached.

They blame us. Of course, there was nothing that any of them could've done to change what happened, but they dang well needed something to blame.

"He's dead," Pit began, staring blankly at his grandson's body. "He's dead, Luke. He's dead with a hole punched in his chest. Why aren't we burnin' those Coats to the ground? I want their bones, Luke."

"Buck."

"Why are you calm 'bout this? He was your family too. Or do you just don't care 'cause it's wasn't K–"

"Buck." Drifter repeated the name, this time with a sharpened tone. "Don't you dare say that. He was like a grandkid of mine."

"But Matt *was my* kid," Shepherd said. Some voices grumbled. Others rumbled. His was the sound of a machine without oil, guttering out sentences in a deep tone. "He deserved his family, his own piece of the world. Not some plot in the ground before his old man. No one deserves that. I –" The lines on the man's face grew dark on his hard features. He dipped, cradling the body in his arms. "We're burying him here on the Homestead. He deserves to be with rest of his folk."

Drifter nodded and led the way.

Tucked in the far edge of the Homestead and below an overcrop was a graveyard for the family. Among the gravestones were lovers and kinfolk lost to sickness, age, or bullets. Some were marked, etched with the names of people Appetite did and didn't recognize, including an aunt he hadn't had the chance of meeting. Others remained blank slabs pressed into the old dirt, curling ivy and white flowers being their only decoration.

Wordlessly, Shepherd began digging the fresh grave. Appetite couldn't help but notice he was digging beside his wife, Audrey. Shepherd had dug her grave himself, too, in the cold of winter and pelting rain, shoveling through the frozen dirt to lay his sweetie to rest. He wasn't the same after that, nor did anyone expect him to be; but this felt different. Where before he raged, this time he was quietly and softly broken as he shoveled the plot.

Uncle Montgomery "Moses" Caldwell wandered in his hempen robe over to speak some words over the grave. His black robes and long grey dreads decorated with flowering weeds and bronze chains fluttered in the air around his neck. He stepped through the graves, careful of the mounds. Where the other brothers were territorial, vicious, or sly, he spoke of peace and honest work. That didn't mean he was a foolish man in this harsh world. Appetite knew underneath the gentle smile, soft voice, and warm eyes was a man who knew where to shoot to kill a man. First and foremost, however, he was religious, with a simple but large family in the Valley.

Moses straightened his back, pulling a leather-bound book from the back pocket of his robe and saying a few words over the body.

It was the briefest of ceremonies.

When it came to funerals, the Caldwells didn't dwell on it long. They didn't dress up, they didn't linger. As quickly as they dug the hole, put the young man in, and covered him with dirt, they were saying goodbye. One at a time, they placed a flower on his grave, picked from the nearby wildflowers growing in gardens around the cemetery. They each took one of the five colors, one for each branch of the Caldwells. Before long, the plot was covered from stone head to dirt toe with them. Uncle Moses bowed away, leaving a cyan flower signifying his family. Perhaps if he had died peacefully, they would've stayed longer and talked about his life and achievements, but hey didn't dwell on things that they couldn't fix; not when there were things that they could.

They left Pit, Shepherd, and the rest of the Hound branch of the Caldwells to their sorrow in the cemetery. Drifter pulled Jo and Appetite away from mingling with the rest of the family, staring with those hard eyes over his shoulder at the group of men and women huddled around the grave.

"It's a dang insult."

"What?"

"They sent us the body this mornin'," Drifter said. "Like they're better people after they killed Pit's boy. Like it was some sorta mistake. Like it was some sorta joke. This ain't a joke."

"Pa, calm down," Jo said in a low, careful voice.

"I'm tryin' to keep face, Jo. I really am. But I'm close to losing it in front of everybody." The thick accent of their clan continued to grow harsher and harsher in his tone, his face turning redder than a fresh radish. "What were they doing out there anyway? They know not to mess with things they can't handle. Everyone knows the rules. Everyone."

"They're young, you can't expect them to follow rules. I didn't at their age." Appetite felt small all over again. For a second, he wasn't the massive man over three hundred pounds and close to seven feet tall. He wilted to the small chubby boy with a mop of red-brown hair faltering under the gaze of a father on the porch after doing something he wasn't supposed to. *Done messed up now,* he thought as he saw his father's face remained unchanged in his wrath. Appetite coughed, trying his hardest to stand up straight. "I was just sayin' that young people aren't known for playing by the rules, Pa. No need to give me the death stare."

"I–" Drifter frowned, shaking his head. "Sorry 'bout that."

"Perhaps you need to sit, come on. We'll make something."

The throng of the rest of the family hadn't subsided. Though the Hounds remained under the cold overcrop, everyone else was scattered again among Appetite's and Drifter's yards. Doc and Big Thunder sat at a plastic table with their children and grandchildren, a miniature clan within a clan. Their discussion of theories and politics served as a stable ground in these reunions. Today, they spoke in hushed tones instead of their normal heated voices. Appetite almost wished they bickered instead. This odd brooding didn't fit the family. *It's what the Bluecoats want,* Appetite thought. *We aren't ourselves.* He pondered that thought all the way to the porch. The Caldwells didn't brood, stew for revenge, and fight things they didn't have a chance of winning. They wrangled a good time out of nothing, even at the worst of times. He stroked his chin again.

Appetite lumbered onto the porch to rearrange the plastic chairs. Drifter heaved a radio onto the table before sitting down and turning the big black dial. He tuned the radio signal for a moment, lingering over one channel, then the next. He settled on where he always did – Loner's radio channel. Loner broadcasted from his outpost, serving as a news and music outlet. An old song filled the air, one of Drifter's and Pit's favorites – not a sad song; some might even call it upbeat. Though he was a quiet hermit, Loner knew his family and what they needed from him. *Thanks for that, Evan.* Perhaps they weren't as good at putting stuff behind them as they thought. Drifter reclined in chair, color returning his face with each second.

Jo appeared again with a pitcher of lemonade for the three of them. She smiled and sat down. "There's our pa," she said, putting a hand on their father's shoulder. "Calm down."

"I didn't mean to blow up on ya. It's been awhile since we lost one of our own folks. Kinda a sour spot." Drifter poured himself a lemonade. He drank the whole cup. "There's things that I haven't told you. People you don't remember. I ain't ready to talk 'bout it yet. Some people don't like us very much because of what we can do. We're different. Something they don't want to talk about." Drifter eyed the crashed, rusted spaceship on the edge of the Homestead. He hadn't ever talked much about that ship; all Appetite knew was that Drifter and his brothers came to the planet on it and never left.

Drifter poured another cup. "That life ain't for y'all. It's something we left behind."

"We're still caught up in it though." Appetite shrugged. "This is gonna hurt. It always does." He looked over the throng of people back to the cave on the other side. The crippling fear of his own child in that graveyard filled his chest once again, deep enough to claw a hole in his ribs. *What would you be doing right now if that was the case? You wouldn't be just sad. You would want to boil their bones too.* "I've never asked about the Bluecoats, Pa. I know who they work for."

Drifter's body grew rigid for a second, followed by a savage toothy smile. He said nothing.

Up until now, the Civilization hadn't messed with C'dar or, more importantly, its people. The Bluecoats were their military, their strong arm. Their presence on this planet was scarce enough to be considered a police or military force. They brought things to the planet, and they suffered through the thefts. This was different. They wanted them gone this time. Appetite remembered the fear on Kindle's face when she saw the Major. Appetite felt it too. He remembered the dark words of his mother in all this. They had clung to him that night as tight as they did now.

"You think they want us dead?" Appetite asked. "For what? For being their–"

"Experiments."

Kindle stood on the foot of the porch with tired eyes. She hadn't slept well; he saw it in her eyes. She wandered over to her grandfather, wrapping a single arm around him. She did the same to her aunt and finally came around to him. She plopped in the chair. Appetite rubbed his fingers through her hair, grinning. "Hey champ. You missed the funeral."

"I know. I'm here, ain't I?" She shook her head. "What are we to them? The Bluecoats?"

"A mistake." Drifter shrugged. "They meddled with my parents and their parents and their parents and created us after a time. Hadn't thought much 'bout it. Didn't care. We're kinda the smudge on the Civilization's swanky record. Didn't think that it was important enough to get their attention like we have. But eh. It is what it is." His face turned serious for a moment. "I appreciate what you did, Cassie. You kept them safe as best you could. You got a lot of this old man in ya, that's for sure."

"Yuuup," Appetite said with a sigh. *Too much of her grandpa, some might say.*

"But be careful from now on, y'hear. Don't go running off like that without your pa or myself. I would've been happy to check out the lake with ya if you only asked. We gotta stay together. It's our only strength."

"What are we gonna do now?" Kindle asked.

"That's a fair question," Jo said, sipping more of her lemonade and leaning forward. "It won't be long before the family turns to you, Pa."

"I've been thinking 'bout it. Wood mentioned something interestin' before this all happened. They brought stuff with 'em, right? We can give 'em hell for messing with us and maybe get a lil out of it too. Make it worth our while, I say."

"Ain't nothing wrong with that," Jo said with a grin.

"Ain't nothing wrong with that at all." Appetite heaved his daughter upwards with the ease of a man handling a child. She groaned. "You need to pay your respects. I'll go with you if you want."

Kindle shook her head. "I want to stay for a bit longer. I – I can't go right now. I can't see him."

"You couldn't have done anything better, sweetie." Jo grabbed Kindle's hand, smiling. "You did the best you could. Better even, from the sound of it. You can't save everyone; a good way to drive yourself crazy is thinking like that. I know from experience." Appetite saw the brief longing in his sister's eyes of a lost past and a simpler life. The love of her life rested in that place too. *We're a mess, aren't we, Jo?* It made Appetite think of his love – not dead, but as lost to him as if she was. "You can't change what happened. You have to live on for the sake of them. That's the best you can do."

The rigidness locked into Kindle's shoulders softened with the thought. She had seen death before; it wasn't something completely unknown out here. That didn't mean it didn't hurt any less. This was someone she had grown up with, much different than seeing an old relative you hadn't known pass away. She had watched her cousin die. Moments like that stuck with you, made you who you are. She softened a little more, resting and breathing. She wasn't ready to go to the grave still. Appetite respected that.

"Hey champ, wanna walk your old man back to our place? Starting to feel like I'm lookin' right now." He gave her a small nudge, groaning and leaning forward. A sharp crack of twisted plastic rippled underneath them. "Alright get up, don't think this chair can take much more, buddy." He shooed Kindle out of the chair before heaving himself out of it. The chair didn't last long after that, falling apart and leaving its twisted remains crumpling to the porch. He stared at it for a moment and shook his head. *We need better chairs,* he thought with mild embarrassment.

Only a few of the family members had the audacity to laugh; the rest knew better. Today, Appetite let it slide. Kindle almost didn't though. Her nostrils flared and she balled her fists. He shook his head, catching her by the arm. *Not worth it today, too tired for that crap. Let 'em laugh, give them something to talk about.*

Appetite waved his goodbyes and headed back to his home, Kindle in tow. The family was slowly gaining their livelihood back. Big Thunder had brought out crates of beer and moonshine, and it broke the monotony of today's drag. Laughter rose among his people, contagious to the rest of the branches of the family like a happy sickness. They would recover.

Right now, Appetite needed to get away from it all. There was too much going on in his head. He loved his family but having too many people around made his head spin. Loner was onto something with the staying to himself thing.

Weary, Appetite and Kindle returned to their cabin. The thick walls gave him some degree of quiet; only the loudest of shouts from his increasingly drunk family members seeped through. Kindle said nothing for a while, walking to their lone dining table. She swiped something off it and handed it to him.

What's this, kiddo? He thought to ask. The words never came out. Her stone-serious face squeezed it from his mouth. Her eyes were sharp enough to cut glass.

Appetite held the letter she had given him, feeling the oddness of paper in his hand. The letter was unmarked, a water stain on the page as a signature postage. He caught a faint whiff of old wood, fungus, and swamp water on the page. Familiar smells. His heart lurched in his chest. How or when this letter got here, he didn't know. Weirder things happened around the folks where this letter came from.

"It's from my other grandpa, isn't it?" She had read the note, knew the name at the end. She asked all the same.

Appetite gave a soft nod, opening the letter with careful fingers. She said nothing else as he read the note. "He wants to meet at the Bayou."

She had never been. In her fifteen years on this planet, she hadn't gone down the mountain to see the Breauxs. She had heard stories of them, met with other families within the swamp. She avoided her kin, despite his best efforts to change that.

Appetite swallowed, feeling a tightness in his throat. An odd feeling all together. He could digest and swallow anything but this. He put the note down on the end table, the pristine cursive handwriting of Remy Breaux etched into his mind. There was a transcendental way the man spoke in a letter. When he asked you to come, you came, much like anyone on the planet would for the Augur of Owls. Crocodile's Walk and its Crocodile was available to everyone on the planet on one condition: no weapons, no violence. That alone made visiting a scary thing for the Caldwells; that, and they didn't quite like things they didn't understand.

"Do you want to go?" Appetite asked carefully.

He expected her to say no. Maybe any other day, she would've. Today, she thought about it. Her eyes flicked to the people outside. "They're my family too," Kindle said in soft words. "I might never get another chance to meet them."

Sad but true. "It's better late than never. It's about time for you meet the Crocodile."

Chapter 5

A Somewhat Quiet Kinda Hoedown
Drifter

"Good times and bad times aren't mutually exclusive. When you havin' a bad time, sometimes you need to have a good one to balance it out." — Bobby Joe "Big Thunder" Caldwell

Bringing Bobby Joe Caldwell was a dang good idea, if Drifter thought so himself. They needed someone with his demeanor. Big Thunder was a very lively and excitable type of fellow, given to outbursts of all different types; he flicked through the radio channels like a child, unable decide what channel he wanted. On the opposite side of that boat, Pit brooded in the back of the truck, squeezed into the back corner like he always did in a bad mood – a bad habit that the old man still carried hard. He hadn't uttered a full sentence since they started this little journey. His mood had improved a little since the funeral – he had only wished death, plague, or fire to everything in existence once today. Probably the best Drifter was gonna get outta him now, but he enjoyed the time with his brother all the same. It reminded him of old times, long before they settled on the planet.

Dusk Mountain Blues

Good ol' times and more to come. That's why they were here, after all – to have a good time. Sometimes you needed to get out of the house and do something.

They drove down the main road, enjoying the day and looking for some mischief. It had been quiet, all things considered. The beds of their trucks were filled with surplus: ammo, weapons, and salvage of value from the Old World. That along with their illegal *beverage* trade was how they kept afloat in complete solitude. The Caldwells and the Breauxs were the only two major families and served as the pillars of humanity left on the planet, besides the growing military presence. There were other people on C'dar; nomads and scavengers, for the most part. They didn't stay for long – either the planet got them, or the people did.

Over several decades on the planet, they still hadn't found everything of value. Whatever happened here had left marks on the world forever. The further away from the Dusk Mountains, the deeper the scars on the world became. Buildings rose all around them, broken and slanted with old shattered windows and chunks missing from their bodies like half-eaten corpses. More scraps of old rusted cars, hollowed out shuttles, and ancient first-model mechs littered the former city, gathering flora and ivy on their metal. A few determined hills devoured most of the city now, cutting through the once-metropolis with mounds of dirt and lines of trees.

Drifter didn't know anything about how the Civilization and their colonies tore this world to pieces; nor did he care much, if he was gonna be honest. He'd found this planet off sheer dumb luck, filled with things the Civilization hadn't cared about in years. Still, there was history involved here, things that might be mighty helpful one day.

Drifter focused on riding the hills, feeling the all-too familiar ups and downs underneath his wheels. Of course, this was a bit dangerous. His truck wasn't built like Pit's jeep or Big Thunder's weird flying thingmabobs. It wasn't made for this type of travel. The motor wheezed and the tires groaned with each conquered hill. Big Thunder cheered after every one, grinning and howling like a young child. Drifter spun around a corner, slamming into an old fence and crushing it as though it wasn't even there. Though it dented the truck a bit, it was worth the small happy howl from the back of the truck, the first sound Pit had made that hadn't been an angry growl or a curse. Already, today was a success.

"Oh, you're not asleep back there," Big Thunder said, leaning backwards and staring at his other brother with his dark almond-shaped eyes. He was a thick man like

Appetite, though a bit rounder and a lot shorter. He often reminded Drifter of a barrel. Every hair on his head and in his thin patchy beard had remained the silky black texture of his mother's, a woman Drifter never knew. None of them shared both father and mother, which was why they all looked remarkably different, but they were brothers all the same. "Good to see that you're still with us, pal."

"I'm still with ya," Pit muttered. Drifter hit a hard bump. "Alright! Alright! I'm here. Don't go off the deep end on me."

Drifter grinned, adjusting his rear-view mirror. What he saw was an upright Pit growling, brow furrowing, and teeth bared. Age hadn't done much to him either, come to think on it. He was as mean, angry, and intimidating as he was when he was in his teens and twenties. It made Drifter feel a kinda way, like time was reserved for creeping up on him alone.

He knew that wasn't true, all in all. He had a lotta years left on him if his father was any indication, the bastard. Sometimes he wondered if he was still alive so he could stomp on his throat. He shook off the thought. There was a time and place to think about that.

"You need to get outta the house," Drifter said. "Get your mind on something else for a while."

Pit nodded. He sat a little straighter in the backseat, stretching his legs. "It doesn't get easier."

"It doesn't," Drifter agreed. He remembered Jo's husband and son, his first grandson. He would've been a little older than Kindle if had made it. "It really doesn't." That wasn't easy either. His brother and the rest of the family had brought him out of that stupor. He turned the wheel of the truck, leading them down a steadier path. The roads smoothed out to a broken asphalt road. "Sometimes, I wonder why we're still here...but we can't think on that."

"Where we goin', anyway? We seem mighty lost out here in the middle of nowhere." Big Thunder kicked his feet out of the window. "Won't be long til some ferals come in on us. I worked a mighty long time on those brews back there to get 'em up and ready. Do ya know how much work goes into just a single keg of my stuff back there? Months, sometimes years' worth of work. Ain't gonna lose it to some wildfolk."

"Some people call us the wildfolk."

"Anyone that says that don't know real wildfolk. They'll strip you dry. At least we don't take the bones." Big Thunder laughed.

"Aye guess you're right. We have a little bit of class left."

Dusk Mountain Blues

Drifter turned the truck, cutting through the suburbs. Despite his jokes, his brother wasn't wrong. Danger lurked in the huddled shells of dead cities and towns that once held life. A tall spire, a former business building, stretched into the from the dead city and around it came more hordes of the wildfolks. Drifter tapped against the wheel. They were watching, he knew – on the roofs, within the buildings, through every crack on the street. They knew their own kind, feared them. They weren't that much different, all things considered. Smaller animals feared the predators whose mouth they could fit inside. Drifter tasted their apprehension in the air, smelled their rank odor against the dust cloud kicking up underneath their wheels. They weren't going to attack. If they did, it would be the last mistake they ever would make.

I want them to try. Drifter licked his teeth, his long tongue lolling out the side of his mouth. A bit of green acid dribbled down the side of his chin, burning a small hole in his blue checkered shirt. *I want them to try their hand against mine and see who'll win.*

The car grew oddly silent. Big Thunder exchanged his over-the-top smile for one of guile and mischief; there was a familiarity in that one. It had gotten him beaten. It had gotten all the brothers into mighty big trouble. Black cats, broken mirrors, walking under a ladder – nothing brought more bad luck than that smile.

Big Thunder reached to his side, fingers barely touching his pistol; Drifter shook his head. He would start all kinds of hell when no one else wanted to. With a single bullet fired into the air, every frustration they had growing in their chest would have an outlet. There would be bodies around them in this dead city. There wasn't that much time. Where they were going was gonna be trouble enough.

"This ain't nowhere near Pete's post," Pit muttered.

"We aren't going to Pete's today. We gotta keep him guessin'."

"I've always hated Pete," Big Thunder added with the calmest of venomous disgust. "Owes me some beers."

"Who doesn't owe you some beers, Bobby?" Drifter asked.

Big Thunder's smile grew. "It's not *what* you owe me, it's *how* you owe me. I'd be willing to let things slide if he didn't dodge me. I might've promised that the next time I see him, I was gonna break his skinny neck on my knee. Who we going to instead?"

"Old Coyote's place. He got something for me – well, not for *me*."

"Ain't that where the Bluecoats trade though?" That caught Pit's attention.

"Is it?" Drifter grinned.

He knew it was. The Old Coyote didn't play for either side. Drifter respected the man enough to give him space from this war when it came to that. Sometimes, though, Old Coyote liked a good ol' fight in his place it brought customers and livelihood to his old, stale world of trade.

Gotta give 'em what he wants. Things to sell and entertainment. What could be better than that? The trick was gonna be finding him; never stayed in one place, the ol' kook. Thought if he wasn't worth finding, you weren't smart enough to barter with. After a while, Drifter caught on to his vagrant ways. It took one to know one. Back in his twenties, home was a four-letter word without a meaning.

"I can't lie to you fellas, I'm expectin' trouble when I get there, and I expect you guys to go a little wild and have a good time. Know when to quit, got it? Don't need to make an enemy out of him."

Slow nods filled the space afterwards. Big Thunder Bobby exchanged a look with Pit over the shoulder of the seat. Drifter eyed him too. There was relief there in those harsh red eyes, the color of the tip of a burning cigar. They melted from red to orange, dripping with a dark contempt.

I'm gonna have to stop him from burning this place to the ground. Drifter rolled the thought in his head, chewing the bitter thought in the hard edges of his mind. *We ain't that much different than those wildfolks lurking in the shadows.* Given the chance, they too would rip the meat off a bone until nothing remained. They were animals, a plague, a force of nature on the slowly civilizing Dusk Orbits.

There was no place for people like them anymore in a world like that.

Ø

They found Old Coyote's pop-up shop by the edge of the Fleetbroken Sea this time. It had gotten its name from the countless salt-bitten and wind-eaten spaceships poking from the sea in metal glaciers. Red light gave the water and the fallen ships a blood-stained hue.

Drifter found himself pleased; he didn't get to go to the sea very often. It was far away from the mountain, and he didn't have enough gas to be gallivanting around like that. The water was a reminder of softer days. He hadn't ever seen the sea on the planet they'd lived on before.

Lived, that was rich. He hadn't *lived* on that awful prison planet of sand and dust. They had been sold into it, one by one like cattle to pay off a debt. In the end, he bought his freedom with his family's blood and slept well at night. Standing on a pier while feeling the salt rough against his skin and sour in his mouth reminded him of how far he had come. He listened to the waves rolling in as he parked the truck in the small dirt lot.

Big Thunder and Pit whistled their approval at a few shuttles coming in and out of the lot. Most of the patrons recognized them; ain't hard to remember a few old men rolling around in an old truck when they could be flying. He had a bit of a reputation here.

Drifter plucked the keys from the ignition and stepped out. The whispers rose all around them in hushed layers. Pit and Big Thunder began unpacking the cargo from their truck, heaving the ship fuel and bigger items first on their backs. Drifter took a few of the weapons, inspecting the guns for anything he wanted to keep. In the end, he took one of the refurbished rifles for himself. No reason to sell such a mighty fine gun to someone who wouldn't appreciate its beauty. He placed it aside, packed the rest in his signature beat-up black duffle bag, and slung it over his thin shoulder. All packed up, they approached the Huntsman's Cabin on the sea.

The shop wasn't a big whoopdedoo. The walls and the roofs of the Huntsman's Cabin were made of a thick, collapsible metal, tinged with red rust and bullet holes. The small shack had seen worse days, though, in its hasty construction from planet to planet. This time, at least, the walls and foundation looked stable instead of slumping in on itself as though it was standing on pudding. Old Coyote had the decency to put the windows in this time, normally foregoing them altogether out of sheer laziness. The energy field within the bar itself protected the bargoers well enough from the elements, it seemed. Despite this and without fail, he managed to put up that stupid neon light sign right above the two swinging wooden doors. Green and white flashed at eye level, burning spots in his sight. The urge to rip the sign from the bolts only intensified when a light sparked and went out against his face. Drifter growled, stooping under the low-hanging frame.

The wave of smoke and cheap beer hit him in the nostrils first. The small shack was already crammed from wall the wall with patrons, growling and muttering under their breath. If you couldn't speak softer than the jukebox, Coyote figured you didn't have enough courtesy in your blood to live.

Drifter liked the music; the old kook had good taste in that, at least, but not much else. The lighting was bad. The planks creaked under Drifter's sneakers, tempting to buckle with every step. Not for the first time, Drifter wondered how the building stayed together. He shouldered through some grisly-looking men taking drinks and exchanging wares to approach the counter. One of the men turned, frowned, sipped from his tall, cloudy mug; and then grinned with all brown teeth, a purple tongue poking from the empty spaces.

"Ay, don't I know you from somewhere," the purple-tongued man barked.

Drifter eyed him. He recognized him as Staff Sergeant Bills, the highest rank of the Bluecoats that was on the planet before Debenham and Xan showed up. He was a thin, muscled man with dark blonde hair the consistency of badly cooked spaghetti. Drifter and the family made him look an absolute fool time and time again. He was a weaker mutant, a poor attempt to recomplicate where the previous Chairman of the Civilization succeeded, and it showed. Seeing him out of his uniform and in beaten, poorly stitched fatigues, drinking and muttering, was quite the hoot.

Bills stared, drunk eyes flickering up and down Drifter's body. Recognition slowly dawn on the Staff Sergeant's brutish face, a sneer ripping through his hard features. He straightened his body, reaching for the pistol sitting on his hip. Didn't recognize Drifter well enough, apparently; that little weapon wouldn't even scratch his hide, even when he looked like a normal, hardworking fella. Stupidity glistened in those dark eyes, the obscene willingness to act on whatever pride held him together. "Luke Caldwell, what ya doin' here?"

Drifter smiled. "Staff Sergeant Lincoln Bills. Pleasure as always."

"Ya show yer face here outta all places. Here, where I drink, where I–"

"Voice, Lincoln. Voice!"

Old Coyote came out from the back room. He stumbled, leaning on his right leg–the last thing made of flesh on his entire body. Drifter assumed for a long time that he was a 'roid made by the Civilization, but learned later that he was, indeed, human, once upon a time. There was little to show that now. Aside from that last piece of bone and flesh, his body was made of a flexible metal alloy, each with perfect parts that made no hissing or cracking.

A bright green light searched the two men, flickering back and forth. Old Coyote tugged his leather cowboy hat over his optics and muttered with his husky, synthesized voice. He plucked the burning cigarette from the small slit on his head that served as his mouth, smashing the butt into an ashtray. "Didn't expect to see you here, Drifter. Whatcha got for me this time?"

"Quite a bit actually. My brothers are unloading it as we speak."

"You're gonna trade with this ruffian?" Staff Sergeant Bills barked.

"I'm trading with you, ain't I?" Old Coyote snapped. "Now sit down and drink your beer before I take it away. Adults are talking."

Bills frowned but shut his mouth all the same, nursing his drink and hurt feelings. *Always the one to bark first, ain't ya?*

Drifter heaved the duffle bag over his shoulder and onto the counter. Old Coyote took it with every intention to be unimpressed. He unzipped the bag and whistled. "What's the occasion? You never part ways with your weapons, not of this quality. What's going on?" Old Coyote's voice took a low, serious tone. "What war do you wanna start?" The question came out as serious as a heart attack. When it came to Old World weapons and drink, there was no equal. Drinks were okay to sell. Guns weren't.

A sold gun from Drifter was the harbinger of the devil; everyone on the planet knew this.

The Bluecoats in attendance stopped their drinking, their drunken banter, even their breathing, it seemed. Only the music rolled through the bar and trading post. They sat in stunned silence, eyes caught on the dusty old man with the knife to the world. Staff Sergeant Bills was the one the broke the silence with a laugh.

"This is about that mutt of yours that you lost to Debenham, ain't it?" Staff Sergeant Bills barked another laugh. "How does it feel to be outta your depth, old boy? How are you -?"

Drifter didn't say a word when he smashed the man's own beer glass into his head. Shards of glass sprayed on the ground and the counter. The Staff Sergeant howled, holding his eye in pain, almost kicking off his stool. Drifter caught him by the hair. A cold, quiet rage filled him as he smashed the man's head repeatedly into the counter until purple blood oozed off the table and onto his black and white sneakers. Drifter yanked the man's head up by his hair, allowing the open wound on the man's ugly face to close. Staff Sergeant Bills had suffered burns, cuts, bruises, everything across the planet. His healing ability had saved him from a lotta those. This was an experiment, a thrill for Drifter to test how far he could go. A soft kinda savagery filled his gut with each satisfying crunch of the man's skull.

"I don't want to hear your voice anymore," Drifter said, whispering in the man's ear. "This don't involve you. So shut ya trap 'bout my folks."

"That's enough, Luke," Old Coyote groaned. I don't want any trouble in the place."

"Tell that to them."

The rest of the Bluecoats squad in the Huntsman was standing now with guns raised. Drifter looked from person to person, amused at their quaking expressions. The door swung open, revealing Big Thunder and Pit standing in its frame; the tension in the room rose.

They hadn't heard what Bills said. Good. Better that Drifter started than either one of them. This way he held the reins, had control over how this went down. *A quiet kinda hoedown.* Drifter rolled his shoulders, smiling at the only backup he needed.

Old Coyote sighed and lit another cigarette, a habit he still had despite not even having a human tongue or mouth to taste it. "Just try not to break anything important...or whoever's still alive is gonna pay for it." And with that, he returned casually to the back room.

The brawl started all at once.

Fists began to fly first. Big Thunder roared into the brawl. Though shorter than most opponents he faced, Thunder knew how to fight. He swung, his meaty knuckles connecting with one of the nearest men's face and shattering his jaw into pieces. Within seconds, he was surrounded by men, each falling left and right to his blows. The more he fought, the louder his punches sounded. As his muscles began to warm, his skin took on a yellow-gold color, resounding blow after blow.

Drifter tossed the bloody pulp of their Staff Sergeant to the ground; his healing mutation hadn't stopped him from losing consciousness, it seemed. Shame. That was fun while it lasted.

Drifter approached the chaos with a few causal steps. A heavyset man went for a swing at Drifter's face, only to be caught by his knuckles and have those digits crushed. Bigger men always thought that it'd be smart to fight him, that he was an easy picking. The boys at the mines learned the hard way after a while that there was no messing with Drifter like this.

Wordlessly, he tossed the man over his shoulder and knocked him out cold with a swift punch. Fighting was a quiet type of hobby for him, like knitting a sweater. The more that came, the more fell to his fists. Thousands of days in the pits was edged into his body. A group full of drunk spacemen wasn't gonna be much of the problem; that is, until the weapons came out.

A blue beam brushed past him, searing his cheek. Drifter touched the burn mark for a second. *Get a real weapon,* he wanted to say, but his mind was too focused on the attack. He stepped around a table, kicking it over for cover. They couldn't put their lasers on maximum heat unless they wanted a fire, and they didn't want that among the pile of crap they put themselves in.

Drifter loaded his revolver with six causal clicks. *Only six today. Ain't gonna need much more.* He peeked over the cover and fired, the heat of the gun feeling nice against his knuckles. Five in the chamber, one in the grave. They wanted to bring out a gun, they needed to know the consequences of that. Another bullet and another body slumping dead on the floor. The rays of blue rained in earnest after that.

Drifter rolled from cover to cover, being wary of when to use his bullets. Energy guns had their own weaknesses. While they didn't need to reload like Old World weapons – unless the batteries were completely spent – they did need to cool off after a few shots. Every gun was different, depending on the manufacturers of the cells. The key, Drifter learned, was learning which cell went with each gun by ear. Though a dangerous strategy in its own right, it was the best he'd learned to deal with the technology. Drifter popped out of cover, hearing a sharp hiss from one of the men's weapons. Drifter saw the brief slither of steam and shot another bullet. Dead. A clean shot through the chest.

There were a few spacemen left in the Huntsman now. Drifter saw Big Thunder, skin the color of an overripe grapefruit, laughing over limp bodies with raw knuckles. Pit stood over a few other men; his serrated hunting knife freshly pulled from a dead man's neck. He too laughed his amusement, a slow huffy laugh more akin to a *woof*.

We're monsters, aren't we? The thought struck a dull satisfying chord in the back of his head, better than the songs escaping from the speakers of the jukebox. Drifter eyed the five remaining members of the squad, scattered in the small space with the same look of apprehension glued on their faces. This was the moment that made men heroes; it was also one that made cowards. Drifter wasn't a betting man, but he knew which one they would choose.

Four fled the moment Drifter stepped forward. A shame, but he didn't have enough ammo to kill them all anyway. They left one brave man who was too drunk or too stupid to realize he was outmatched. Drifter thought to let him go, let him live his life. He even played with the idea as the stupid boy raised his weapon and shot, a bright red laser shooting from its barrel. The ray came close to hitting, burning through the flesh of Drifter's shoulder in a searing pain. With a bit more clarity and a lot less fear, he might've done the deed. *Brave kid, wrong place.*

Unflinching, Drifter shot the boy in his chest. Not a cough or a gurgle. Like that, they were done, and the room was quiet again aside from the light sounds of bluegrass.

"Does it make you feel better?" Old Coyote asked after a long while.

"It was never 'bout feeling better." Drifter took a soft look at the heaving Pit in the corner. If he had heard what the Staff Sergeant had said, nothing on heaven and earth would've stopped him from burning this place to the ground. This way there was only dead bodies and burns. "I'm sorry 'bout this, Coyote, in a way. They came all this way to trade with you. But now, look at it this way – their stuff is yours now. Plain and simple. They'll think we stole it; you get free stuff. Win-win."

Old Coyote folded his metal arms, looking at the carnage before him. First and foremost, he was a businessman. Everyone knew that the moment they walked in here. When given a choice, he would take the most profitable option; here, the most profitable had option arisen. All he had to do take the stuff that Drifter was offering, plus the things he came to sell, and leave this backwater world before the bloodshed started.

Without an expressive face, it was hard to tell whether he would rat them out or take the deal. Either was a possibility now. The old cyborg sighed again, tugging the cowboy hat on his head.

"You crazy bastard," he said after a time. "'ight. I'll take your offer. Don't seem like I got much of a choice, now do I?" He walked over to the unconscious Staff Sergeant, frowning. "Tell me what you want so I can get off this planet. I ain't getting caught in another one of your wars."

Chapter 6

Crocodile Walk
Kindle

"In the deep swamps of C'dar lies a people older than the Civilization itself. They are the Breaux, an ancient clan native to C'dar. They seemed to have adopted a civilization remarkably close to an Old World culture from North America, but they aren't human, mutant, or artificial intelligence; only mimicking our forms for our comfort. Anyone that has seen their true forms have been remarkably quiet on the subject, much to my displeasure. Their power – and forgive my scientific mind for saying so – is rather close to magic, beyond any understanding we have so far. We have no understanding of their Flame and its opposite power, the Shadow. I would advise anyone to avoid confronting them." -- Chairwoman Dr. Elizaeen Authford, Author of the Civilization's Guide to the Dusk Orbit Planets

Kindle had a hard time deciding which was paler: a glass of milk or her pa's face. She watched his expression as he drove one of Vermin's miniature tanks down the mountain, up the valley, and through the plains heading to the swamp. She always assumed that he had a good relationship with the Breauxs. Apparently, that didn't mean that the superstitions didn't scare the living daylights out of him.

Kindle couldn't ignore her own heart throbbing in her chest. Ever since she was young, she was told that at any time she could go visit her mother's family; how they said it, though, came with this thin ribbon of fear and reverence for the Breauxs. She had heard so many superstitious stories centered around the swamps that it created its own folklore in her head, to the point that she was afraid. From tales of the Shaman, the Crocodile, the Flame, and its Darkness, she had learned everything there was to know about them that was written down.

Going to see them was a different thing.

Appetite being all dressed up and looking like a different man did nothing to quell her beating heart. He wore his nice pair of raw denim jeans, a pressed button up shirt, and fine hard leather boots shined to a sheen. He had put his long hair up into a tight ponytail, wearing his "going to do business" cowboy hat as the icing on the cake. There were very few occasions where her father put this amount of effort into his appearance; it just wasn't who he was as a person. To see him stiff and muttering, his slow voice incomprehensible in the seat beside her, his eyes remaining focused on the road ahead... *He really doesn't want to go.*

With the Bluecoats roaming, he thought driving the tank would be safest. The travel wasn't a long one by any means, taking a little less than a morning to come down from mountain and trek to the wetlands. Once they made it to the swamp, however, they would have to do the rest on foot; the Breuxs and the rest of their people had a zero-tolerance policy on weapons. From the look on her father's face, it seemed he would rather tear every gun on this small tank off with his hands than upset Kindle's other grandfather.

"Pa?" Kindle asked, trying to swallow her own fears. "You okay?"

"Hm?" Appetite's eyes widened for a second, the sound that left his mouth a high, startled hum. "Yeah, I'm fine. Completely okay, why do you ask?"

"I don't know, you seem to be ready to jump out of your skin."

Appetite tapped his fingers against the wheel. "Do I?"

"You're sweating," Kindle said, arching an eyebrow. "And you're stalling."

"I haven't been in a while is all. They're nice people. Good, no matter what ya might've heard from everyone else. They have their way. Ina was special to the Breaux – the Shaman, the teller of the Flames."

He spoke her name. Kindle couldn't believe it. He had *said* her name, without heat or poison of any kind. Kindle never asked stories about her, not even how they met. The way he spoke her name opened doors in her mind that she had locked shut for years.

"Are you ready to talk 'bout her?" he asked, his voice soft. "I mean you're heading to her home and it's about time we talked at least a little about her. I never wanted to force the issue or nothin', just…" He sighed, his heavy chest deflating. "Ask away."

She didn't start firing questions out immediately. Instead, she looked out the small glass window to her right, watching the world roll by. Among the odd atmospheric environments, the Ghostwalk Swamp might have been the oddest on their world. The closer and closer they approached this frightening land, the more that the colors around looked bleached to white. They began to see some of the eerie silver-leafed, white-barked willows marking the territory of the Ghostwalk Swamps. The color of the grass transitioned from green to red to blades of grey. A hard-sour taste was in the air too, even within the safety of a vehicle. She had passed it on her travels with her cousins, uncles, and grandpa from time to time. Every time she thought, *I'm gonna do it.*

Today, she couldn't turn around. Today, she had to walk into the Swamps where her mother once stood and it terrified her. *She's been gone so long I have too many questions.* Kindle quietly choked on the bones of her words. *Where do I start,* she wondered? She frowned.

"You look like her," Appetite said in a low voice. "Ain't never been happier with genetics."

"I'm getting your height and I have your eyes."

"Probably the best two things I got," he laughed. "But really, you look like her. She was...I suppose *is* still the most beautiful woman I've ever seen. She's also the strongest fighter I think I've ever seen. She had a temper, don't get me wrong. It was a thing that my pa found perfect for me. I needed someone to balance my...tolerant nature at the time. I took too much crap and let too many people roll over me. She stopped that."

"How did you meet?"

"We tried to kill each other."

"What?"

"I wanted something from an abandoned colony. Ina wanted something from an abandoned colony. I don't even remember what it was. She almost killed me. Happy it was there though. I wasn't happy at the time; probably wanted whatever that stupid thing was." Appetite gave a soft, distant laugh, one reserved for fond memories. "Ain't nothing quite like having the person you fall in love with you try to kill you with a flaming axe. Please don't fall in love with anyone with a flaming axe. It's complicated way to start off...well anythin' really. But, that's how we met.

Over some doodad that neither of us can remember now. It was simpler times." Her pa relaxed a little in his seat. The stiffness in his body began to leave bit by bit, returning to the Papa Woody she always knew. "We came to an agreement. She got to keep whatever she wanted, and she didn't kill me. I feel like I got better of the deal since I can't remember for the life of me what we were even fightin' over."

Appetite slowed the tank down, crawling up small hills and through thick thatches of the willow trees. The world around them grew darker. Habit made Kindle believe that it was the canopy of the ever-expanding swamp above them – her mind knew otherwise. Just outside of her window, she begun to see the *barj*.

The *barj*, the Shadow of C'dar, drifted above them as a thin black cloud, inking itself across the ice-blue sky and white-green leaves. When the ground grew soft and treacherous and the sound of water began to rush under their treads was when the shadow became an absolute blanket. The afternoon sun above them was gone, leaving only the fireflies and torches to line the way.

I don't think I can do this, she thought, looking at the black of night in the day. *I can't do it.* She trembled; fear caught tight in her chest. She knew she had to. Not because her dad would force her; he would turn this tank around the moment she gave the word. For that reason, she knew she had to go. She had to.

They donned rubber waders before exiting the small tank through the sizable top hatch. She expected a powerful stench from the swamp to choke the life out of her. What she got was different. Yes, there was a stench from the marsh gas, but not nearly as bad as she had expected. There were other sweet smells mixed in with the methane; one caught her interest and her memories. She searched for it in every breath. Was this not her first time here?

"Pa?"

"Yeah?"

"Where was I born?"

Appetite laughed a weak chuckle as though he had been caught. "Not too far from here."

"Why not the Mountain?"

"Bad luck, she said. Too far away from the Swamp. Guess she was right; we got the luckiest kid in the world."

"Then why did she leave?" The words came out much more bitter than she intended. She pressed her mouth into a hard line.

Appetite sighed, following her off the metal ladder and into the shallow water below. This was the hook he was waiting for all day. Now that it was caught in his mouth, he struggled with what to say next. He beckoned her over, wading through the still waters and swarms of massive mosquitoes and multi-colored flies. He led her to what she thought was a few unremarkable wooden posts stuck into the water. She soon realized that he was leading her to a bridge, each with long wide steps that ascended a few inches against the sheet of white lily pads marking the deeper lagoon.

Appetite helped himself to one of the many torches on the side of the path. He lowered the torch closer to her than himself, as though protecting her. She appreciated it as the black *barj* coalesced around them.

"It wasn't you," he whispered, his voice soft against the croaking of frogs. "That was a choice she made. Ina...always had her own way of doing things. That wasn't a bad thing, but she liked being on her own. I thought everything was fine. We had nine months to think about it, y'know. I guess that wasn't enough for her. I don't think anything was going to be enough to keep her in one place."

"So, she just left me."

"She left the both of us." There was the hurt, that blow to the chest. "She couldn't handle standing still, even for me. I wasn't asking her to. I don't think she ever got that. I was asking her to get to know you and try to be a family. I wasn't even asking her to stay. But to her, that was half-stepping. She couldn't have her foot in both rooms."

"Was she right? Could she have done both?"

"I – " Appetite pressed his fingers against his nose. "No. She couldn't. Her father tried to tell her that she could. In a way, she was right. Seeing you in this world brought those fears to life. I think seeing you was the first time she was ever afraid. For the first time, there was something more important than her place in her clan…"

"Were we? Were we more important, Dad?"

The blackened water stirred beside them, splashing on the red wood of the bridge. Appetite raised the torch a little higher, hearing a small hiss of steam. Kindle looked down for the first time into the depths. A large, wide shape moved beneath their feet, shaking the little bridge with each sway of its fins. A trickle of fear froze Kindle in place. The creature rolled one of its pink eyes upward, annoyed at their heated voices. It made no further sound as it swam back down into the depth where it came.

"What was that?" Kindle whispered, hoping that it was part of her imagination.

"A *barjka*," Appetite said, also peering down into the black. "They aren't…aggressive…usually."

"Usually."

"Can't say I'm an expert." Appetite glared own, a bit unsure. "First time seein' one myself up close."

"What if it…"

The bridge shook violently again underneath their feet as the creature swam back up. It rammed its weight into the supports, cracking it with powerful waves. A sound, very close to a roar or a screech, filled the air as the creature breached the water for a split second.

While it had legs like a crocodile, its body resembled something of a sea or desert whale of C'dar. She saw the creature twisted up into the air through the darkness, its massive, red-fleshed belly contorting into a spiral and landing back into the water. It grew quiet again before the second breach. This time she saw its head better – narrow, sharp, and a little too small for its body. Pink eyes filled with a predatory hunger locked onto them.

Kindle stood; painfully aware they had no weapons on them. *Suppose we should've been quieter,* she thought as the creature doubled back around towards them. She saw her father readying himself for a conflict, the red fur of his mutation rolling up his thick arms. They might not have brought weapons, but he was as much of one as anything. The *barjka* cared little at the obvious challenge and attacked.

Kindle couldn't understand much of what happened next. One minute it was attacking, the next it was shrieking. A massive spear came hurtling through the air above them, the smell of cold trailing behind it. Blood sputtered from an open wound in the creature's stomach as it splashed back into the water. She thought it was dead then, only to see that it was only – rightfully – mad. It lost all interest in the bridge, searching for whatever wounded it.

Kindle searched too. On the surface of the water, a dark-skinned man stood on a small wooden boat, adorned with decorative wood-and-porcelain painted mask of reds, yellows, and oranges. The man on the river looked unimpressed at the massive beast swimming at him at full speed. He casually plucked up another one of his spears.

The man held the purple-tipped spear for a second, checking its weight. In the face of certain death, the man kept calm, the ethereal darkness of the swamp bending around his muscled arm.

What can one spear do?

The *barjka* leapt at him, a maw of a thousand teeth opening to consume man and boat. The man catapulted the spear with all his might, sending it whistling through air. The spear tore through the creature, cutting through its entire length. Both halves of the monster slammed hard against the water, rocking the spearman's small boat. He wiped the purple blood from his dark chest before rowing over to the bridge as though he hadn't just killed a massive beast.

Upon closer inspection, it became obvious that this man wasn't quite human like them. Yeah, he looked the part – just like the mutated Caldwells – but anyone with eyes could see that while the people of the Mountain crash-landed here years ago, the Breauxs had history with the land. There were things that looked off; the texture of his skin, the color of his eyes, the sharpness of his teeth. His limbs looked a little wrong on his shoulders and hips. In certain lights, he didn't look human at all.

The man plucked a stubborn piece of purple meat from his black beard, stepping off the boat and onto the bridge to inspect the damage. He turned, frowning at Appetite with those slightly alien features. With the back of his hand, he hit her father on the back of the head. "What have I told you 'bout coming 'round here all loud, boy? Gonna get yourself killed."

"It was my fault, sir," Kindle said. It was. She had shouted and put them all in danger.

The man looked at them with those pupiless, whiteless purple eyes. He wandered over to her, rolling one of his shoulders. His dark skin was marked with looked like thousands of scars and odd white war paint. The long, angular features of his face gave him an almost predatorial appearance, not helped much by the slight scale-like markings. Somehow, despite only having a few inches on her, he felt imposing in ways that not even her father or grandfather did. A small smile etched its way across his face, his eyes softening with each passing second. He shook his head and wiped the remaining blood from his cheek.

"It's 'bout time we meet, Cassie. I've heard a lot 'bout you. Remy Breaux," the man said, extending a hand. "And I guess I'm your other grandpa."

Kindle blinked at the long-fingered hand for a second. *This* was her mom's father, the Crocodile of the Swamp. She took his hand after a time. "Nice to meet you," she said, her voice dancing awfully close to a question. "Sorry 'bout almost I' you killed back there."

"It's not the first time," Remy said, staring very pointedly at Appetite. "And I'm sure it won't be the last. C'mon. No point of sticking around longer than we must.

Male *barjka* don't travel alone, and I don't have enough spears for all that."

Ø

The Crocodile Walk led to a sizable village tucked into the Ghostwalk Swamps. Kindle's eyes wandered from place to place, trying to digest the sheer awe that she felt. Each of the homes was set in a small platform of wood and metal, floating like the lily pads that surrounded them. They moved inch by inch within the circle of an enclosed pond, the flexible bridges moving with them. Every island came with its own portable generator for electricity and an oddly shaped crystal to keep the darkness of the mysterious *barj* at bay. The homes weren't small, either; even the smallest on the edges of the village, made of a darker, harder wood, was two stories. Large dragonflies and moths zipped around each of the torches running parallel to the long red bridges.

As she walked, Kindle noticed the little things that marked the Breauxs – and any family aligned with them – as opponents stronger than even the Civilization wanted to mess with. There was wonder in how everything worked, and a level of raw power. Kindle felt both like she belonged and she didn't.

Remy led them to what was the largest of the homes in the swamp. It was three stories tall, wide, and made of a slick black stone and dark brown wood. The windows on each floor emitted a warm light from the lanterns tucked behind their clouded panes, giving the house a mystical look from all sides. White and green ivy climbed up the walls, steps, and bridges, covering the house with warm-colored flowers that invited them in with their pleasant scent. The porch reminded her a little bit of her and her father's cabin, wide and with plenty of chairs and a large oak front door. Men in white painted wood masks and clean black clothes bowed as they approached, movements soft and silent. They looked as part of the home as anything else, statues of flesh and bone ready to kill any person in their way.

"I'm sorry 'bout the quietness. It's been a while since we've had visitors."

"We aren't your first?" Appetite asked.

"No," Remy said. "You know that we don't take a side in your conflict with the Blues."

Appetite tried to not let his annoyance show. "I'm as patient as any man, but ain't much time before they decide that they can take ya too."

"True, true. But until then we aren't going to antagonize them the way you do. We don't have the same negative history y'all have with them. Remember, our kin were once a colony in the First Civilization, before the Fault that destroyed everything. In many ways, their respect stems from things they don't understand, the forgotten things they lost in the Fault. Until that respect fades to history, they will not step foot here with weapons. Like you."

"I still wouldn't trust them...Remy. What'd they come for?"

"Who's better to come to when you know nothing of the land? Major Debenham isn't a dumb man. He's even kind and understanding under all that exterior."

"You didn't see the hole he made in my cousin," Kindle snapped.

Remy gave a soft snort. "You act like the Caldwells haven't done worse."

It took everything in Kindle's body not to say anything. She gritted her teeth, chomping hard on the swampy air. He wasn't there. He didn't see the man...that *cyborg's* satisfied expression as he punched through her cousin in a spray of blood. She had seen Mastiff's face with its perfect, pristine horror, dead before he even touched the ground. It haunted her at night; clung to her waking steps, too.

Kindle swallowed her hot anger, wandering behind the two adults in a cold silence. Remy eyed her with those violet eyes, expecting her to say something. She only followed them up the stairs of the massive porch and through the front door. Her fingers and her teeth ached by the time they were in the softer air inside the Crocodile's manor. The heavy door closed behind them with a loud boom, leaving only the three of them and a few of the Crocodile's security details within the parlor. Remy stopped in the center of the room with a smile on his face.

"Neither of you took that bait. I'm surprised." Remy shrugged, waiting for a response. He didn't get one. Mildly disappointed, he kept walking, that grin on his face refusing to dissolve. It only made the anger kick harder in Kindle's chest. Appetite shook his head.

He led them to a small area on the side of the parlor that looked to be some sort of study or lab. More wooden masks in thousands of colors filled every wall, staring down on them with hollow eyes. Purple candles tucked in long metal rods burned green flames all around them and served as the only light in the room. A few of the windows remained open, letting in the darkness of the *barj* and the whispers of the wind. The middle of the room only had two items; a black cauldron with a fresh flame of its own, and a long table blanketed by glass jars filled with oddities.

Without pause, Remy walked up and began tossing herbs and other, more grisly items into pot. "The Flame is going out."

"What?"

"The Flame is going out. You've noticed that the *barj* has been getting worse, spreading to the edges. It's getting worse."

"'cause Ina has been off planet for too long." Appetite sighed.

"That isn't your fault. I am offering some advice...for a simple request." Remy stirred the pot with a slow, lethargic motion.

"I know what you want. Ask her. Not me."

Remy frowned, tossing a long claw from the *barjka* into the cauldron. The liquid hissed back in a cloud of hot steam. "I know what it looks like. I'm not using either of you to handle my problems here. The long and short of it is that there's your problems, and there's the planet's problems. Both can essentially destroy everything here. I'm willing to help with both of those, since you and your family are so willing to cause all kinds of trouble. All I'm asking for is for someone to take the Flame. A part of it at least."

"Again, I'm not going to say yes or no for my daughter. Ask. My. Daughter. Explain it to her. Ask for her help. She came 'cause she wanted to come and meet your family. And—"

"Pa., I got this." Kindle lightly pushed her father aside, taking the helm. "I came to meet you and get to know my... mom's...side of the family. I guess I came 'cause I knew one day I was gonna have to. But if you know anything about this Major Debenham, I want to know and I will help ya if that's the price, Granddad. What exactly do you want? That's why you asked me to come, right? That's the only reason."

"Don't question my loyalty to you," Remy interrupted. The playful and aloof tones in his voice were gone, leaving only cold solemnity in his words. There was a sincerity there, almost a concern in his voice. "I care for you and Woodrow. I've been here for longer than you can remember, my grandchild. I would do anything to protect the both of you. But there are things that are important to me, too – like the very land that keeps you and your family alive on this planet. So before you start judging me on not stepping into the politics, think about why we are staying out of it. And honestly, this is for the best. You're powerful, Cassie. Stronger than even Ina. So, swallow that Caldwell pride and listen to what I have to say. I'll help you if you help C'dar. Simple as that. I would much rather have a place where my granddaughter lives."

Kindle felt her face go warm from embarrassment. What did he mean about the danger to the planet? How was that connected to her mother's disappearance? Everything suddenly felt small, so small that the room spun. She felt herself stumbling forward, head swimming. Her father's big hands steadied her back into reality. Even now, he didn't say a word for her. *What does he mean?* She wanted to ask, but the words in her mouth felt heavy.

"Alright," she managed to say, lowering herself into a nearby chair. "What do I need to do?"

"At this moment, I only want one thing," Remy said, dipping a ladle into the hot liquid of the caldron. He poured the mixture into a small wooden bowl. "I want you to drink this."

Chapter 7

Shadows in the Well
Appetite

*"Shadows in the well have stories to tell.
From the warm midnight gales to the stones of hail.
Only a few know what tales they sell."*
--The Augur of Owls

Appetite didn't feel like he belonged in the room with Kindle and Remy.

No matter how much he tried to adapt, dip his toes into the into the deep unknown of their world, he knew that this wasn't his place. Old superstitions worked hard on him, like a pick chiseling its way through ice. He liked to think that he was more tolerant than some members of his family, but that deep root of fear and respect for things they didn't quite understand clung to him with every passing moment.

He walked through the moving bridges of the Crocodile's Walk and through the sprawling village of Willow's Grove, hauntedly aware of the eyes that followed him with every step. They too had their superstitions about him and his. They called them monsters, animals wearing the clothes of humanity. Such was the way of people, he supposed. *You can't get to know someone if you're too scared to speak,* his mom had always told him. So, he was going to take the time to get to know the people again.

A lot had changed in fifteen years. The village had become very much a city in his time away. There were plenty more of those floating houses on the lake, and more of the bog had been cleared away than he remembered. As he walked, he noticed small changes in how the place made up. He wandered around for a little over half an hour searching for the marketplace. His memory worked against him; where his footsteps felt familiar, his eyes knew nothing of where he was. This didn't bother him, though. He let his feet carry him from one island to another, recognizing a few things now; the immaculate shrines, the massive mess hall, and finally the market stalls teeming with people. A dull bolt of familiarity struck him, one that he promptly swallowed. He didn't want to think about that right now.

The market, too, had gotten bigger since the last time he visited Willow's Grove. Where before they'd had only simple weapons, food, and supplies, now they had local spices and exotic fruit found in the nearby area. Once upon a time, Appetite had known them all by name. Now his mind only clung to the ones he remembered the taste of, of course: the spicy golden chili peppers; the sweet, hard-skinned pink fruit known as the *kao;* and the sour tastes of their swamp grown citrus. The memories made his stomach grumble.

The butcher was still here today, as mean and grumpy as ever, his beard wild and straggly against his dark skin. He had the thick arms of a birch tree, covered to the elbow in green blood. Today, he was chopping up some massive scaled animal with a cleaver as sharp as sin. The older man glanced over, a small amount of recognition glittering in his eyes. He came down with another powerful crunch, severing the twitching head from the scaly body.

"Thought you were dead," the butcher said with a sour amusement, not even looking up with his pupiless orange eyes.

"Same to you. Heard you got pretty sick, Elijah. Never heard anything else 'bout it though."

Elijah shrugged. "Eh, didn't like the idea of being dead that much. So I got over it."

"Can't much blame ya. Any news around here?"

"Sit down, boy, I know you're hungry. I'll have my boy whip you up something."

He wasn't wrong. Awkwardly, Appetite sat in yet another chair much too small for his massive body. It seemed that Elijah had learned his lesson about serving

Appetite: if you can't accommodate his size, make sure the chairs are sturdy enough.

Appetite slumped in the chair, arms over the counter, watching the stoutly-built butcher move from behind his counter to wash his hands clean of blood. His boy, Santiago, was a grown man in his twenties now; he stirred a pot over a cooking fire, stoking the flame. He'd only been five, last Appetite saw him. Now, he had all the looks of his father, with all the short temper and half the age. Pushing with a tad more vigor than he probably needed, Santiago stabbed a whole metal stake through a slab of meat, heaving it over the cooking flame.

Elijah patted his son on the back with fatherly pride. "Like father, like son, eh? Ain't nothing quite like it."

"Ain't nothing quite like it."

Santiago rolled his eyes and continued spinning the spit.

Elijah finished off a few cuts of meat before sighing. "A lot has changed since you left. You know they blame you for the situation we're in, right?"

"For the Flame?"

"Yeah, and for losing their pride and joy."

"I didn't lose her. She left on her own."

"Do you think that she would be gone if she had never met you?" Elijah rose an eyebrow, waiting for a response. He didn't get one; he wouldn't get one. "Whether you're at fault or not, it don't really matter. You're the one they blame. Ina..." Elijah stumbled over her name like everyone did around him.

Even in my own head. Appetite hated that her name had become that small stone that tripped every sentence. She wasn't dead. At least, he didn't think so.

"Ina meant something to us. More than her title or her connection with the Flame. She kept us grounded when her dad couldn't – or rather wouldn't. Remy isn't a people's person. It's the nature of his job, I suppose."

Everyone knew that they needed the other half of their power, the Shadow. The *barj* came from it. It was said that when the first Civilization came, it was this that kept them bay. There was also a price, an elusive one spoken of in whispers. *I got the jist of it though.* Some superstitions had a kernel of truth tucked in there somewhere. Remy the witch doctor had his followers and served his people well. He would do anything to insure the safety of his people and the planet. One thing Appetite had learned on the mountain with his own family was there was always someone who thought they knew what was best.

He shook his head. "Who's causing trouble 'round here then?""

"Ignace mostly. You know how he is."

Appetite grunted. Santiago stoked the flames again, its tail licking up and up towards the young man's face. The smoky smell came next, drifting in his direction. The constant pain in his stomach stirred.

"Don't cook his steak too much, my boy," Elijah said. "He likes his a little bloody, am I right? He likes everything like that."

After a few minutes, Elijah sent his boy off to help other customers and handled the food himself. When he was done, he put the food on the plate and cut the first slice off with a sharp knife as if to show his point. "You're different. You mellowed with your age as many tend to do." He cut another piece with a soft click of the knife against the wooden plate. The red juices flowed a little over the lip and onto the counter. The hunger throbbed hard in Appetite's stomach, the smell catching the wind on just the right angle. "Don't mean that there's not a little bit left in ya it seems. Enjoy yourself."

The butcher pushed the plate along with its fork and knife and continued wordlessly back to his work.

Appetite hadn't thought about Ignace in years. The last time he had heard from him was when he'd almost crushed the man's skull with his bare hands. He remembered the man's hair rough against his large palms, his fingers digging into the skin, muscles, and bone. There had been a certain fear that he gorged on that day. Ignace stopped being the brother of the woman he loved, the one who hated him, and he hated in return. For long minutes, the man was no different than an aluminum can – an empty one at that. He remembered the satisfying crunch, the shrill voices of his men and women clamoring for him stop with empty words and threats. The man's eyes threatened to pop out of his head with each tightening finger. The smug look on his face was gone, replaced with only sheer and satisfying terror. The younger man Appetite kept inside, the silent brutal towering colossus of a man who hated everything, stirred in the back of his head with a satisfied grin. That was a long time ago. But he knew that Ignace remembered just as clearly.

As long as they were in the same village, he might as well pay the man a visit.

Appetite cleaned the plate as he always did, leaving not even the bones, and left the butcher and his son to their work. After buying pastries from a small bakery run by a confident old woman, and a beer from a rambling old beer seller to wash it all down, he strolled his way through the market. The memories came back to him with every step. In the newer parts of the village, he could ignore the feelings. Here, in places that he recognized, he started to feel the threads of familiarity. Buildings he had been into, people he knew, things he had bought or tried out. It like coming home all over again – with everything good and bad that came with it. Old memories surfaced and danced in his head as he finished his beer. He almost wished that he could get drunk enough for this; at least then he could blame that for what he was going to do next.

People were things of habit. They didn't move or change their ways unless they had to. Ignace Breaux wasn't any different, caught in his slow loop of doing the same darn thing. The small glimmers in the faces that recognized Appetite turned from mild amusement to fires of hate the closer he got to the totems. The tall, multi-tiered, painted wooden structures stared down at him with pale white eyes cut from chips of bone, hidden within the long leaves of the willows. A small clearing was cut out in the middle around a simple gazebo.

In the center a man sat watching the fire with hard eyes. Men and women in long red-and-orange robes surrounded him, meditating over a large bonfire.

No amount of meditation could stop this man from his ambitions.

Ignace made him wait. Appetite knew he'd heard him come up. For one thing, he wasn't was a stealthy man; when you were the size of small truck, you tended to make a sound everywhere you went. The man ignored him, let him stand there like a fool – but he'd learned patience a long time ago. Appetite finished his beer with slow, obnoxious slurps. There wasn't much left, of course. He had to make it last. *I can wait here all day.*

In the end, Ignace was the one that blinked first. He stood, taking in a lungful of smoke through his nose and breathing it out in a cloud of grey. He turned, smirking with those pearly white teeth peeking through those smug lips. "My, if it ain't my sister's towering behemoth. Didn't recognize you without her collar around your neck."

The scarred man walked over with a grin plastered on his face. The sneering confidence hadn't changed over the years. He sauntered over, looking up the length of Appetite with those hard-red eyes. He stared up, his twisted lean body underneath the robes of red and orange.

Appetite noticed a little trip in his step. Ignace didn't see the softer, patient man that he become; he saw the man that gave him that ugly red spiderweb scar on his face and the dent in his skull that hadn't healed right. Memories worked the same way for everyone when seeing someone that hurt them.

Ignace pushed his kinky black hair from the good side of his face. "I vividly remember saying that you shouldn't bring yourself around here."

"Not even minutes in and it's already 'bout you, Ig."

"Don't call me that."

Appetite smiled.

"Why are you here, bull? I thought you weren't going to come back."

"I thought that too." Appetite vividly remembered the promise after Ina vanished. He wasn't one to take stuff back. "But it ain't right to not let my daughter meet the other side of her family."

Ignace paced. "Yes, your daughter," he hissed with slow words. "I've heard she was here too."

A cold, soft anger rose in Appetite's stomach. "She ain't in this, *Ignace*."

"I ain't gonna hurt your *whelp*. Why would I... unless..." He stalked around, brushing against Appetite's side with every bump. "Oh, unless it hurts you."

"*Are* we really doing this?"

"Oh stop, Woodrow. You act like I'm the *monster* here. I won't let you tell me what's best for my people."

"Ignace," Appetite shouted, his voice rippling through the willow leaves. The sudden anger startled Ignace to the point of jumping back a few inches. The men, his posse, lept into action with their spears pointed at Appetite's back. *Don't wanna do that gentlemen. Don't let the nice clothes fool ya.* "I'm here to give ya a warning. I've always known what you've wanted, and you thought that you were going to get it. Ya didn't, did ya? You were always second place to Ina. Always. Her not being here hasn't changed anything. The Flame isn't yours nor will it ever *be* yours. You will never be a leader. So, whatever you have planned, keep that between you and your pa. Got it? As long as my little girl's here, you don't move a muscle. I don't care what you got planned, leave Cassie out of it."

Ignace cocked his head back a bit startled. He had experienced Appetite's rage before. In his anger, these spears, guns, or whatever they had at their disposal meant nothing to him. Appetite waited for the man to respond with the blankest expression he could manage.

That smirk progressed across the dark man's face again. "You really don't know, do you? You have no clue," he said in the softest of whispers. "I guess it doesn't matter at this *very* moment." He gave a low, hot glower underneath his heavy brows. The smile didn't regress. If anything, as the seconds stretched into long minutes, it had gotten worse. A thick orange pulse rose from Ignace's shoulders; heat pressed against Appetite's body. "Welcome back down from that precious mountain. Perhaps you will find that more things have changed in our fifteen years apart."

The odd heat disappeared in an instant. Ignace folded his arm within his robes, his men resting their weapons all around them. Appetite eyed him, unimpressed despite the sweat now soaking his shirt. This wasn't something he hadn't seen before. Living out in the Dusk Orbit planets and traveling with Ina gave him all types of experiences. *Flexing ain't helping much. You know what I can do.*

"You won't have to worry about me," Ignace said. "Besides, I think in a few days or so, you're going to have your plate pretty full. Have a good evening, Mr. Caldwell. It's always a pleasure to see you."

The orange-robed men left without a word. Appetite watched them, heart thumping in his chest, as they left him to wonder what in the blue blazes Ignace had to be so confidence about.

Ø

Appetite returned to the manor in the dead of night to find Remy in well over his head.

He had never seen the man with anything other than a calm expression on his face. Tonight, Remy stood with his back against the door, purple eyes weathered like rust on an old car and shivering as though the evening air was cold. Appetite tried to ignore what he felt clearly on the air the moment he stepped foot in the manor. A thick layer of warmth and muck clung to the air, choking them with arms of humidity. A lance of panic rose through Appetite's chest. Fear for his child's life was followed hand in hand by an immeasurable amount of rage.

"What happened?" he began, feeling the arms of his shirt rip from the bulging of his muscles. Small rips became larger ones as he grew, feeling the hot surge of power from a full stomach. Words became difficult to string together in his mind, replaced only by savage grunts. "What happened to my little girl?" he managed to mutter. "What. Happened?"

Silence.

Silence for too long.

The anger took over. One second he was at the door, the next he was leaping across the hallway. His thunderous footsteps broke the wooden planks, the mass of his body ripping through the decor as though it was nothing. He was on Remy in seconds, long before any of the maids, butlers, or guards could hope to react. Appetite slammed his fist into the wall a hair's breadth away from the man's head, punching a hole clean to the other side. Remy didn't flinch; he only raised his head as though seeing Appetite for the first time.

"She's alright, she's alright,'" Remy said, looking up into his now painfully red, glowing eyes. "I promise. I would've told you right away if something bad happened. Just unexpected. I didn't factor in whatever mutations your family have - that's not important and you're not listening anyway. She's in the spare bedroom resting."

Appetite pulled his fist from the wall, splinters of wood stabbing into his knuckles. The anger remained. *You promised she'd be safe. I should'nt've have come here. I shouldn't have come.* A roar escaped his lungs, the sound of death to the manor, even to his own ears. Remy looked for a second at the beast heaving down his neck in puffs of heavy smoke, tongue lulling from his unhinged mouth. Appetite backed up with a few steady steps, reeling himself back. He heaved thick breaths to try to get his mind back. He let the rigidness in his body leave with every second. *I need to see her.* He pushed Remy aside, no longer hearing the clumsy apologies at his back.

He stomped through the house, feeling ragged and broken. He knew the way; that much hadn't changed. Around him, he heard the stirring of the house guards. They were too slow to stop him from almost eating a man alive out of trust. Now, they were wary and ready for him in case what he found wasn't satisfactory. Nothing in heaven or earth would stop him if there was a single hair wrong on his daughter's head.

He stomped up the twisting stairs, the flameless torches throwing his monstrous shadow up and across the windows and the underbelly of the second floor. He slowed himself, becoming mildly aware of his weight creaking against the wood, the lava of his anger cooling into a hollowed rock in his chest.

He reached the spare bedroom; the thick, black wooden door was closed. Another one of those ominous red masks hung from a small knob on the face of door. This one looked down from its post with a scowl in those painted yellow eyes. He wouldn't have gotten close to this supernatural totem in his right mind but parental protection broke through that. He began to hear things - soft whispers and chuckles on the wind - the moment his hand touched the doorknob. He had heard them before with Ina.

The Ember Gods, the murmurs of the Starcall, she had called them. Superstition ran thick in his subconscious mind, threatening moments of hesitation. His conscious mind willed it away. His daughter was behind that door. Nothing was going to stop him. He shouldered the door open.

A blast of heat hit him from the other side.

He stood in the frame of the door, staring into the lightless room. The familiar smells barraged him. Where he expected the smell of sickness or rot, he got a peppery aroma touched with nutmeg and sugar. What looked like fireflies or wisps bounced and danced around the room. On the other side, the *barj* accumulated in the corner as though it was a remorseful child in timeout.

Appetite walked in, eyes flickering back and forth. Nothing *looked* off, only felt it. The room barely had any furniture and a single window. On the far side of the room, Kindle was sitting up in a bed much too big for her. She looked a little pale, her hair was a mess, and the odd vents in her skin were open. Other than that, she looked fine... aside from one detail: she was holding a fire in her hand. The flame was a torrent of different shades of red, woven together and beating with a certain life.

Kindle caressed the flame with her fingers, lacing its embers through her fingers. It disappeared like a real fire, rather than the thousands of fireflies it was made of. She stared up, eyes pale but smile vivid. "I didn't know I could do this," she said after a time.

Appetite deflated. Any residual anger he had rushed out of his body. He ran to her side, sitting on the bed and reaching for her free hand. He took in a sharp breath. "What happened?"

The door shut behind them. Remy had entered; he moved to speak. Kindle shook her head at him.

"I got it," she said. She extinguished the flame. "I got a little overconfident, I reckon."

"Looks like more than a little," Appetite replied.

A weak smile from her. *Good.* "Okay, okay. More than a little."

"What did I tell you 'bout that, knucklehead?" Appetite gave her a light tap on the head. "Wanna talk about it?"

"Not right now," she gave a smile. "I... saw her."

"You saw who?"

"Mom."

"Where?"

"Through the Flame." Kindle went to grab a cup from the table. Her father met her halfway, putting the cup of water - or, at least, he thought it was water - in her hand. "She's far away."

"How far?" He cursed himself for asking.

"I don't know. Maybe a galaxy or so." She drank some of the water as though that was a good enough answer. Maybe it was. "I saw ships too."

"What kinda ships?"

"Fighters and cruisers, I think. Fleets and fleets of them on the distance. Bluecoats mostly."

"That's enough, Cassie," Remy said, stepping in. Appetite gave him a hard stare at the interruption, but he had regained his nonchalant attitude. "Drinking too much of the Spark might have caused you to see some things; it's nothing to worry about. You need to go back to bed. There's much you need to learn before I let you head back to the mountain. They're going to need you. So, rest."

Kindle finished her water and rested her head on the large back pillow. She muttered something under her breath for a while before nodding off. Remy approached from the other side, though with a little caution and respect this time. Grandfather and father watched her drift off to sleep; Appetite held her hand the entire time. When she was sound asleep, he rose gently from the bed to let his champion sleep off whatever crap she had experienced, beckoning Remy to the same. The lean witch doctor dipped his head and followed him to a small corner of the room. Neither seemed remotely impressed by the other. They waited for a little longer to let her sleep to settle in.

"The Flame is the life of the planet," Remy said in a whisper. "Have you ever wondered why C'dar was different after the first Civilizations fell? Why even despite the apocalypse at their own hands, this planet survived? That's why. The Flame allows us to eat, breathe, to live on this planet. It allows us to grow. To have a Handler of Flames or a Shaman is needed on the planet, at least for a year or so. Fifteen years without one has put strain on the planet. People blame you and your family for it."

Appetite knew that Remy wasn't wrong. He chose to say nothing.

"For the sake of the Willows, I'm going to ask you to leave. The tension is too great."

"I get the importance of all this," Appetite said in a soft voice. "I really do. But I'd rather watch this planet die than my daughter. There are thousands of these. She's the only one of her."

"You care for her." Remy sighed. "You have my word. Nothing like that is going to happen again. You, however, need to get that tank off our lawn and head back to the mountain. I got some news that you'll want to hear. Word on the streets is that your father has started a war."

Chapter 8

Sensible Brooding
Drifter

"Tread lightly from here. Tread lightly and triumph." -- Jo "Rancher Queen" Caldwell

They returned with their loot the next day to find that Shepherd had done somethin' real stupid.

He knew that Spencer and the Hounds weren't the most stable of the family. The Caldwells had to have some degree of madness to survive here on this planet with not a lotta people but a whole other lotta things that could kill you. Drifter wasn't one to judge about that. That being said, the Shepherd was closer to a raider than anyone else in the family; he had done terrible things. This one ranked in the top ten - no, about top five - of the silliest things he had done.

Heads lined every post leading up the mountain, crows poking at their empty eyes. Shepherd hadn't discriminated in his rage; men, women, synthetics, organics, mutants, humans, were all equally put on display. From the look of it, they appeared to be a small squad caught in the wrong place at the wrong time - not unlike those green boys they stole the 7-A from.

Dusk Mountain Blues

There was no denying it now. They were at war.

Pit, despite his best efforts, couldn't contain his glee at the grisly site. He rose from the back seat, pushing through the mountain of spoils and grinning like a mad man. That was the reason they gave them the collective nickname of the Hounds. Dogs are loyal, emotional, passionate creatures. They also hunted, mauled, and killed once they found a scent. From the grandfather to the sons to the pups, they shared those single-minded traits - with minor variations here and there.

Drifter cursed under his breath. *What did y'all do,* he thought, clutching whitened knuckles against the steering wheel. He knew Pit hadn't planned this, he didn't really have...what's the word...the *foresight* for that. At the very least, they could've been smart about it, not parade their spoils to decorate their home. They never did. *Gonna have to fix this too.*

No one noticed that Drifter wasn't too happy about it.

Big Thunder turned after a while, seeing the unhappiness creep on Drifter's face in a stark contrast to their giddy brother. He flicked his eyes back and forth from one brother to other, obviously a tad confused on how he should feel. He kept quiet; a smart move, all in all. Drifter hadn't the time nor the dang patience to talk 'bout his feelings. Right now, Drifter was too busy mentally trying to find a big enough shovel to dig themselves out with. They sat in an uncomfortable silence, driving through the valley of the dead and ascending the mountain.

When they made it to the summit and to the Homestead after a few empty minutes, it appeared that he wasn't the only one upset about this. A few of the family had already begun discussing - very heatedly, might he add. Drifter parked the truck by his garage. He jangled the keys from the ignition and opened the door with a bit more anger than he should've, stomping around the back. The crowd of his kin fell into silence as the patriarch quietly unpacked the loot from the Huntsman. A few of the nephews and nieces helped, taking the various crates to the warehouse behind the cabin. Their little arsenal for a rainy day.

Drifter motioned for Doc, Moses, Jo, and Shepherd to stay off everyone without a single word. Everyone knew better than to test him in one of these moods. He tried his best to keep cool, but his anger sputtered outta him like oil. What tipped him over the edge was the satisfied expression on Shepherd's face. The boy had lost his son; he was willing to give him a pass in his grief. Not if he was going to be smug 'bout it though. So, he did what good family member would do: he popped the boy right in his mouth.

The punch came hard and unexpected, as one does when you sucker punch a fella. Shepherd fell to the ground, nose delightfully busted and crooked. He cursed, growling, muttering, clawing at the dirt with blood trickling off of his chin in ribbons of red. Pit opened his mouth but shut it quickly with a glance over his shoulder when seeing his older brother's death stare. He knew that his son deserved that one.

"*You don't think*," Drifter thought - or, at least, he *thought* he thought it. He heard his voice echo against the trees; flocks of birds flew up from their nests. He had shouted, apparently, since everyone was looking at him with mouths agape.

Drifter felt his knuckles sting a tad from the blow, his throat a little raw from the shout. No one said a word for a very long time. Drifter peeled back his thick film of anger only a tad as he paced. "Did you think that maybe, just maybe, there might be reckonin' to whatya did, hm? Think 'bout that. There's a reason I went all the way out to vent my anger, boy. You might've just led them right to us!"

Drifter trembled. In all his born years, he hadn't experienced anything like this. Shepherd sat in the dirt, holding his nose, eyes alight with deep recognition. The display of anger had given the Bluecoats a breadcrumb trail up Dusk Mountain. The Dusk Mountains served like a natural defense for the family, but Doc and Loner had made sure they had other defenses besides - they didn't wanna have to use those. The mountain and the natural traps had always been enough for the idiots before; now, Shepherd might given them the key to the front door.

The idiot. A single punch suddenly didn't feel like punishment enough. Even as the Hounds carted him away, he thought to chase him down and give him another swing.

"Remember when your ma died to those off-world pirates? I told ya, we'll get revenge for her. I promised ya. It didn't happen overnight; it didn't even happen over a year. Guess what, it happened. We took our time. We take our time here, Spencer!"

"That's enough, he gets it, Pa." Jo grabbed Drifter by the arm. "He knows what he did wrong. But what's done is done. How 'bout you cool off, eh?"

Drifter felt his thin body being dragged away from the rest of his family and onto the porch. His body continued to tremble, but the fog of anger retreated. He took off his mesh ball cap and slammed it into the dust. He took a breath - the thick kinda breath meant for a truly rare type of frustrated. His daughter eased him back into his rocking chair and fetched him a cold cup of water and a few aspirins. Slumping in his seat, Drifter downed the medicine and the water in a single gulp, unsure of which his body needed more.

He met Jo's eyes and groaned; she had the look. The look that Mary had when she was fixin' to say something he might not like. *Here we go.*

"You know we get it from y'all, right?"

"I know," he grumbled. "You want better sense for your kids."

"You know. Apples and trees and whatnot." Jo sighed. "We can't help it."

"All I'm askin' for is that if you're going on a killing spree, do it right. There's a time and place for that. A sensible type of brooding. I thought I at least taught 'em that, y'know."

"It's something I picked up after a time. You're really good at it, Dad."

"Am I?"

"Sometimes." Jo smiled. "But really, we're in trouble now with that little stunt he pulled. Where were you guys all yesterday anyway?"

Drifter squirmed. "Shooting some Bluecoats and taking their stuff."

"You do see that Spencer thought what he did was a good idea because of stuff like that, right?"

Fair point. Drifter relaxed. Jo knew how to put things into perspective. Even when she was a kid, she knew how to correct her ol' pa. Still, he wasn't going to apologize, nor did she expect him to. The fact remained that they were in trouble, and no matter how well-intentioned her nephew was, he screwed them more than he could possibly imagine.

Drifter filled the cup with a little more water, kinda hoping there was something stronger in his small cup. He needed to cool down. "Where's Evan and Wood?"

"Wood's heading back. Evan said he's coming up the mountain too. He's got something he's been working on. Not to mention Doc's been working on a few things. Nothing like funerals and imminent danger to bring our families together. I take it where I can get it, though."

Jo spoke Appetite up; they heard the familiar roar coming up the driveway. Not even a few minutes after she said it, the small brown and green tank came rolling up the side of the mountain. He didn't stop for a second, hardly noticing the crowd. Drifter watched his big son climb out of the side and land with a thunderous crash. A few of the cousins laughed under their breaths as they usually did when seeing Appetite move. Never to his face, of course.

Though normally patient with them beyond what was acceptable, his darkest mood stripped that away.

He charged into the house and came back only minutes later dressed down in sweatpants, a tank top, and flip flops - his comfort clothes. He charged towards them, his hair wild and his beard long against his collar bones. He heaved a heavy breath. "What's happening?" he asked in a slow, measured anger.

Jo shook her head. "Spencer killed a bunch of Bluecoats and put them on display."

"Of course, he did." Appetite frowned. He took a deep breath. "Cassie's stayin' for a spell at the Willow's Grove."

"Don't seem so happy 'bout that," Jo said, folding her his arms.

"She's her own girl, but...don't trust her stayin' close to Ignace. But I can't do much about that." Appetite pinched the bridge of his nose.

Jo folded her arms. "That pompous son of a gun still around?"

"And you haven't killed 'im yet?" Drifter found himself adding. *Ah, see, bad habit.* "Don't say it, Jo. I heard what I said."

Appetite gave a puzzled look but didn't ask. "She's going to stay for a while. What are we doing 'round here?"

"Tryin' not to die." Jo shrugged.

Appetite laughed. "That's all any of us tryin' to do, I reckon. What's the plan, Pa?"

"We haven't gotten that far yet." Drifter pinched his nose. There was a lotta things they *could* do; there was a lotta things *needed* to be done. They had prepared for this eventuality for years. *And they called me paranoid.* Nothing came easy. They get here easy. They didn't stay here 'cause it was easy. They learned what worked and how to survive, preparing for the day that the colonizers would grow interest in C'dar. *Only a matter of time. Only a matter of time.* "I need some company, y'all alright coming along? I know you've had a long day, Wood, and your patience for your ol pa's gettin' thin, Jo. I honestly need both of ya if you can manage the time. If I stay around them, I might do something I regret."

"We might have even more company."

Drifter furrowed his brows, seeing a man in a tattered cloak coming up the mountain. He leaned heavily on a twisted old rod fashioned from parts of a car axis. He wasn't a big man, or tall, much the same as Drifter himself. There was something about him, though; even in his tattered wandering clothes of tan and grey pants, and a yellowed t-shirt that might've been white once with a few too many holes. Puffs of grey-green smoke left his respirator, billowing around and through the fabric of his hood. Two small, rusted red drones buzzed around his head and a long, bare skeleton 'roid followed him closely.

Loner, the youngest of Drifter's children, silenced the light hum of conversation. He wasn't one to leave his cave at the bottom of the mountain; unless he went on a scavenge for parts, or to work on the radio station network. He wandered toward them, his small mechanized army making a bit of a ruckus in this awkward silence.

Drifter grabbed him into a hug; the man smelled of oil, rust, and sand. He loved him.

Loner huffed a little, patting his ol' dad on the back. "'Ey, pa. Jo. Wood." His hugs continued around their small family.

"Hood off, son." Drifter smiled.

He hated it but he did it anyway; Loner tossed off his hood. Though younger than both Appetite and the Rancher Queen, Loner had inherited Drifter's apparent ability to lose all the color in his hair in his mid thirties. There were a few persistent flecks of weak darkness in his hair, cut messily short by what looked like a knife. His eyes were a shade darker than the rest of the family's blues and rimmed with dark circles. He hadn't been out much lately, judging by the milky color of his skin, almost sickly against the metal of his respirator.

He huffed again, deep, measured, and a little uncomfortable out in the open. "'Right, you guys got me outta my cave. What now?"

"The 'roid is new," Jo said, drawing out the conversation. Loner hated talking about himself.

"They can't speak yet, trying to learn itself. New AI I'm messing with. Jesse. Say hi." The bare 'roid of black bones looked as startled as a machine could. It waved awkwardly after a time. "Good. Good."

"Don't overwork yourself, Evan." Drifter found himself saying. "Last time…"

"I know. I know," he muttered. He stuffed his hands in his pockets. "What's happening? I heard about Matt."

Jo took the lead. "Let me bring you up to date."

And just like that, their little clan was together. Drifter and his three children walked through the Homestead, inspecting the defenses and checking the inventory. The anger he felt hibernated, and the whole situation dissolved into shallow puddles in his head. He listened to Jo's explanation on what was happening with her own life;

Loner and Appetite listened and then shared what was happening with them. All the years of raising them in that small cabin gave them a close bond with one another. Kids were cruel at any age and in any galaxy; and his children knew that too well. They learned to deal by working as a unit. That hadn't changed in their older age. They were a pack - his pack of smart, witty, and resourceful men and women.

Drifter led the small crowd across the Homestead, checking things here and there. The watch towers were back up. They hadn't been up in years, not since the pirate problems they had a while back. Doc's kids and grandkids had worked on setting up the fences and the turrets. The familiar sounds of metalworking and woodworking - the buzzing of saws, the beating of hammers, and the humming of drills - filled the area. While Doc and Vermin worked on that, Drifter couldn't help but notice Mirabelle taking what seemed to be parts of a reactor. The young woman, just as thick as but darker-skinned than her father, carted the pieces onto her small floating shuttle, wordlessly smiling from ear to ear. It might as well have been her birthday with how well she was taking this.

Big Thunder and Moses's countless children and grandchildren scurried around the Homestead, ranging from young kids to teens to grown adults older than

Appetite. They had started earlier than Drifter and hadn't stopped; through them, the Caldwells' genetics would survive into the next few centuries at least. Drifter saw the children's several mothers (a habit they gotten from the father they shared, and the cause for their vastly different appearances) huddled up and talking amongst themselves.

Big Thunder was instructing any kid that could hold a weapon on safe gun rules under the massive oak tree. Moses preached by the crashed spaceship, their ark, with a small congregation, speaking words of equal parts wrath and mercy. Drifter couldn't help but notice the similarities of how the brothers handled the topics. Eerie how similar their words were. Drifter let that thought sink in for a while and found the hole a bit too deep for his liking; he put it away in his head and kept scrolling.

"Pa."

"Yeah," Drifter said, turning to Appetite. "Gonna have to ask whatever you were asking again. Wasn't paying attention."

"Where are we going?"

"Oh, nowhere in particular. Been thinking about what we're gonna do next." Drifter wasn't actually telling the whole the truth; he was, in fact, pondering anything besides what to do next. He pinched his nose and cleared his head. There were plenty of things on the table now. First and foremost was to check on Big Thunder's distillery. The moonshine was their primary source of bartering, after fuel and salvage - it was by far the most consistent outta all of them. Before the Bluecoats even attempted the mountain, they would go there to cut the Caldwells off from potential allies. *Maybe they'll do it to try to stay in the law. They would've come up here before if they weren't so worried about that.* Luckily, the Caldwells didn't have to abide by the law; they would cut corners if they had to, cheat if they gotta. That was the difference between the two factions. The Bluecoats believed they were in the right and legal. Drifter knew that him and his kin weren't.

"Gather around everyone," Drifter barked.

The family stopped what they were doing. Guns were put away, bibles were closed, and all manner of talking stopped. The throng of family made a tight circle around him. Drifter couldn't help but noticing the Hounds standing a little further away. He sighed. Right now, he couldn't afford alienating them. Besides, they were some of the best gunmen in the family. Drifter found himself wishing a little that Kindle was here. Pit, his brother, he could handle. The Hounds as an angry ball of revenge, he couldn't. Shepherd stood in the forefront; broken nose taped but dribbling a bit of blood on his lips. He still hungered, biting at bones without meat on it. *Might can use that. Gotta use that, stoke that flame.*

"As we all know by now, we done got the attention of a Major of the Civilization's Bluecoats." Drifter took a deep breath. "I know, I know. We're all partially to blame, me included. We poked this cage enough times. Now the cage's open and we're gonna have put the beast down." He cleared his throat. "First, we need make sure Thunder's distillery's 'right. There're too many things there that they can't have. Secondly, our homes. They're gonna come for me, I know it. Y'all already done a good job startin' it. But take this seriously. These ain't people we want to mess with. We hit them hard before they hit us. Got that?"

"What's stopping them from coming up here right now?" one of Moses's many grandkids shouted. Zeke, maybe.

"Nothin' to be honest. That's why we're gonna keep people here. Two teams: one for the distillery and one for the Homestead."

"Where are you gonna go?" Bulldog asked. He, of course, expected him to stay at the Homestead. It was his home after all. Drifter smiled at the young boy through the crowd.

"I'm gonna go with y'all. It only makes sense."

The Hounds nodded. *They wanna fight, let 'em.*

"Of course, y'all gonna have to listen to me. We didn't get this far being dumb. If I ask you to do it, do it. Don't ask me question, don't say the word 'but', don't even look at me the wrong way. You do it even if you don't agree with it. Y'all gotta trust me - *all* y'all. I didn't bring my brothers here to let us lose all we got."

"I gotta question, Pops." Appetite raised a single finger. "Why exactly do you think they want us gone? We're just a backwater planet full of nothing but old stuff."

The five Patriarchs - Drifter, Pit, Big Thunder, Doc, and Moses - knew this answer. Drifter saw his brothers' faces change within the crowd, some soft, others harder. There were pieces of their past, things they kept from their children and grandchildren. Not out of secrecy; not entirely. There were things a man couldn't find a way to talk about. The Space Prison of Taros and the Desert Prison Planet of Daedal were his childhood, and the reason he could do what he did. The dark metal cells, the hours in a glass pod filled with stasis liquids, the silver sands of windy dunes in his mouth, the hammering of ore for days at a time. Those things he wanted to spare the next generation of. How could he tell them that their mutations were no different than a farmer growing the perfect breed of corn?

But they had the right to know where they came from, right? The very thought terrified him.

"I -" He took a deep breath. "The Civilization made us. Sold by our pa, Max Caldwell, to the prison Taros and its scientist for his own dang crimes and debts. We were rats." Drifter remembered those young years as though they were yesterday. He tasted bile in mouth. "After being experimented on for several years, they threw us on the desert prison planet of Daedal. Mutants like us slipped through the cracks during prison planet riots all across the galaxy. Now the Civilization's stable under a new Chairwoman, they're tryin' to clean up their own mess. We're part of that mess. Besides, this planet ain't a bad one for them to get their hands on. Could be great for a new colony. But first and foremost, it's about cleaning up the previous government's mess. That's the long and short of it. Anyone that wants to know anything else, feel free to ask any question 'bout it, but you might not want to know the answers. We are what we are and they don't like it very much."

Everyone in the crowd stiffened. It was one thing hearing bits and pieces from their own fathers. Saying it aloud in its entirety came with a certain indescribable shame, like being stripped away by the elements. Drifter swallowed his pride for a moment, taking another deep ragged breath. "We don't like talkin' 'bout it, but it's part of us. You have every right to know why you're being hunted and why we're different. Should've told y'all sooner, but it is what it is."

"Well…" Appetite said after a long silence. "That explains quite a bit."

Jo nodded too. "All because we're a little different from them."

Drifter felt himself grow cold and distant. "Everyone git now. We got work to do and it ain't gonna fix itself. We're leaving in a bit." He took the stunned the silence as a chance to slink away.

The soft memories of a hard past came rushing back at once. He liked to think that he got it out of his system, made peace with it. When the words came out of his mouth, he wasn't the experienced ol' man. For a few seconds there, he was that little boy with clay-red hair wandering Taros for a glimpse of a dad that sold him. He stepped away, slipping through the mass of kin and to the other side without another word.

He made it to his own porch before he allowed himself to break a little. Mary Lu sat in her rocking chair, a long-crocheted blanket of purple and white over her lap. She smiled at him, and somehow, it made the feeling in his gut ease a little. She turned to him with those soft, knowing eyes. With her right hand, she patted on the rocking chair beside her, beckoning him to come over. He did so, slumping into the comforts of wood and mindless rocking. Mary Lu grabbed his fingers and said nothing. She never needed to.

Chapter 9

Simple Gatherings
Appetite

"You can always tell who a person is by what they bring to a dinner." --Major Steven Debenham of the Bluecoats Airmen

Appetite hated stormy days. Something 'bout them never settled well with him. The pelting rain against his wood cabin, the crackling of lightning and pounding of thunder, the howling of wind down the side of the mountain - it all gave every storm this ominous presence on Dusk Mountain. He remembered being afraid of this kinda weather when he was a kid, wandering these very halls to his parents' room on the other side; years later, here he was, wandering the same cabin with the same feeling in his stomach. He felt like a dang fool every time.

"It's only rain and bad feelings," he grumbled under his breath. "Only rain and bad feelings."

As a family, they decided to stay at their father's cabin while he was away to look after their mother. The party assigned to the Distillery left when the sun cracked over the grey horizon. He remembered hearing the trucks roll off early this morning in several small groups, each armed and ready for a race if they needed to escape. Appetite watched them leave from his window before nodding back to sleep for a while. When he woke again, they were gone and it was raining.

The loneliness didn't help much. His mother, brother, and sister eased it, but he missed his partner in crime, his buddy, his friend; Kindle was out there somewhere in the Swamp with Remy and Ignace. He hadn't decided which one was worse after the last debacle. She had urged him to leave, though. His history with everyone there only served to put his daughter in danger. Papa Bear that he was, he couldn't savor the thought. With the danger everyone was in and her not being here, he thought his mind might explode.

Not even an hour awake, his mind wandered to stress eating. He muttered curses to himself. *Fine way to eat my folks out of a house and a home,* Appetite mused. He supposed it couldn't be helped.

Appetite wandered to the kitchen to see Loner already awake. He was hunched under the small dining room table, naked aside from a pair of boxers and the respirator on his face. His long flesh colored tail slapped against the floor in frustration as he too muttered out his thoughts. Using the prehensile nature of his tail, he picked up a tool with it . to help with his tinkering, his weak lungs wheezing hard from the work. It was odd seeing his tail. Loner was often pretty ashamed of it, keeping it wrapped around his waist underneath his clothes. Other family members had more or less extreme mutations. He had every right to feel the way he did, but Appetite wished that he could show his younger brother how talented and cool he was.

Appetite approached his brother, putting a big hand on the slim man's shoulder. Loner jumped, hitting his head on the underbelly of the dining room table, screeching like a small animal.

"Woody, don't do that!"

"Sorry. Whatcha doing up this early?"

"I always get up this early," he muttered, crossing his legs. "What are *you* doin' up this early?"

"Why d'ya *think* I'm here?"

Loner snorted. "I wouldn't mind breakfast." He put down his tools, unfolded himself, and squirmed out from underneath the table. It reminded Appetite of a small animal leaving his nest. *No doubt I look about the same.*

"Any reason you aren't wearing clothes?"

"It gets hot when I'm workin'."

"What are you working on?"

"Jesse's mind core." He shrugged. "They need their sleep too. Also, it helps me think."

"Didn't look like it."

"Frustration helps too. Helps me think."

Loner wandered to the fridge. He pulled out a bundle of frozen chickens, an arm full of tomatoes and carrots, and a couple of eggs from Moses's farmlands. He turned, grinning underneath the thin plastic of his respirator.

Appetite rolled his eyes and waddled towards the counter. When their parents were gone, the cooking often fell on him. He began to wonder what they did for food in their own homes down the mountain. They knew, though, that if they ever asked, he would make them a meal without question; that was what families did for each other.

Appetite washed his hands and got to work on breakfast. "Two rules," he said, heating up the oven his father had made and finding some of the metal pots in the cabinet. "No work at the table, and you're the one that's going to have to wake Jo up."

Loner winced at the thought but said nothing; rumbling, he padded off, his little three-pronged feet making small taps into the dragon's den. Waking Jo had to be the worst chore either of them could ever conceive of for the other - being notoriously stubborn awake must've given her an unbreakable will asleep. Sending Loner to do it might've bought Appetite enough time to get some of the cooking done.

Grinning, Appetite began his much easier and much more mindless task of cleaning and cooking.

With the care he would give his own kid, Appetite moved each piece of Loner's workstation onto the living room's table. He had broken somethin' with his "sausage fingers" before - one of the few times he had ever seen Evan upset with him. He'd learned to take things at a slower pace after that. He left everything exactly as he picked them up, not even an inch outta place. *Treat their stuff like you want your stuff to be treated,* his pa told him after he broke that device. Funny how decades later, he still remembered.

Loner's tinkering safe and outta the way, he began breakfast.

Thawing and cleaning the chicken took most of his time. He found himself staring out of the window, mindlessly watching the rain pour over the lip of the roof. Streaks of lightning cracked over the grey sky in large forks, streaking across the charcoal black that was now the sky. He sliced one chicken, cutting it into his family's favorite pieces. He kept one whole for himself - he could eat more, but he didn't need to be greedy. A bit of oil heating in a pan and and a deep pot, a lot of cracking of eggs, and a bit of slicing of tomatoes - breakfast was on its way. This was usually a good feeling for him, but this stormy weather only made things worse. He only hoped the generators held.

"You're not alone, Woody."

Appetite wheeled around to see his mother sitting at the table, smiling and clutching her cane. The soft sea colors of her eyes roared with a distant understanding. She leaned forward a little, her hair in a thin curtain over her eyes. "The rain always did bother you. Somethin' bout it always got to ya. Keep in mind, though; gut feelings ain't something to be ignored. What's on your mind?"

"It's -" A pop of oil coming close to his face interrupted him. He kept to his frying, stoking the meat with a set of tongs. "Cassie's out there in the swamp. Pa defending the brews on the other mountain. They're fine, but I can't shake the feeling -" *Bang.* A crash of thunder this time, accompanied by a high snap of lightning. "Can't shake the feeling that something big's gonna happen today. Somethin' mighty big."

Mary Lu nodded. "I feel it too." She tapped her fingers against the ball of her cane. "How long have you been having this?"

"Hm?"

Dusk Mountain Blues

"These feelings. How often do they happen?" she asked after a long while of waiting for the rain to peter out. "Do they come with anything else?"

Appetite frowned. He hadn't thought much about it, but he was picking up what she was putting down. He couldn't put words to what he felt - it was like asking a blind man to explain shapes. His mother watched him go through his thoughts with a calm, measured patience. It made him feel proud the way looked at him. She didn't rush him, didn't so much as make a sound. He focused instead on making the breakfast, thinking of dropping the topic all together.

"You don't think its - y'know - I'm - it's nothin' like that. It's a feelin', that's all. Don't happen much." He pushed the thought into a corner of his mind. "I don't feel comfortable talking 'bout it."

His mother nodded and let the topic go. She knew when he was uncomfortable talking about a thing, nothing would break him outta of it.

"That's not unlike your pa." She smiled. "It's alright. I do want to ask you how you feel about what he revealed the other day."

"'Bout the experiments? How we got the way we got?" Appetite licked some chicken grease from his fingers. In all honesty, he hadn't wanted to think about what his dad and his uncles had gone through. He had heard stories. They always left a sour taste in his mouth. "We can't change what we are. It's all we've ever known." He flipped over the quartered chicken in the pan and checked his deep fryer again. He tossed the eggs into the pan, followed by the tomatoes, and scrambled it all together. "Were you…"

"Experimented on? Yes. But my abilities were there before," she laughed. ""It's amazing how cruel a person can be when they're faced with something they can't understand. If it wasn't for your dad's…stupidly reckless plan, I wouldn't have gotten to this old age. I wouldn't have had the pleasure of meeting my children and grandchild. But, all in all, I'm happy that the family has taken it how they have. It gave them a little more to fight for."

Appetite found himself respecting his mother more than even before. She didn't look like a woman that had seen hardships. *Who does, though?* he reminded himself. With care, he took his scrambled eggs, plated them on the three plates, and carted them over to the table. He set the table in silence, his mother watching him. The proud look in her eyes made a good feeling rise in his chest. "Eat 'em, Ma."

He placed the other two plates on the table before finishing up his significantly larger breakfast. Another rumble of thunder boomed throughout the room followed by a sharp bang within the house. Jo shouted a curse back. This went back and forth until Loner dragged her by her arm out of her old room to the table, his two drones wheeling behind him. One buzzed a little louder than the other, lightly smoking.

"You didn't flash her, did ya, Evan?" Appetite asked, frowning.

"She wouldn't wake up."

Jo growled. "If punching a sick man wasn't okay, I would've punched you in your stupid, skinny ribs."

She looked a mess collapsing in the dining chair. Her hair was all over, her eyelids heavily lidded, her face slumped and tired. Appetite brought them some coffee in large tin mugs. Rare stuff, really - it was one of the few things they didn't have the means to grow. Until another shipment came from off world, they had to be sparse with it. Appetite never really cared for the stuff. Didn't give him the jolt of energy it gave others. *Probably for the best.* There were two types of people in the galaxy: people that didn't need their morning coffee and people that did. Appetite respected that.

At last, his breakfast was finished. He pulled his whole chicken (though a little underdone) from the vat of oil, scrambled the rest of the eggs and tomatoes, and carted his bounty to the table. Everyone else had already begun eating. Jo was scarfing down food. His mother ate politely at a measured pace, and Loner sat with his respirator aside and eating happily. Appetite pulled up his chair and started to sit down. Lightning snapped; thunder boomed...the door knocked?

He stood there, confused for a second, ears straining against the rain and the wind. It wasn't his imagination. There was a knocking at the door. He put down his silverware and wandered out of the kitchen. "Put some pants on, Evan," he said on his way out to the main living area.

He came to the open door to see Zeke standing in the doorway. The teenage boy, all red faced and pimply, stood with his hands in his pockets. A few of his older cousins stood behind him, armed with rifles pointed at a much shorter third man...in a blue coat.

The cold feeling rippled through body, the one he had been feeling all day.

Second Major Debenham stood on the porch, wiping his muddy boots on the wood. Appetite almost lunged at the man. "Good morning, Woodrow. That's your name, but you prefer Appetite, right?"

In all his years, he hadn't felt a simpler rage.

"Don't...don't do that," the Major said, putting up a finger. "Some of your people have already tried." He pointed out hundreds of holes on his coat. "And I chose not to act. So please, don't act rashly again. You saw how that goes." The Major patted Zeke on the head. "Mind if I come in? I brought a little something for your trouble."

"Let the Major in, Woody." His mother's calm, leveled voice on the inside of the cabin surprised him. "Don't attack him."

Appetite sent the armed men away. If the holes in Debenham's coat were any indication, it would take more than what they had to kill a man like this.

The cyborg major dipped his head, walking through the frame much too short for him. Reining in the urge to crush the smaller man, Appetite moved aside. Major Steven Debenham placed his coat and his hat on the rack by the door, revealing his metal arms and metal eyes. He shook off some of the water.

"I brought a little something for breakfast," the major said conversationally. "Good thing, too - no one tells you that scaling a mountain works up an... nah, I'm not gonna say it. Mind if I sit down?" Appetite took in a deep breath, but Debenham interrupted him. "I know what you're thinking. You can search me if you want to. But if I made it this far without killing any of you, do you really think that I need a gun or a weapon of any kind to do it if I wanted to? So, let's pretend that I'm not murderous killing machine bent on wiping out the Civilization's mess across the galaxy."

That's a fair point. Appetite grumbled. "This way, Major."

"Please - call me Steve. Only my airmen call me Major. Boots on or off? It's raining bad out there; don't want to track in the mud...cats and dogs, like my grandpa used to say."

"You can keep 'em on. I'll clean it later."

"You really need a doormat. Would've brought one if I'd known. You don't think to bring something like that. Guess we take stuff like that for granted." He took off his boots anyway. Appetite couldn't help but notice the knapsack over the man's shoulder. "Alright, time to eat."

Appetite led the major into the kitchen where his family still sat. Jo and Loner had finished their meals; they stared up at the Bluecoat standing in their presence. His ma didn't raise her head; she sat plucking the remaining chicken from her plate.

"Augur of Owls, Rancher Queen, Loner. I've heard much about all of you. Been giving some of my airmen trouble; more than trouble, some say. Again, I'm not here for that. I'm here to be cordial and eat at your table." He took the knapsack off and pulled out its contents: a large tin container, a sizeable bag, a canteen, and a small flat circular device. "Don't worry, it's not an explosive. Your kin checked it. Not that I can *have* explosives - lost the quals. Long story. Actually, it's not a long story more than an embarrassing one. Just...let me open it."

Major Debenham popped open the sides of the container with satisfying snap. He popped off the top, revealing a normal, perfectly brown ham-and-hash brown casserole underneath. "I made this at camp. It's not as good as I would've made it at home with the wife and kids, but eh. It is what it is." He took the small circular device and hovered it over the meal. It began to burn bright, heating up the small container, melting the hardened cheese against the shredded potatoes. He held it in midair and used his other hand to open the pack. The scent of fresh coffee grounds rose into the air. Once the meal was finished, he brewed the coffee using the same device and a strainer he produced from his pocket. "Aww, here I am rambling, and you haven't eaten your breakfast yet and your food done got cold. Want me to warm it up for you?"

"No."

"Come on, it's safe. I promise. All of it is. I wouldn't *poison* you with *food*. I'm not a savage."

"Then what are you?" Jo snapped. Appetite was surprised that didn't happen sooner.

"A man doing his job." The major exhaled an exaggerated breath. "I do take pride in my work, but I like to think I'm fair. You see, my job is to rid the galaxy of threats to the Civilization, specifically lab-related threats such as rogue A. Is, androids, cyborgs - like myself - mutants, and other types of experiments done by the last Chairperson. It took me a long time to find the former Chairman's mutants from the Daedal. I didn't expect an entire family, a clan per se. I admittedly got curious. So, I'm here."

"Will this change a thing, *Steve*?"

"No. No it won't."

Appetite tore into a chicken leg, practically ripping the meat from the bone and crunching into the marrow with a single bite. *Steve* was right about one thing: his food had grown cold. Brooding, he continued his breakfast without a word. No one said anything for a very long time.

Major Debenham must've seen Appetite's discomfort; he leaned over and used his warming device without a word. The skin of the chicken crisped up and the eggs warmed within seconds. Afterwards, he cut off some pieces of his casserole and plopped it on both of their plates. "I'm not a monster, believe it not. This is the first mission I've actually gotten the chance to talk to people that wasn't completely savages. I mean, you are. But you're not. So, I'm giving you a heads up and I'm gonna see what you do."

You had every reason to attack here instead of the distillery. Why? Another boom of thunder. *Why waste the time?*

The Major forked up another piece of hash brown casserole and plopped it in his mouth. "Why would I come all the way here and not bring my people? 'Cause I knew that the *Drifter* would be elsewhere, and I couldn't help but take that chance. There're just some people that you can't ignore and he's one of them. After you've done my job for as long as I have, you see that there's patterns. First few, I tried to work my way up. You don't do that. You work your way down. Who's at the top? Your husband and your father." He relaxed his shoulders further as though he finally found comfort in his chair, his metal eyes eying them in a glow of green lights. "Right now, as we speak, Captain Xan and dozens of his boys from his strike team are headed your way. I, believe or not, am an observer in this. I'm not even supposed to be here."

"You're here to stall." Jo stood up, pulling a gun from her side. "What's stoppin' us from keepin' you here?"

"Nothing, I mean, aside from the fact I could kill you all in a blink of an eye if I *really* wanted to. But that's complicated and messy. Just look at your mother's face. She's seen someone like me before; haven't you?"

Appetite turned to his mother's face. There was something there he hadn't seen before. Mary Lu kept the pleasant smile on her face, warm and grandmotherly, the one that he had always known. Deeper though, there was a frosty glint to her features. She never broke eye contact with Debenham. She placed down her fork.

"Somewhere along the line you've met someone like me. Not as dashing and ruggedly handsome, I hope, but someone, nevertheless. Stop your children from doing something stupid for their sake. They'll get their chance at me. Right now, I'm eating breakfast and you're on the clock. So instead of thinking about how to kill me, start thinking about how you're going to get this information to your dear ol' pa."

He's right. Appetite let his mind slow down and focus on the real problem. This was a battle in itself. The Major wanted to get them nervous, throw them off their game. Appetite extended his arm. Jo stared at him, exchanging thoughts with a simple glance. *Patience, Jo, patience.* Out of all of them, that was one virtue he learned. That was his strength. *Slow and steady, Woody, slow and steady.* They had a way out of this, but they needed to play it smart. Appetite straightened his back and took a bite out of the Major's casserole. *Huh.* "Not bad, Steve," he said, his low voice turning sweeter than syrup. "The food I mean, it ain't bad."

"Eh, like I said, would've been better. Had to use what I had." The Major's face changed a little, noticing the shift in the atmosphere. Jo relaxed and seated herself, Loner kept quiet, and the Matriarch of the family laced her fingers together. He'd lost his momentum here and he didn't quite know where and when.

Appetite widened his grin and helped himself to several spoonfuls and bites of food.

Major Debenham cocked his head. "What are y'all planning? I had you on the ropes until now; what changed?"

"You don't know Drifter like we do. Call it a matter of faith." Mary Lu pulled herself to her full height. "Do you mind, Major, taking me to that window after you're done with your meal? I'm in need for some air. There's nothing quite like rainy air for the old lungs."

"Of course, ma'am." The airman's confusion deepened. To his credit, he kept his smile and finished his food. Like a true gentleman, he got up and offered his arm to the old lady that he would have no problem killing if he wanted. "This planet is really beautiful. You should consider yourselves lucky. There's some nasty planets out there."

"Yes, there are. Daedal was far worse."

The Major stiffened. "That planet isn't a thing anymore, ma'am." There was an odd genuine tone to his voice...almost apologetic. "I handled it myself."

"That's good to hear, sweetie. When did that happen?"

"A few months back."

"And that's how you found us. There were records there." She smiled again. "Also, I can't help to notice your accent. You're from a back planet too. We tend to have this drawl our voice. Where are you from, sweetie?""

"A small planet named Kalis. Ain't - " He caught himself. "It's not big, out on the edge of the Civilization planets. I don't like talking about it that much. But I can hear the similarities between us. It's truly a shame, all and all, what I have to do."

"Then why do you do it?"

"For a better galaxy."

"It's always for the better of the galaxy, isn't it?"

The Major and his mother took their conversation to the window and opened it up, exposing them to the rain and wind of the outside air. As much as Appetite wished to hear their discussion, there were things that needed be done. He gave a subtle nod to Loner, who made a clicking sound in the back of his throat, a simple command to call over one of his drones. It buzzed around and hummed; from there, Loner whispered a few words.

Appetite didn't know much about the drones and how they worked; but he did know that they could send a message.

The next command was soft snap of Loner's finger. The small red drone phased into a deep camouflage known as a hard-light shift. Only a very light outline remained. Loner nodded softly towards his brother and clicked his tongue one final time. The drone zoomed towards the open window.

Here's the tricky part. The faint outline of the drone drifted. Mary Lu kept the Major distracted, making small talk with very soft words against the wind. Seconds passed. More seconds passed. Major Debenham looked over his shoulder for a brief second. If he saw the drone, he made no effort to stop it; it zipped outta the window, into the rain and the wind. Worst come to worst; it would find a nearby family member to tell them what they learned. *It's a good plan. Be careful, Pa.* It was the best they could do on such short notice.

Mary Lu closed the window herself. "How about I make us a pie, Major? You came all this way and brought somethin'. The very least I could do is return the favor. Come sit and enjoy a little time off."

Chapter 10

Brimstone
Drifter

"Yeah, we got moonshine at the Drum...but that's not all we got there." Luke "Drifter" Caldwell

Yeah, 'bout time for it.

When ya live as long as Drifter has, you start to pick up when things are 'bout to go wrong. There was a pattern to it that young people couldn't quite see without experience. The tune was always the same; good things happen, good things keep happening, everything goes according to plan - and then always, like a swift kick in the balls, everything hits the fan. Didn't mean he liked knowing. Being young came with a certain invincibility when the inevitable cosmic shift happened. All Drifter got now was an uncomfortable feeling when they reached Big Thunder's home and distillery, the Drum.

The Drum was tucked deep within the forests of the Dusk Mountain valleys beside a freshwater stream. Raindrops pattered against the canopy of pine needles and oak leaves in a steady stream above them. The weak grey light that did manage to peek through the clouds did almost nothing to brighten their road ahead. The thick layers of moss and mud gave their trucks and small tanks a bit of a struggle on the way. More than a few times they had to stop to fix a truck wheel or push them outta a ditch or a sea of a puddle. A trip that would've normally took them a couple of hours took well over a day, leaving the family tired and weary. Drifter could only hope that the Bluecoat was having as bad of a time of a time in their travels. *Sure hope so; at least we know what we were getting into.*

They continued down the rugged, beaten path, the sound of water in the air and at their back. It was a dang beautiful place, even when it was dreary, dark, and miserable. He loved this planet and he loved his family.

Today he rode with the youngest of his brothers, Montgomery "Moses" Caldwell. They had used their nicknames as armor on Daedal - a tradition they gave to their kids, and them theirs. Montgomery got his from his quiet, refreshing outlook on religion and his calm demeanor. And he split open a desert with his mind once; it kinda stuck after that. Drifter had seen this look before, the one that had his brother locked up deep in the mines. It was the very same look he had before his abilities manifested and he tore that man to pieces with his mind. He drove, the thick thatch of his dreads hanging down around his face. He knew that he would have to draw his gun today and was making peace with it. *Moses without the flowers and the robes.*

"Monty," Drifter said, "you didn't have to come. We had it."

"Not a matter of what I wanna do. This is my planet too."

"Your promise."

"I remember saying that I won't pick up my gun or take a life for any personal gain. This isn't personal gain. It's survival."

"When you start makin' exceptions to your own rules, you start seein' exceptions everywhere. I - you're better than most of us, Monty. You always have been. You don't gotta -"

"Luke." Moses's voice grew colder than the rain and much harsher. "My family, my wives, my kids, my grandkids... they're important to me. I'm willing to fight for them."

"Even for yer greedy older brother."

"Even for my greedy older brother." He laughed, flat and cold, not at all like his usual laugh. "I'm serious, Luke, we've never seen anyone above a Captain back here. I don't think I get it. Why come so far? There's gotta be somethin' else they want. Somethin' they lookin' for.

Somethin' more than finding some smuggling boys and girls on a planet. We ain't *that* important to bring someone only a couple of steps down from the General himself. They want something on this planet, mark my words. There's somethin' else afoot. I feel it. Can't back down from duty."

Moses's different-colored eyes flickered from side to side, taking in the world around him. The forest thickened and so did the rain. Grey and rusted memories of the Old Planet began to bleed through the colorful nature. They began to see parts of the devastation of the old Civilization tucked in this valley; long-buried spires, buildings broken into cliffs, rusted vehicles touching the clear water...an old world, half forgotten, conquered by nature. Now that he thought about it, experienced it, it wasn't so odd to think the Bluecoats might've lost something on this planet that they wanted. Among the things the Caldwells found during digs, salvages, and raids, there was more than enough to survive on. *Ya might be onto a thing there, Monty. But what do we got here?* Curiosity piqued the old man's interest. He turned his attention back to the road.

Cut from an old factory, the Drum sat within an old warehouse on a small, rocky hill. Big Thunder and his boys and girls had taken it and made it their own. restoring it from the ground up to the best of their ability. From there, they filled it with the thing that Thunder liked the most - booze. Moonshine and beer, mostly. Good stuff, too - he processed, brewed, and bottled it all in the facility. The upper portion of the Drum served as the living quarters. The lights were off on that floor. A bad sign, all and all; the young kids were usually upstairs during this time. The only reason they wouldn't be if they were -

Crap.

"Monty."

"I know."

Up ahead, Thunder stopped and pulled aside; he crept out of his truck, weapon drawn, and extended his hand behind him before clenching it. Every vehicle in the caravan lost its power. Without the loud engines and the bright lights, only the sound of the storm and the river remained. No birds. He stalked through trees, squelching through the mud, rifle up. Bobby had been a member of the Daedel security team; they'd shoved a rifle in his hands as soon as they were big enough. He knew stuff like this better than Drifter ever could. Better for him to take the lead in times like this, Drifter reckoned - he wasn't below giving the reins of this bucking horse to someone that knew how to ride.

Drifter watched Big Thunder stalk through the trees with a few of his sons and daughters, following what appeared to be a small red drone. From back here, they reminded Drifter of a small hunting party searching for a buck. Pit and his boys followed suit, hunting dogs for the hunting party.

Drifter grabbed a revolver and a rifle, jumping out of the truck and landing with a satisfying *plop* in the mud; it came up almost knee deep. Rain dripped down his body. *Should've packed a good raincoat and a good pair of boots.* Too late to worry about it. Better muddy than dead.

Up ahead, the Hounds picked up a scent; they sprang into action. The first bullets were in the air within seconds, bursting through the bark of the trees. Flashes from the guns' barrels lit up the dark as bullets ricocheted in all directions. Bluecoats surrounded them on all sides, firing both conventional and laser weapons from the cliffs above. The family fired back into the emptiness.

The Bluecoats had the advantage on that high ground. Down here, all of the family were sitting ducks for the gunmen above. Didn't help that neither side could shoot their way outta paper bag right now. Maybe it was the weather. Drifter couldn't make heads or tails outta of it.

Drifter stepped outta cover to show the young people how to do it. His fired his gun and - whaddya know - he hit some men. They toppled over the side, landing face first in the mud. With a few shots, three men were dead and two 'roids disabled from waist up - but he missed the last bullet completely. Rain. Gotta be. Messes with a man's aim. He scrambled from cover to cover, reloading his six shooter and eying the attacks on the treeline. They didn't have enough bullets to keep going like this. They needed to -

A bullet hit him on the shoulder. The pain rose through his right side and spread upward through his body. Blood pooled against the already wet fabric of his white t-shirt, dying it red with every second. Judging from the pain alone, it wasn't a confirmed hit; more like a nasty knick. Didn't help his mood any. Those bastards shot him. He threw his revolver to his left hand. As Thunder once said, "Better to know how to shoot with both hands and not need to than wish that you learned."

Drifter fired off a few more shots toward the trees, holding his position as the pain crept up his neck in a fire. He ran through the road, Moses not far behind. *Why'd we stop, Bobby? What did that drone tell ya?*

Must've been Evan that sent it, maybe as a warning. But he couldn't think 'bout maybes. He needs some definitelys.

Growling through some mighty fierce aches, he headed for where he last saw Thunder in the treelines. Rain dashed against his face. The taste of tree needles was hard and sour in his mouth. Moses and a few other men followed behind, laying down cover fire.

Drifter turned, slipping against the mud as he saw a platoon of Bluecoats charging at him. Trying his best to slow himself, he grabbed onto a nearby tree with his injured arm, wheeling around it and shooting with his offhand. He missed gloriously. *That* he could blame on the rain.

Moses stepped ahead in the nick of time; he raised his hand and pushed forward with his palm, and a powerful, purple sonic boom rippled through the air, uprooting trees and men alike. He pulled his fingers back, holding everything in place with that odd purple energy, then ripped them from the air, slamming them into the ground with a sickening crunch.

One second was all it took for the frightening mind juju to grip the men and crush them like a can.

Moses brought the lumps of meat back into the air, suspending them in a whirl of energy once more and slammed them down again for good measure. Or... perhaps out of habit. He levitated the meat pile up again...

"Monty, enough!" Drifter yelled.

His brother didn't move immediately, drawn into the temptation of his power. Spittle dripped from the side of his brother's mouth, foaming white at the corners of his lips. Drifter eased over, motioning with his hands for Moses to take slow breaths. The color of his eyes had already changed to that sickening pale white, empty of pupils. Thick purple whelps bubbled on the surface of his skin, contorting his features.

All at once, he lost his interest. He dropped the people - or what was left of them - onto ground equally soft and mushy as their remains. He took a deep breath. After a few more, he returned to himself.

A chill deeper than anything the rain could cause ran down Drifter's spine. Seein' this mind stuff (telepathy? telekinesis?) always disturbed him. He supposed turning into a giant lizard was equally unnerving to some people.

"Stay with us. We're gonna need you," he said to Monty. *Look forward,* Drifter wanted to say, but he found his tongue stuck on the roof of his mouth. He *thought* he had the stomach for this kinda thing.

Tired and a little thunderstruck, Drifter led them through the dark trees and up the hillside. They were heading towards the back end of the Distillery, which wasn't nearly as impressive as the front, only sewer drains and garbage bins.

Once they arrived, they saw Thunder standing with a small group of boys and girls around him. His oldest (the first of many and should be considered an accomplishment considering how many siblings she had to deal with) stood beside him. Eleen - a spitting image of her father with her dark hair, and sharp eyes, and lean features - stood hunched over, panting and muttering under her breath. By the look on Thunder's face, Drifter could see there wasn't good news.

"Three problems," Thunder growled as they approached. "There's explosives on the road, they're in my Distillery, and Toby's trapped inside."

"Don't worry about it. I got him," Drifter said, "Anything else I need to know 'bout?"

"Except the shooting and the bombs? Nothin' much. Someone saw the Captain 'round here somewhere."

"Once I got Toby, we're getting out of here. No need to lose any more kin off this."

Thunder mumbled something under his breath, holding what Drifter now saw as his ruined arm. "'right. Y'know what we're gonna have to do."

"I gotta back up plan. Do what you hafta do."

Dusk Mountain Blues

"Get it started. I'll be out in a few. Make sure Moses don't overextend himself."

Another pack of soldiers rolled over the hills to the south. Drifter loaded his revolver and prepared to shoot, but Thunder pushed him off towards the Distillery; he needed to think about Toby first.

Drifter left Thunder to fend off the soldiers, rushing through to the back door with the sound of gunfire rippling behind him. He yanked the door open, the smell of dust and days-old garbage hitting him in the face. The smell of smoke lay soft within the rotten stench of the single-passage dark corridor of the back entrance. After running for what felt like a small eternity, the corridor spewed him out into the massive main room of beer, moonshine, and an ever-growing inferno. Drifter cursed. Some idiot tripped the failsafe. Not entirely from the look of it. *How'd they managed to do that?* Perhaps someone saw it and managed stop it, or Thunder hadn't quite rigged the place right, but it wasn't doing what it was intended to do.

...And that was explode.

The Caldwells had learned things on their time on this planet - most importantly, don't leave behind anything they can use.

Though this was Thunder's largest home and main factory for his products, it wasn't his only one. Still, this was gonna be a loss. Hundreds of thick wooden kegs lined every wall, stacked upwards and outwards to the window. Some were filled with drinks, while other kegs were only to get certain questionable merchandise off planet. Over a dozen metal fermenters and stills glimmered from the warm light of small fires peppered throughout the main room.

Drifter blinked away the pain in his sweat-burning eyes, stepping in with care. The place was swarmed with Bluecoats. *Whatdya lookin' for, ya morons?* That creeping hunch that Moses had in the truck resonated in his head like an echo in a cave. They *were* looking for something on the planet; getting rid of some backwater mutant clan was an added bonus. *But what?* There weren't too many things on this planet that he didn't know about. What made them think that they had found whatever they were looking for? Drifter shook off the thought. *Toby. Gotta find Toby.*

Drifter eyed the top floor, which overlooked the main floor. Tucked tight within the crevice of a few stacked boxes he saw the little man, shaking and afraid. He had found a good hiding spot, at least. No fires had started up there, and the failsafe still had a long time before it truly went off, but that didn't mean the Little Thunder wasn't in danger. Smoke and little lungs didn't play well together.

One brother had already had to bury a grandkid. He wasn't gonna let it stand twice.

How I'm gonna get up there? There was bound to be another way up. There had to be - the rest of the kids had made it out. Drifter crept around the corners, low and tight. The Bluecoats weren't lookin' for nobody, so they weren't gonna find nobody. That was usually how it went down at least.

Slithering through the shadows of machinery, he listened. The Bluecoats talked amongst themselves, frustration and worry from the creeping flames littering their words. The lean figure with a few more stars on his fancy lil' coat barked some orders to the rest.

"It has to be here. It's *no* way that these hoarding hillfolks haven't found it yet. Search harder. I'm not gonna be the one to explain it to the Major - or worse, to the Chairwoman." They were opening up kegs now; a dangerous thing. Big Thunder liked rigging things. Call it an odd pastime of his older brother. Sooner rather than later, they were gonna trip something they were gonna wish they hadn't.

Right now, I wish they wouldn't. When they did, he might want to be miles and miles away. Drifter gave a low groan in his head. He had to hurry.

He slipped through the darker side of the room, narrowly escaping the sight of an annoyed, stocky man in a stupid hat. After a little searching, he found a small ladder to the second floor. Drifter cursed. There was no way that he could use that without being seen. He thought himself a mighty fast climber, but he was an old man now, and it wasn't the quietest way to get up there. Besides, Thunder had a few children that didn't have use of their limbs; he would've built another way up.

I should know my way 'round. He knew that his patience made him the best one for this job, but gosh darn it, he wished that he knew a bit more about the actual layout. Winging it was only fun when it was just your own life in danger.

Again, he swept his gaze around room, taking everything he could. If the solution was a snake, it would've bitten him. A simple door leading to a wrapping ramp was only a stone's throw away, light still on from when the others escaped. At least he didn't have to climb. *I'm not as young as I once was, after all.*

Waiting until the Bluecoats were distracted, he dashed through the door and up the ramp to the second floor.

A second problem arose once he made it up. He'd wondered why Toby hadn't moved, despite being younger and pretty fast, able to make it to the ramped corridor with ease. Underfoot was metal mesh flooring meant for overlooking the main floor. Each step came with a loud *chink*. Tip toeing did nothing to stifle the noise. To a little boy seeing a bunch of strangers with guns below him, the sound might as well have been a siren sayin' *shoot me*.

There was no way around it. The young boy turned his head, finally seeing his good ol' uncle tiptoeing across the metal floor. Drifter crept forward, putting a single finger on his mouth telling the boy to keep quiet. A wide smile stretched across the little boy's face. Drifter smiled back, taking steps forward. *Chink. Chink. Chink.* Three steps. A little closer. *Chink. Chink. Chink.* A little more. *Chink.* Whispers below. Drifter felt his muscles tighten. *Chink.* One more step. The muffled sounds below grew a little louder. Dipping low, he joined the little boy underneath boxes of what appeared to be tools.

Drifter gave a brief glance over the railing. The Coats had noticed the sound but couldn't figure out where it came from.

"'Ey, Little Thunder," he whispered. "Your grandpa and mom's worried 'bout ya. How about I get you out of here, buddy?"

Toby nodded. *Smart kid. 'Course he is, he's a Caldwell.* Drifter swept the boy up, and his little arms locked around his neck.

"Up ya go." He heaved the thin boy over his shoulder. Toby remained silent. Drifter took tentative steps backwards, the vague taste of thick ash and alcohol in his mouth. The fire was getting stronger by the second, touching on the outskirts of an inferno. He kept Toby close to his shoulder. The less the little boy breathed in whatever was in the air, the better.

He took more steps back down the corridor, his heart slamming into his chest. *Clink. Clunk. Bang.* The smallest part of the railing fell away, tumbling down to the bottom and onto a soldier's fancy blue cap. He looked up.

Drifter wasn't a man to believe in luck, whether good or bad; things either went your way or they didn't. But seeing every eye slowly inch up to the second floor over one single screw-sized debris made him re-evaluate his outlook.

He grabbed Toby a bit closer. Getting this boy to safety took priority over ripping these men's faces off. They blinked in confusion, recognition dawning on their faces minute by minute. They knew who he was.

The leader of the pack recovered first, drawing his laser rifle up. An order was on his lips, but he was a little slow on the draw; Drifter shouted first.

"Get on my back, kid, take my weapons and hold on," Drifter said, taking advantage of the stunned hesitation. "Hold on tight."

Toby knew what was going to happen next. He scrambled onto Drifter's back faster than a squirrel scurrying up a tree with the weapons around his small shoulders. Once Toby was tightly secured, Drifter vaulted off the ledge.

They were falling for a brief second, the rain of lasers flying around them. His muscles strained tight against his body, bones cracking and reforming underneath his skin. From there, he grew.

He landed with a powerful thump on the ground. The wooden floor shattered beneath his landing. His mass took up a little under a quarter of the room, his long green tail wrapping the full length around. No matter how many times he had done this across his decades, the feeling of transformation felt as foreign as the first time.

The little boy on his back cheered in excitement. No doubt Bobby had filled the boy's head with all kinds of stories about his great-uncle Luke.

A few lasers smacked hot against his skin, the red rays exploding in bursts through the lizard scales and insect carapace. The heat left his scales glowing red and painful.

Mutant Killers. High-heat lasers meant to cut through him. This time, they were prepared for him.

The leader stepped forward, his entire forearm hissing open into a well-fashioned bullet gatling. The thick shadows from the rafters fell over the man's scowling face. There was an odd red sheen to his eyes, a strange color to the beads of sweat rolling down his face.

Drifter grinded the inner workings of his teeth, slamming his tail into the ground. This was Captain Owen Xan - and he was a 'roid.

He looked, smelled, sweated, and breathed like humans. Some androids even ate and drank. Make no mistake, though, they weren't human. Given a directive whether by their creator or by their own judgement, they would kill anyone without a second thought. Drifter winced. He could only assume that the gatling wasn't for show.

"I'm going to ask you once, stand down," Captain Xan said. "Tell us where it is."

Drifter didn't know what *it* was, and he didn't care right now. He growled and snapped his teeth.

"Have it your way, animal."

The rain of laser fire began again at the tip of the captain's head. Drifter kept forward, shouldering the blows. His exoskeleton and scales were a bit weaker on the front of his body, but he couldn't risk turning around.

He took every explosion, the heat melting away his skin. The pain rippled through him, resonated with him. He couldn't take this for long. The pain ran through his body, bursting against his skin over and over again in rapid succession. He pressed forward, the thought of the little boy melted into bone by those rifles or that gatling giving him strength.

Family was his reward for surviving that planet. Family was his life and his joy. He would do dang well anything for them, whether that's stealing or killing. They wouldn't take another one of his kin away from him. No, not with the idea of Pit's boy in the dirt still fresh in his head.

Drifter let out an ear-splitting roar.

He leapt over the crowd, through the pipes of the distiller and fermenters, crashing through a few kegs on the other side. Clear alcohol sprawled against the surface, spreading out. The fires soon drank it up the liquid within seconds, adding even more flames to the mix. *Perhaps the explosion idea wasn't Thunder's best.*

Toby yelped in excitement the way only a little boy could as the inferno grew. This was one of Bobby's brood, alright. Good. An excited boy could make good decisions; a scared one couldn't. *At least one of us is havin' a good time.*

"Keep yer head down," Drifter growled in his best impression of a responsible adult. "You don't wanna breathe this in."

Drifter headed towards the barred front door, grabbing the boy. The heavy sounds of his massive claws scraped against the wood as he increased his speed, pushing all four of his legs further and further. Only a few minutes into the transformation, his body strained to keep up the speed, and everything already ached. *Gettin' old, ol' boy. Ya gettin' old.* Beast or man, that fact remained the same.

Anytime now, the flames were going to find their mark. He didn't want to be here when that happened.

He shouldered through the front door with all the power he could muster through the pain of the still-pelting lasers on his back. He howled, splinters of wood stabbing into the now soft parts of his melted skin. The door wouldn't budge. The bulk, the scales, the monstrous mix of a lizard and a bug, underneath it all was blood, muscle and bones. Those things made an old boy feel a little less invincible. One more shove. One powerful lurch - and then the door left its hinges.

The air gave the fire a much-needed meal to go with its drink.

The failsafes went off all at once. An ear-splitting sound rippled through the once quiet valley. Drifter pulled out another leap, using all his muscles to jump onto the cliffs. He ran through the forest with Toby still attached to him. He was looking back, Drifter knew. That was his home in flames, crumbling to the ground. The excitement had died for him, leaving only the ash to remain.

Drifter remembered having those feelings as a kid. He'd hoped for them to never taste that sour bitterness so young. *Homes can be rebuilt. You can't.*

"Uncle Luke."

"Yeah, Lil' Thunder."

"They're still alive."

Drifter turned his head. The boy's eyes hadn't failed him. Among the ruins of the Drum, Captain Owen stood with his team. A light blue force field enveloped the area, leaving none of the men to die in that horrible explosion. At the very least, it slowed them down. Force fields of that strength came up quick enough and held their shape for a bit. They didn't come down easy from there. At the very least, anything the Bluecoats could use against them, whether they knew the value of it or not, was destroyed.

The Caldwells needed to clear their heads, create a better plan. *Think we might've underestimated the Coats here.* It was time they formed up and retreated. There was a time to fight...and a time to turn tail and run.

Chapter 11

Moth Wings
Kindle

"I've had the pleasure of the first taste of the Flame. That was when I realized we weren't that much different from moths." --Remy Breaux

Kindle watched the end of the world and thought nothing of it.

The memories of it came and went through her waking hours and her sleep. The Flame, as the name suggested, found places of warmth within C'dar's memories. Sometimes that was good - hands huddled around a bonfire, laughter in the air. Much more often, though, it was the fires of war the visions latched onto.

The world remembered the day it died. It remembered the bombs, the warships of the warring colonies that brought the first Civilization to its knees. Kindle saw the orbital strikes from the Dreadnaughts, the crash of a Cruiser off the shores, the missiles and the raids from the A.I. Darts. She tasted the horror on the air, the desperation locked into the people fighting the war.

The vision was old now. She'd combed through its contents hundreds of times by now, sitting in her bed among the fireflies and the thick smell of swamp water. Kindle blinked the visions away from her own head. After a few deep breaths to anchor herself to reality, she tore the sheet from her bed and walked to the window, flinging it open.

The almost eternal night of the swamp and the *barj* made it difficult to tell what time of day it was. The rain didn't help much. Over the crown of trees, harsh lightning streaked, and leaves spun violently in circles. An unsettling feeling churned in her gut. She hadn't ever thought that she would feel the way her pa did about storms; it never made sense until now.

She leaned over the pane of the window, gathering her strength bit by bit through the humid air. Wind whistled through the willows of the swamp, splashing her face with much needed droplets of water, cooling her down.

Remy warned her that this would happen the deeper she dove through the Flames. Soon she would be able to block it out. That couldn't come soon enough. Trying to block it all out felt like trying to stop a speeding truck with her hands.

Just when she thought she was in the clear, another vision swam into her mind. This one felt different than the ones of the past. Urgency ran through her, quickening her heart. She saw a quick glance of a valley, pines and oaks standing tall. She heard a river rushing beside her, the smell of its freshwater odd against where she knew she really was. She turned to see the very thing that drew her here.

The Distillery she saw now wasn't the one in her memories, the one filled with her uncle's laughter and her dozens of cousins. Embers of the once-massive building still burned. Blurry figures stood in the middle within a dome of blue lights. Kindle tried to search through the vision for clues. She came up empty. The vision dissolved seconds later.

Is someone dead? Who was there? What *happened?* She needed to find out.

Grabbing her revolver Coal from her nightstand, she hurried out of the room. She realized it must have been afternoon. The workers and servants of the lavish manor buzzed from room to room. Kindle stared over the lip of the railing of the second floor, looking down. The chatter rose at the sight of her. Heads turned every time she made eye contact. She knew that look; everyone did it when they knew something they didn't want to share. She took to the steps, descending down the spiral with her shoulders squared, back straight. The crowds parted around her. The chatter stopped. Eyes found her and quickly lost focus. She ignored them all.

Cassie Caldwell was on a manhunt for her grandfather. No matter what they needed of her, family came first. Whatever Remy wanted; it would need to wait.

She found him in his lab. The empty-gazed wooden masks gave her no pause today. Black wax candles burning an odd purple fire sat around his cleared desk. A thin, lavender holographic screen stretched over the entire length of the room; a foreign alphabet cascaded down it in a waterfall of text, and Remy's eyes gleaned obvious information there that Kindle couldn't see.

He hadn't noticed her. She took a few more steps, getting a bit closer. He spoke to whoever he was speaking to with audible clicks from the back of his throat. In the shadows, he looked more alien than he ever had before. Kindle swore she saw a few green tentacles draped over his chest like her grandpa's snow-white beard.

Remy's my pa too.

"Grandpa?" she asked in a tentative voice. She searched for a little hardness in her voice and found nothing of the sort. "I'm leaving."

Remy snapped his fingers and the screen dissolved in a burst of white light. He swiveled in his chair. A spark of what looked like amusement glittered in those purple eyes.

He leaned forward. "Any particular reason why?" he asked, tilting his head.

"My family's in trouble."

Remy paced around the room. "Saving your family won't really matter if the world dies while you're not looking, my dear."

"You think I care 'bout that right now?"

"It's this wonderful thing called priorities. Young people don't seem to see its value very much."

Kindle opened her mouth for a comeback. She tried to think of witty retort. When nothing came to mind, she snarled out her frustration. The only comfort she found was in the cool finish of Coal.

All logic told her that it wasn't Remy's fault that this was happening. He more than likely didn't have a stake in all this. The apathy soured her of him further. She understood his concerns and wants; that didn't mean she had to like it.

She cared about her grandpa and pa more than the planet at this very moment. That wasn't going to change. And he couldn't stop her no matter how menacingly he sat in that stupid swivel chair.

"I'm leaving," she repeated. "You can't stop me."

"Yes, I can," Remy said with a shrug. "But you're gonna stay of your own accord, because I have something you want."

"What?"

"A way to save them." Remy put his hand up. Kindle hated that she couldn't charge through the conversation anyway. "They're alive. I had one of my ships scout ahead. Your family handled themselves well against the Captain's platoon; only a few of them were injured in the attack, and they gave them quite the beating along the way.

"Drifter's in pretty bad shape, last time we saw. He helped one of the little ones out of the building. An... unfortunate underestimation almost got him killed. To think that the Civilization developed a fully functional, sentient 'roid - and a mutant killer at that..." Remy approached his desk, tapping his finger against the wood. "But it is what it is. They handled themselves and that's all that matters for now." He kept his hand up. "But how long are they gonna hold out, Cassie? How long before the Major gets involved and decimates everyone you love? What will you be able to do with that little pistol alone? You're a good shot, but taking down a cyborg and an android meant specifically to destroy your family.... that's not gonna work."

"What are you gettin' at?" Kindle snapped.

"I'm *getting* at the fact that you're going to need all the help you can get to beat them. You have a rare opportunity to learn something from us, Cassie. Until Woody, we didn't mingle with your family even when they crashed on that mountain. Honestly, I didn't care much about them. I daresay they weren't interesting to me at the time. Then slowly my interest rose.

"They - or, I suppose, your family - grew more and more powerful, like a primitive race finding metal and inventing fire. Before long, they had their little community in the mountains, the valleys, the forests, the plains, with scavenged and invented technology of their own. They were everywhere, and with them came the trouble of your Bluecoats. Still we didn't interfere. We stayed here." Remy gestured to the place around him with his arms as though showing it off. "But sooner or later, they were going to tip the scales against your family, and this is where it happens.

"But you can be the stone on the other side. You can be the Shaman. You can make this difference that you couldn't before."

Kindle took some steps forwards to the middle of the room, her hand easing off Coal. Remy rocked in his chair; she tried to read his expression. He was smiling, but there was nothing there, not in his eyes or the curve his lips, like a man pretending to understand what the expression meant. The shadows of the *barj* danced around his hard features, the purple candlelight appearing to stretch his already long face.

A coldness swept the room. She took a sharp breath and another step forward, her bare feet against the cold hardwood floors. She straightened her back. Like her grandpa always said, *when you're feelin' low, act tough*. She walked to the center of the room; a sharp breath caught in her lungs.

"What do you get outta this?" And with that courage, a few orange flames flickered into life around her. Warmth filled her. "What are you tryin' to teach?"

"Fear, understanding, light, and darkness. That's what I'm tryin' to teach you. The moment you stepped in here, you made your choice. Whatcha do with it will be up to you." Remy stood up, straightening his dark purple vest and smoothing his slacks. "I'm going to go for a walk. Care to join? I have things to do around the village and you can't stay cooped up in this house forever. I'm more than sure that's not the type of life that you're trying to live."

Kindle sighed, letting go of the tension in her chest. The candlelight died again, leaving the thick darkness of the shadows in its wake. The electric lights hummed on soon after, filling the lab with a clinically cold white light.

Dusk Mountain Blues

The *barj* remained, inky black stains against hard, dark wood floors and walls; they inched towards her for a brief second. In that moment, they felt more alive. She swore she heard a heartbeat within them.

She choked down her fear. *Fear, understanding, light, and darkness.* The words repeated inside her mind in a loop even after they left the lab. What did he want and what was she going to get?

She followed Remy through the crowded main parlor and out into the village square. From the center, he took her down what felt like the longest floating wood path in the entire village. Oddly enough, the storm lightened at their arrival, leaving only small traces that it had even been there. The sun peeked from the canopy above, rays digging hard against the thick layers of leaves. The air was cool and fresh from the morning with the odd hominess of the swamp.

Kindle allowed herself to soak in the details of the bayou, the tall trees swallowing the water with green touches and brown teeth. A little further away she saw old half-sunken shacks and unfinished barebone homes reclaimed by nature. One ivy-covered mansion had become the den of quite a large creature; it lumbered through the beams of the first floor with its thick dark brown fur and harsh purple eyes. She didn't want to know more about whatever that was and hoped with all her might that it didn't want anything to do with them. They passed it without incident.

Willow's Grove behind them, they continued onwards. The water of the lagoon gave way to a winding, muddy uphill path. The air around them thickened to an uncomfortable warmth, choking her with every breath. Sweat dripped down her face and pricked her eyes with its salt. She pushed on by focusing on the things around her; thick brown posts were hammered into the ground and adorned with red roses, yellow daisies, and the occasional odd blue colored flower. Up further, a few were even stone, carved in the harsh lines of a foreign language. They came upon the summit of the muddy hill, a clearing surrounded tall pale-barked trees with soft blue leaves on all sides.

"Watch your step. It gets kinda bad up here." Remy flicked his wrist, extending a long wooden pole from a bracelet he wore. A large purple sphere-shaped drone rose from the tip of the staff like a gout of flame from a wizard's palm. Light emitted around them from the AI's eye as it swept the area. Soft audible beeps followed every sweep. *A scan. For what?*

"Have you thought about why I let you keep your weapon? Or even why I let your father bring it in here? I figured at some point I would have to teach something of our means of defense but yours will do for now." Kindle didn't like the way he said it, teetering close on disgust; but she let it go. "It's best for you to be comfortable. Do you have ammo? Is it energy or traditional?"

"Good ol' fashioned bullets."

"Petro," Remy called out. The drone turned. "Outfit her with what she needs."

The drone, Petro, hovered over. "Weapon?" it asked with a smooth, soft voice. Somehow it sounded familiar.

Kindle pulled her weapon from her side. The drone scanned it for a brief second, whistling a faint song while it worked. Materials began to form in its translucent stomach. It spun metal with the ease of crocheter with yarn, light bending to create shells for her weapon.

She hadn't heard of any drone that could've done that outside of the Civilization. Doc and his family would've known what it was called, but Kindle was drawing a hard-blank right now; her mind was too preoccupied with why she needed the weapon in the first place.

Petro dropped quite a few shells in her hand. "Ask at any time during the trial if you need more," the drone said. "Good luck." It whistled its way back to its master.

Kindle blinked in amazement, stuffing the spare shells into her pocket. She would've found Petro amusing if it hadn't just dropped ammo into her hand and wished her the best - for what, she hadn't a clue.

She thought to ask; she even would have if her grandfather didn't blow a dang horn.

The horn was made of black bone, cut into a twisting spiral and tipped with gold around the mouthpiece. Foreign symbols on the side glowed whiter and whiter with each subsequent howl. The sound pulsated through her chest, bumped and burned hot in her ribs. When Remy put the horn down to his side, his lips were red and a little broken on the lower lip.

Another sound followed after the horn's died; a powerful stomping and the crunching of wood and stone. She looked at her grandfather again, expecting an answer of some sort. Again *nothing*. He wouldn't say what was going on. By now though, she knew what was happening. She also knew when a wild animal was headed her way - her pa taught her that, at least.

Survival took over from there.

Kindle wheeled around towards the sound of uprooting trees. She'd watched Pa and his brothers deforest some of the valley for their farms when she young. She remembered large trees crashing into the dust against the weight of Doc's harvester mechs on those warms days under the sun. She remembered the amazement and trickle of fear she felt as they fell, or worse - crunched under the spinning blades.

To this, that memory of fear felt like nothing.

The monster hacked through the land with little effort, and nowhere near as clean as the machines. It came through the final patch of trees with an explosive burst of bark, needles, and leaves; Kindle's eyes widened at the sight of the grueling, twisted monster stampeding after her. The black mass of flesh, similar to a large lizard with shining wine-colored scales, whipped around on the tips of its claws. It blinked at her, oversized head tilting. The motion reminded her of grandfather.

This thing ain't your grandpa. This thing's gonna kill you.

The first shot was often the best shot. She unloaded with Coal. The first few shots ricocheted off the scales, bouncing dangerously close to her own feet. The only thing it managed to harm was the creature's demeanor; before, it was angry but curious. Now only hot rage remained.

It charged at her with its full vigor now, snapping its jaws at her with its hundreds of teeth. Though strong, it wasn't fast by any means - the run to the clearing must've taken a lot of its energy. Kindle needed to keep moving. She focused, a cold concentration falling over her. The creature swiped with one of its red claws, trying to cut her in half. She danced back and landed a few shots in the inner side of the beast's belly. Pockets of blood hit her on the face; she felt the warmth and taste of it in her mouth. The creature howled and thrashed.

A claw sailed through the air and caught her on the face. New blood - *her* blood - sprayed from an open wound on her forehead and down her right eye. She kept moving, heart pounding in her chest as she ran in circles around the creature, reloading for another round. The lizard - dragon, wyrm, whatever - kept its assault. If anything, it grew more and more ravenous with every attack. She rolled through her next attack, firing at the creature's head. One bullet caught what she was aiming for this entire time: the eye. It exploded in a bubble of blood.

The creature howled its pain, doubling over and writhing in the dirt. *Can't do much about your eye,* Uncle Monty's son Tiger had said after Kindle accidentally shot it out, and then laughed it off. *No shame aiming for it when you have no other options. Sometimes you just gotta take a cheap shot.*

Kindle went for the killing blow to the back of the neck. The shot had no business missing. Kindle stepped back a little too late. She sailed through the air, her legs swept underneath her by a sweep of the tail, and landed on her back. Pain shot up her entire body. Tears rolled down her face. She squirmed, subtly aware of the heavy scaled tail to her right and the recovering beast looming over her.

Coal was still firm in her grasp - one thing that her family had drilled in her head was to never let your hand leave your gun. She tried again, firing at a range so close she felt the heat of her own discharge. Again, the bullets didn't hit. This time she saw why - while it had scales for physical defense, it also had adapted another defense. The scales on the back of its neck flared up, emitting a light blue pulse of energy; some sort of kinetic barrier similar to a portable shield. The eye shot was more luck than anything. It wouldn't allow her to get away with that again. Kindle would've been impressed if she didn't fear for her life.

It's a wyrkel. And like none she'd ever seen before, probably bred for this trial. *That means...*

She knew how to kill it.

The *barj wyrkel* snapped down with his maw. Kindle rolled to her feet, narrowly escaping the hundreds of teeth. "Petro! A spear," she shouted. The *wyrkel* clawed at her, tearing through the cloth on her shoulder. She cried out in pain. She had to keep moving. The big bastard smelled blood now and with blood, a meal.

It jumped forward, trying to crush her with its weight. She barely managed to dodge this time, twisting her body at the last second; in that one instant, Petro the drone dropped a lance in her free hand. She spun it upright, the crystallized purple tip shining, scattering light from the torches. She went to stab it and got what she expected in her gut the entire time: the fire from the lizard's maw.

Blazes struck her in full force, and she smiled. Energy weapons. Bon fires. Extreme sunlight. Heat of any kind gave her strength. She pushed through the inferno using her pistol arm and her shoulder. Smoke hissed from the odd holes opening on the surface of her dark skin, tickling the skin and muscle it ran by. She'd learned to get used to it at young age; this time, though, something was different.

More than strength and speed filled her this time. There was a primal energy attached to the underbelly of the rest of what she already felt. A memory of a woman's face flashed before her eyes, a comforting, familiar face traced with tears - there and then gone in a second. In its stead was a power like she'd never felt before. She stepped forward one step at a time, absorbing all she could to get close enough to.

Dusk Mountain Blues

She pivoted her body at the last minute as the dragon fire stopped. The *wyrkel* yelped, noticing the tip of the spear a little too late. Mimicking every day she spent spearfishing with her father, she plunged the spear into the dragon's throat.

Muscle and gore plopped against the dirt and her shoeless feet. The spear had gone clean through the shattered teeth of the *wyrkel*, up through the roof of its mouth. What surprised her wasn't the strength of her attack - she had done similar things before with enough heat coursing through her. No, the surprise came from the smoldering remains of everything left.

On the tip of her spear was only the *wyrkel*'s head. The rest was gone as though caught in explosion. White fires burned against blackened bones where a body should've been. What was the saying: "don't fight fire with fire." Well, she did. Hers had won.

A tiredness swept over her. She dropped Coal and the spear tipped with the beheaded *wyrkel* to the ground. Adrenaline still pumped extra beats into her heart, but soon that, too, would fade. Her mind wasn't on the battle anymore; it was on that woman she'd seen in that brief moment of power, the soft features of her familiar, dark-skinned face looking down on her, soundless words on her lips and soft tears on her cheeks.

Mom. She hadn't ever seen her. Her dad didn't have a single picture of her. Yet she knew. Every part of her knew that was her mom.

Why now though?

Kindle pushed the thought from her mind. Everything felt a little odd for a second. Her knees quaked, her mind swam; but she was still standing.

Through the mayhem of everything that happened, Remy stood. There was no applause or fanfare of any kind. He stood, head cocked, with a smile on his face - one that could easily be mistaken for pride if she hadn't seen a real one million times on Grandpa Drifter's face. No. He wasn't proud of her. He *expected* her to pass this trial one way or another. What was on Grandpa Remy's face was a hunger, a want, a need so deep it was everywhere in him.

What do you want? she wanted to scream at him. *What are you getting out of this?*

She staggered forward. "Was that acceptable?" she managed to choke out.

Remy laughed. "It seems like there's much more of Ina in you than I gave you credit for. She gave me the same look when I brought her here at your age. You might've killed Yana faster than your mother did Oyi. The result was the same." He shrugged. "How d'ya feel?

Y'know, aside from the beatings itself, you should feel different - like something opened. That was how Ina explained it. The shadow half of the Flame, I fear, is a lot less open about it, so I'm gonna have to take her word for it. So…" he arched an eyebrow. "Tell me. How do'ya feel?

"I feel fine. I just wanna head back now."

Remy put his hands in the air. "Listen, this was tradition for all Shamans. Or, I guess, potential Shamans. I had no intention of letting you die, and you yourself said you wanted to get better at this. You came here wanting to know more and you can leave at any time. You won't though. I have a thing you want. You want to protect your family from the Bluecoats. I want you to help me save this planet from itself. That was the agreement." He squinted his eyes. "Was it not our agreement, granddaughter?""

I don't wanna talk 'bout this right now. Kindle picked up Coal from the ground and plucked her new spear from the carcass. She took in a deep breath, fighting off the heavy fatigue anchoring her every movement. Buried under that fog stirred an uncertain power in herself she couldn't recognize. Reflexes told her to choke it down, keep it controlled. The Flame bucked back, rolling up her stomach and up her chest to the point that it burned. The pains from the cuts and bruises meant nothing in that brief second of dizzying agony. She exhaled, letting the fire cool.

Her mom was right. It *was* like a door being opened - a door that lost its hinges and laid on the floor. There was no closing it now.

Chapter 12

Humility//Hubris
Appetite

"They're strong, Major, but not as strong as they think they are. When it's all said and done, they are relatively human and I am not."
-- Owen Xan, XA-003 Bioandroid, Sixth Battalion of the Bluecoats Fleet.

"Hm. They lived."

Major Debenham put down his fork with a satisfying clank on the fine plate. He licked syrup from his lips, the crumbled pecans littering the stubble on his face. He closed the translucent blue screen of the video feed with a swipe of his finger; the audio died soon after.

Appetite readjusted in his chair beside the good Major, stuffing down a grin. The Drum may have been gone, and the gunfights still raged on, but they did much better than the Bluecoats expected.

The Major leaned back in his wooden chair. For the first time upon his sudden appearance on the Homestead, he didn't look as poised. Appetite reckoned that it was quite the opposite - the anger in the major's eyes betrayed his cool-headed demeanor.

Debenham stood up from his chair, pushing himself away from the table. "You saw this, didn't you?" he asked the matriarch sitting pleased at the other end of the table. "But how far can you see? When will that confidence of y'all's burn out?"

"Steven," the Augur of Owls said in her sweetest voice, reserved for only her enemies, "I let you in my house. Not out of hospitality, but because if you left, you would've tipped the battle. There was no way Luke and his brothers could match you, not yet. But with you here, it gave us a little time. You're going to have to recover and we can plan a bit more. This isn't the end. You know it, I know it. So please, stop acting like you're upset 'cause it's not easy."

"I *am* upset, Mrs. Caldwell. I don't wanna be here. I would much rather be with my wife and my children. I'll admit I find the fighting enjoyable, but at the end of the day, I don't view y'all as meat. However, I can't let you leave. What you're doing here is selfish. You don't see it, but there's an order of things forming. Laws are being made and structure is forming. The Military Fleets, League of Colonies, the Science Committee, even the Churches of the Five Lights and the necessary evils of the Viscount Corporations - the Civilization is rebuilding itself. C'dar would've made a great colony for people but everyone 'round these parts knows about *you* people. My question is *why*. Why do this? For *what*, complete freedom?"

Appetite watched words come to his mother's lips but never made it out. Freedom wasn't some value that the Caldwells believed in; freedom was who they *were*. The crashed spaceship served as a symbol of their escape, their drive to get away from it all. Histories of old-world countries were the first thing that Drifter taught himself to read. He grew up learning of fights for freedom - a tattered and frayed old-world flag even hung in his workshop, one that supposedly symbolized freedom.

You don't know us very well, Appetite thought. And why would he? He only saw them as an obstacle in the way of their peace. He couldn't see how that peace came with a price. *You've only seen good things 'bout them; we've only seen the bad.* One thing Appetite learned on his travels with Ina was that everyone thought their way of life was right.

"It's 'bout time you leave."

Major Debenham blinked at Appetite's cold words. "You're probably right. I've overstayed my welcome." The Major rose from his chair. Standing at his full height, the navy man still had to crane his neck to meet Appetite eye to eye. He gave a deep sigh and gathered his stuff in his pack. "I'll admit," he said, his voice whipped back to his fatherly tone, "you've all gotten far and played me good here. I got a bit too confident in my boys. That won't happen again."

A tense silence blanketed the small cabin as the Major took towards the door. Jo glared a hole in his back as her fingers danced on the handle of her rifle, Prairie. Loner had put his mask back on, his remaining drone hovering over his head.

Appetite smiled. He had eaten a full meal, more than his share - he was at his most dangerous. As good as he felt right now, he figured they were all more than prepared to fight a cyborg of his level. The only reason they hadn't ripped him apart was the safety of their old ma.

However, nothing happened. The Major slipped on his boots, tightly tied his laces, and opened the door.

What met him on the other side was the full force of the Caldwell family. Major Debenham shook his head, laughing all the while.

Appetite followed him into the living room for a closer look.

On the lawn of the Homestead, Doc sat in the cockpit of a massive unfinished mech - one step up from metal skeleton work. Its exposed reactor glowed red in the dark shadow of the overcast sky. The sheer height of it - over 25 feet into the air, and wide too - sent chills down

Appetite's spine. He had seen mechs before, but nothing of this magnitude.

With Doc were the remaining members of the family who hadn't gone to the Drum. They were armed to the teeth with weapons of all sorts, ranging from well-made laser guns to the common shovel. All for one man. One man who looked completely unfazed by his apparent situation.

He can kill us in an instant. We could take 'im, but not without a lotta graves.

Major Debenham readjusted the strap of his backpack and *took* a step forward, towards the crowd.

All Appetite heard at first was the sharp hiss of steam. He hadn't seen the Major leave the door, only a broken floorboard where his left foot once was. Tracking him with his eyes proved equally impossible. The Major moved like a blue streak of lightning, swerving through the crowd with ease. Doc came down with a large metal fist, machinery cranking into motion, but he proved too slow - the fist only managed to hit the ground, shaking the entire Homestead.

The Major ran under the mech's legs, slipping through the gap with little effort. He hadn't a weapon on him; only his cyborg enhancements. Deftly, he dodged an attack thrown his way, never missing a beat. No one managed a sound bullet or laser on the man aside from scrapes here and there on the Major's navy-blue uniform.

Joseph, one of Moses's sons, stepped forward with a pitchfork to try to catch the Major in the leg. The metal snapped on the man's thigh. Maribelle followed up a shot from a plasma shotgun at point blank range and caught only the light of personal shield. Debenham turned to them, a mild irritation in his eyes, and raised his fist.

"Let 'im go," Appetite shouted from the porch.

Appetite remembered the hole that the Major had left in his cousin. The precision blow had left the boy's lungs outside of his chest. *You'd kill us all if it meant you could go home.* "Don't fight 'im. He's playin' with us. Let 'im go or he's gonna kill y'all."

The mob froze in their tracks. Everyone felt it now. Everyone saw him for that moment. This wasn't a normal Bluecoat, the kind that they'd beaten for decades. This man was trained to kill people like them. *A clockwork case. Bug spray to an ant hill.* They couldn't risk it, not without a plan. Patience. Slow and steady.

Some of his family wasn't going to see this as the right call. Some might even hate him for it. But their lives meant more than their pride; they lowered their weapons.

The Major looked at them, smiling. He lowered his fist. "I see. Someone has some sense. For that, I'll let these boys and girls live. See you around, Woodrow."

And just like that he was gone. Appetite watched him jogging through the forested tree line and leaping over the snow-touched cliffs of the mountain. They watched his back even after they lost track of his silhouette. A collective exhale rippled through the mob, sweat beading on dozens of different faces.

Appetite exhaled himself. His large chest and belly relaxed from the tension. A dull headache bumped hard in the back of his head, reminiscent of fear. Not for himself - Appetite never feared for himself. He feared for everyone around him. He hadn't felt this way before, and for the first time, Woodrow Caldwell knew exactly how his father must've felt every day of his life.

Ø

Drifter stumbled into the door, black and bloodied, burns underneath his oversized clothes. Appetite ran as best as his heft would allow him to his pa's side, propping him up with a meaty arm. Warm and sickly sweat soaked through the thin white t-shirt and denim jeans as though he had jumped into a river of his own making. His face lost all color, his bright eyes dulled to the point of emptiness he had never seen in his father. The worst of all of this was the smell: the choking stench of burnt skin and heavy infection.

Appetite carried his father to his recliner, helping him out of his clothes. They needed to treat these now. With the rest of the brothers in similar conditions, it fell upon their children. This didn't feel like a victory, or even taste like one. From the looks of it, despite the Bluecoats not getting their hands on whatever they wanted in the Drum, they barely got out with their lives.

'Nother push like that... he couldn't think about that right now. His pa needed him.

Jo and Loner rushed over, the first aid kit unlocked and ready to go. They treated the burns the best they could. From medical gels to burn treatments to cold water, Drifter braved through the pain with little more than a few whimpers. He clawed at the arm of his chair, nails ripping through the fake leather and to the cotton underneath.

He can feel pain; that's good. Appetite always saw his father as this invincible man. This wasn't the first time he had come home like this - riddled with bullet holes, bruises, or cuts. He was always smiling before, self assured in whatever he was doing. In that chair, he looked his age; and Appetite hated every second of it.

He held his pa's hand. "You're gonna be okay, Pa. You're gonna be okay." No matter how many times he said it, neither of them felt any better. He gave a tight squeeze on his dad's knuckles, earning a smile. A weak thing. One meant for the family, not for him.

"I'm 'right, boy, you can stop worryin'. All of you stop your dang worrying, I'm a little hurt is all."

"When are you gonna stop this tough act, Pa?" Jo took in a sharp breath. "You ain't as young as you used to be."

"I know," he laughed. Weak. Not the same as before. "I know," he whispered.

They sat quiet as church mice as they took turns dressing him in bandages with soft reverence. Their mother's face was the worst. The usual warmth in her hadn't returned, still clinging to the bitterness and a soft, harsh frown on her face.

"You could've gotten killed," she said. "You would've if Loner didn't tip y'all off. Why'd you go anyway? What were they lookin' for at the Drum?"

"Somethin' we got that we didn't know what we had. Don't think it matters right now. It ain't there, or we just got rid of it." Drifter gritted his yellowed teeth for a brief second. He straightened his back in this chair, serious in his mummified state. "I ain't 'bout that. They tried to take more from me and I ain't havin' it. Y'all are *mine*. This planet is *ours*. I won't let them have it."

Drifter blinked a few times, eyes heavy from fatigue and wear. His consciousness swayed but he shook it off. Somewhere in that fleeting moment, he had a thought. Appetite didn't know what it was or what changed, but it startled his father awake.

"I'm gonna look out for y'all," his pops said after a time. He heaved himself up, groaning and muttering under his breath. "Got some thinkin' to do. Check on everyone, will ya, kiddos?"

Appetite knew those thoughts well. The ones that shocked a man awake in the dead of night, ruining a good nap or a good meal. After that shock wore off, the idea stalked every thought other thought in their head.

Silently, Drifter scrambled to his room. Appetite turned to his mom, expecting an answer and finding nothing. She followed him out of the room, the sounds of her cane knocking against the wood.

They weren't gonna get any more insight on his thoughts until he was ready. Not a second sooner.

Appetite shrugged. *At least you're alive, old man, whatever you're up to.* Appetite gathered himself, worry bundling in a tight knot in his stomach. "Let's leave 'em alone. The best thing for him right now is rest. I'll come back to later."

Jo and Loner agreed. They gathered their things in the house, including the Loner's 'roid, Jesse.

"Woody," Jo said as they opened the door and a blast of lukewarm air hit them in the face. Loner made a noise that sounded a bit like a squeal, the whistling wind hitting his bare chest the wrong way. "I think we're fighting this all wrong."

"Whatcha mean?" Appetite asked. The answer came to him a little later with a little more thought. "Oh."

Looking on the Homestead, the answer came as clear as day. The family sat huddled against a roaring bonfire, bandaging wounds and doctoring up. Someone plucked at a banjo, trying their best at a song of some sort. The booze wasn't out yet, so no singing yet. That fact alone told their tales. How they were acting...it wasn't them. They weren't used to getting punched in the mouth, licking their wounds in a dark corner.

Appetite clenched his teeth, grinding hard against his uneven gums. Only sad faces, even sadder nervous stirring, and the saddest strings from that dang out-of-tune banjo.

A sudden anger blossomed where worry once was. They'd made it out alive with little to no casualties from what he could see; they deserved better than that.

Appetite squared his shoulders, coming to his full towering height, and stuck out his chest. Standing this tall, people noticed ya. They couldn't help it. Their heads turned.

The first one to notice him in the crowd was Big Thunder. Uncle Bobby, the usual life of the party, sat mute at the edge of the bonfire. He held the wrapped and ruined stump that was once his left arm without even a tankard of drink. He had lost his home, his arm, his demeanor like Uncle Buck did before. This wasn't gonna happen again.

"Evan. Can ya -"

"Already on it."

"Jo. Can ya -"

"Already on it."

"Well…" Appetite straightened his shirt. "Good to know we're on the same page."

They dispersed on their own quests to fix this mess. Appetite lumbered home, trying his best to look as confident as possible. Keeping his back straight always proved difficult, a habit Ina had beaten into him. "*A big man like you, hunching over like that. Makes you look small and dumb.*" That was one thing 'bout Ina, she didn't pull punches. At the moment, he was happy to have that tutoring. The more he walked, the more he caught the eyes of his family.

Digging deep, Appetite heaved a bag of charcoal into his arms, tucking the bag underneath the top of a grill. Then, with a massive display of strength, he picked the grill and the heavy bag of charcoal together. That got a whistle from the crowd. A little bit of life. *Better, better.*

Once the grill was in place, he turned around back towards his cabin and headed to the deep freezer in the back. He took some wire and thick rope, tied it across his chest and his stomach in an "x", and adorned it with small metal fishing hooks. From there, it was a matter of getting all the food wrapped and pinned to him. This was where his size came to his advantage. He managed to hook over fifty pounds of chickens, veal, bear, sausage, and beef to himself, weathering the intense cold against his body. *Nope. This ain't gonna be enough.* Bearing through the cold, he waddled to a small shack on the outer rim.

The shack wasn't particularly big, but airtight - one small window, thick wooden walls, and creaky floors. Large barrels, gifts from the Drum, lined every wall of the storage room. The largest nice wooden keg was filled with a hard liquor, a gift from Big Thunder a while back for his eighteenth birthday. He wrapped his big arms around the keg, heaving it up and over his head; a small waft of liquid that had soaked through the wood hit him with a pleasant aroma.

His muscles bulged at the weight of it all. It should be enough for now. If he needed another one, he would just have to make another trip or two.

Appetite turned, closed the door to the shack, and wandered back to the bonfire as the herald of food and alcohol, a god of tomfoolery. He slammed down the keg with a powerful thud, kicking up dirt and dust into the air.

"Alright," he shouted. "We're sittin' here being sorry for ourselves and moping. That ain't us. Yeah, they made a fool outta us, almost killed us. We've been in similar situations before. What's wrong is that we're off our game. We're playin' their game, not ours. So, we're gonna have some good food, have some good drinks, and work through this. We ain't gonna sit by and let 'em get to us. Time to man up and figure out what's gonna happen next. Not in this doom n' gloom type of way, either. We're gonna have a good time doin' it, 'cause that's where we're at our best."

His folks blinked at him, confused. They hadn't expected something like that from Drifter's big, quiet, slow-speaking boy. He was the thinker, the planner, the quiet one in the back, not the one trying to rouse them up. They shared glances for a while, saw the food and the drink he carried. Small grins traveled from person to person. They nodded, life running through the once dead audience.

"And if somebody don't rip that banjo from Bulldog's fingers, I might smash it on his head." That got a laugh at out of them. "We're alive. Y'all made it. We're gonna make it." Their faces changed even more to a blossoming adoration, even among men and women older than him. "How 'bout we eat, we patch up, we get better, and we give 'em what's comin' to 'em."

And like that, he broke through. It was like they all realized at once that this wasn't how it was supposed to be. A few men and women stood up, gathering themselves and helping Appetite with this impromptu cookout. Going out and fighting the Bluecoats on their terms, that wasn't their way. They weren't built for that. They were scavengers, bandits, thieves, raiders. On their quest to avenge their kin, they - and even Drifter, to an extent - had forgotten that. They backed themselves into this shallow grave and now they had to claw out of it. Whether that was with a shovel or dynamite, that was their call.

Looks like they're coming back to me. Next time he was gonna have to be on that battlefield with 'em, it looked like. They needed his sense.

By the time they got all set up around the bonfire, Jo and Loner had returned from their quests.

Loner wasn't the type to want to stick around for things like this. For that reason, a few of the family got a little skittish when he was around. They often forgot that he cared. But you couldn't be raised by Drifter and not care for these crazy folks. He wandered to Big Thunder, sizing his arm with a long measuring tape. The stout man frowned for a second until he realized what was happening.

Loner began that very moment on making a new arm for their uncle, talking him through designs with hard light constructions from his 'roid. Experiencing this almost immediately lifted Thunder's spirit. He had always wanted a cool metal prosthetic. Loner would make the coolest for the excitable old man.

He would've cut his own arm off sooner if he knows this was what was going to happen. Crazy old man.

Jo, on the other hand, returned and mingled with the crowd. She gathered all their weapons, making jokes to each and everyone one of them. Putting the weapons away and getting them prepared needed to happen sooner rather than later. It would give her a project to do since her cooking was outta the question. She worked and fixed Ham Bone a few times. When it came to weapons, though, she was the cream of the crop.

Appetite let them do their thing while he did his. The mood rose again. The weapons away, the start of the crackling charcoal grill, and a few drinks being passed around. *There we go.*

Everyone settled in around the fire. Bulldog brought over a table; Appetite tossed all the frozen meat on it after a quick wipe-off. Bulldog's sister Dane was now plucking at the banjo. She was leagues better than her brother, and knew a few songs that the family recognized, too.

A certain degree of hominess fell over them, especially over the Hounds. They were docile, out of their element again. Ever since Mastiff died, they hadn't been the same. Appetite knew it hurt. It hurt when Jo lost her son and her husband, a close friend of his. Scars don't heal well when you didn't slap medicine on them. Words served good for that. He beckoned them over, stoking the flames until the meat thawed enough. The two Hounds awkwardly shuffled over.

"'Ey," Appetite began. "Y'all doing alright?"

"We're managin'," Dane said. She missed a chord in the song she was playing. Told him she was growing uncomfortable. She adjusted her fingers, her dark hair covering one side of her face in a crow feather-dark veil. *Hadn't slept well since this all started.* Haunted was the only thing tougher than scarred. "Is this 'bout - " Dane began to ask.

Appetite wiped his brow of sweat. "No. No."

Bulldog made a face. He did look like his namesake; squashed face, beady eyes, and small nose. "Where's Cassie?"

"She's with her other grandpa at the swamp right now. Learning a few things."

"Ah…" The two Hounds nodded.

"I wanted to pull ya aside to tell you and your family that you don't have to do it alone. My pa ain't that good with things like that, not good at all. What I'm tryin' to say is that, yeah, we're tough, but we don't have to be quiet 'bout it. My pa and your granddad Pit, they aren't used to talkin' bout things. They keep it inside until it boils over outta their control. I want you to know that ain't good. You're better when you talk 'bout it. Cassie likes you guys and I won't want her to come back to see y'all like that. So, don't keep it inside. Let it out. I want y'all at your best too." The two young pups nodded. They weren't gonna do it now - too embarrassed. One day, though, they would. No rush in that.

They shuffled away. Appetite watched their backs. They were good kids.

"Hey, Woody." Appetite turned his head to see Vermin grinning. The tall, four-armed man cocked his head and gave his cousin a quick punch in the shoulder. "What's gotten into you, man? You sounded like your dad. Shucks, you have me believing we can do this."

"'Cause we can. All it takes is finding our footing."

Chapter 13

Red-Touched Dreams
Drifter

"Burned. Bloodied. Beaten. Broken. The Daedal taught me what those meant. Gettin' blasted reminded me of it. Don't like it. Don't like it at all." -- Luke "Drifter" Caldwell

Drifter hadn't woken in days. He figured it was 'cause his dreams were usually shorter than this.

Vivid dreams were a side effect from the *dream waters* of the stasis pods in his youth. This wasn't for the comfort of the prisoners; more for the safety of the officers. Turned out that it was much easier to control a man after hours or days manipulating their dreams.

Decades later, sleep still came with long streams of lucidity some nights he controlled it, others he didn't. In the days locked within his own mind, he experienced a little of both this time - a twisting river of consciousness, writhing and coiling around bends and smashing into the shore of his own noggin. There were places he recognized, places he ain't seen in years.

Then there were places he hadn't ever seen before in his many years in this galaxy. This part of the dream was one of those.

Drifter looked around, feeling the air on his face and water underneath his toes. He caught his reflection on the waves. There was a younger man looking back at him - in his thirties, with long clay-red hair, bright eyes, and sunburnt, pox-scarred skin. Boy, he was a tall one, all wiry muscle and sinew. Had he gotten shorter?

The red flare of his mustache twisted up into an uneven smile of chipped, yellow teeth. He still had that. Good thing, too. Seeing too much of his younger self without seeing something he recognized now would've been mighty disappointing. Drifter straightened his back, grinning like a dang fool.

It's a dream. But dang it felt good to be young again. He forgot that every moment hadn't always come with a small sting of pain. Felt good. Felt real good.

His dream led him to an open field not too different from the one at the bottom of the mountain. A small trail of smoke rose into the air, coming from deep within the sea of the grass. The blades of grass tickled the hairs of his arms as he walked. He heard the faint crackling of embers among the soft whistling of wind. There was a fire somewhere in the distance. The smell caught his nose a few times, the taste of clean smoke bitter on the roof of his mouth. He knew the taste of a camp or bonfire from a wild or house fire. Maybe desperation ruined the taste. He didn't know; he knew it tasted different and that was 'bout it.

He kept heading for the direction, following his nose. *Ain't like my other dreams. Not at all.* He was a few minutes into the dream and nothing had exploded yet.

There was still time for that, he reckoned.

He made it to the campfire without any incident, much to his disappointment. It was a modest little thing; a few decent-sized logs, a flame whose crown barely reached his knees. A small bird of some sort roasted on a spit, turning on its own by a small mechanism.

Drifter frowned, looked around. There was no one here. Dang well shouldn't be without him knowing about it - his brain, his rules. But there was no denying it; there was stranger here.

The beauty of the landscape darkened around him in the way it did when a big cloud blotted out the sun. He was that cloud. An odd sense of urgency hit him in the way the only a dream could. He reached to his side and found that he didn't have a weapon on him. *Huh.* That wasn't like him. For the first time, he wondered if this was his dream at all.

"Oh, it worked."

A dark, swirling shape appeared. It approached from the opposite side of the dreamscape where the plain's grass grew shorter and became the color of wheat, wearing a long, tattered, dirty red cloak, much like Loner wore when he was forced to go outside. The shape didn't appear like Evan - much too short and slim around some areas.

The shape sat down across from him, tossing back their hood.

Kindle.

The sight of his granddaughter brightened the world again; orange flowers even bloomed around the ring of the clearing.

"Hey Granddad, wassup?"

Those simple words pumped even more life into him. This was better than explosions. Much better.

She stopped the spit and pulled the crispy, browned bird from its pike. "You got hurt pretty bad saving Toby," she said softly, voice touching on hesitation. "They got you pretty good."

"Yeah they did." Drifter frowned. His body remembered for a second that this was a dream. A sharp pain flared all over his skin, bringing tears of pain to his eyes. He shook it off. Dreams were for getting away, at least for a little bit. "Are you - "

"Here? Yes. Can't explain, don't got a lot of time." She ripped off a wing from the bird and handed it to him. "Eat up. It ain't real food but it'll help you survive. Give you somethin' to hold on to."

He didn't question it. The dream did feel different, now that she mentioned it. Deep inside he was holding on. Drifter took the roasted bird from his granddaughter and bit into it. Duck, sweet and savory. He hadn't had duck in a long time. Out of all the animals brought over from the Old World, ducks were oddly rare in certain galaxies. Don't ask him why. No one knew or cared that much at this point. *Maybe they should, though.*

Ravenous, he chewed through to the bone and beckoned for seconds and thirds. Kindle smiled and watched. "You look nice, Grandpa," she said after a time. "I've never seen you so…"

"Not old," he laughed. "Well before your time."

She laughed. "I'm glad that I can see it." The look in her eyes and lips changed for a second to an expression Drifter couldn't pin down. "I don't know what's happenin' here. There's things that Remy isn't telling me. He has his reasons and I know that…but there's more. I don't know what to do, Grandpa. Y'all need me. I know it. I've seen it. You almost died, but if I was there…"

"It would've gone the same way."

"You're probably right. Don't seem right."

"Whatever he asked you to do, can ya say it's not important? What did I always tell you? Always - "

"Handle your business," she finished. Kindle brought her knees to her chest and sighed. "I miss y'all already. It don't say much, do it? I haven't been gone for very long, and I'm already pining to be back at the cabin. I don't like it here."

"'Bout time you left the coop though. You've been a good kid. Maybe too good for Woody." Drifter laughed. He tossed the bones into the sea of grass. "But that ain't why you here, are you? You got somethin' on your mind. Or on my mind? I don't know. Either way you have somethin' important to tell me."

"You need to talk to the Hounds and the rest around my age. Pa laid down some foundation but they need to hear it from you. They backed you into a corner before and you reacted like they expected you to. Not what they needed. They needed to see this man. They needed some kindness, not force. They aren't like Uncle Pit. He's much more emotional and it almost got y'all killed. Get to him. He needs to hear that you care; it might get y'all on track."

It was good advice. Their anger and confusion led to more mistakes than anything. Not only that; revealing how they came to be hadn't helped much. The young'uns picked up on the smaller things like that. Drifter knew that despite his best efforts, he'd gotten caught in the moment and almost got them all killed.

They couldn't go on like that. They couldn't pretend that everything was gonna be okay. Some people needed to talk 'bout bad things; others needed to talk more and never could find the words. A well of thick shame bubbled to the surface of his chest. The feeling tainted the dream world this time with a light, grey colored rain falling from a cloudless sky. The campfire hissed steam like a back-alley cat and then choked like a man spewing on seawater.

"I gotta do better," Drifter whispered. "I gotta do better."

"You would've gotten to it eventually." Kindle smiled. She looked up to the crystal blue sky, raindrops bursting on the bridge of her nose and dripping down her face. "It's 'bout time for you to wake up." She stood up, dusting the dirt and grass off her pants. "Stay safe, Grandpa. I don't wanna lose you."

"I don't wanna lose you either."

Kindle walked over, the camp light glowing against her darker skin. She did look like her mom, but he couldn't help to see a little of Woody and a little of himself in her too. She bent down to him and wrapped her arms around him into a strong hug. Drifter frowned, feeling the tightening fingers against his back. *What's going on, Cassie? What can't ya tell me?* She broke away before he could return it and turned from him.

"I'll come back when I can. Stay alive, all of you."

Drifter went to tap her on the shoulder, but she vanished into a flurry of marigold leaves. She was gone as quickly as she came, leaving her old man alone at the campfire.

The dream world rained cats and dogs without her.

Ø

Drifter was back to being an old fella.

It wasn't too bad, aside from being wrapped from head to toe with bandages. The choking smell of antiseptics and burn treatments filled his nose, followed close by an intolerable itch on his right arm.

He looked around. He was in his bedroom, small as it was. The only window in the room remained open, letting raw and unfiltered light blast him in the face. After a few painful blinks, he searched the room. His wall of his favorite guns right over his bed was dusted and unperturbed. Every corner of the room was clean and swept, his clothes packed into a closet on the side. Someone had taken the time to organize his bookshelf and maps.

What was new was that the same person that cleaned his room brought in the flag from his workshop and hung it on the opposite wall in clear sight. The morning light managed to catch the tattered thing at the right angle, brightening up the pinkish-red and dirty white stripes, and the stars on the faded blue corner – most definitely blue, now that he got a good look at in the light. One of these days he was gonna fix it up with the respect it deserved.

He had to fix himself first.

Drifter rose upright in his bed. An IV pulled at his forearm, tucked deep within the folds of the bandages. A soft beep of the heart monitor chimed on and on. He hadn't noticed it at first. Now that he had, he only wished for it to can it. He went to rip every wire off of his body – until the sheets beside him stirred.

Mary Lu was sound asleep on his stomach, curled up and quiet. He often wondered how she slept with his loud snoring and endless stirring and still managed a good night sleep. Ripping out the IV would sound the heart monitor and she didn't deserve that. Groaning, Drifter forced himself to lie down. No sleeping though. He'd had enough of that for a spell. He placed his hand on his wife's head, running his fingers through her hair. There were worse things than being stuck in bed with the love of your life; much worse things.

He lay there for a little under an hour, musing through hundreds of thoughts. In the forefront was Cassie, his little fire, at the swamps. He had seen some weird crap in the Dusk Orbit planets in the times he went off planet – some real weird crap. He even knew of the Flame and what it could do – or, at least, he knew what Kindle's mom had told him. It wasn't so odd that she could speak to him in his dreams. Her words and his worry of her clung deep to his mind. Her advice was what gave him a little strength, beat up as he was. There were things he needed to make right.

Moses walked into the room, gliding in his hempen brown robe. He looked more himself with his dreads up into a tight bun, amaranth stems and marigold petals woven into the grey. They made eye contact for a brief second. He placed down his concoctions and his kit, walking over to check Drifter's vitals. He had learned all he could about medicine, energy, and farming – the good and just things in life. He wasn't meant for killing, raiding, blood and guts. Not his style. Power like his belongs to people like him. Too bad life didn't work on the same morals.

After Moses finished his checks, he unplugged the medical mess set up where Drifter's nightstand once was. "Time to get up; gotta check your burns. Get up, steady now, don't blow out your back."

Drifter squinted. Moses laughed softly and grinned; Drifter did as he was told, carefully wiggling from Mary's grasp. Once he was upright, Moses wasted no time peeling the bandages from his skin. No matter how much care he took, the burns underneath wailed in an intolerable and agonizing pain.

Drifter caught an eye of the dozens of thick burns on his body from the lasers. Pink, black, brittle skin covered every part of body, which was feeling kinda like tenderized meat after a few goes with a hammer. Drifter poked at one on his chest and got a shock of pain for his trouble. Stupid decision.

Moses shot him a sharp glare. "You're healin' okay. It'll scar pretty bad."

"Always wanted some burn scars. You know this."

"Yeah, when you were twelve…"

Dusk Mountain Blues

"It never went away, Monty, but I was never stupid enough to get 'em on my own."

"Glad to see that you got a little sense left, Luke."

They went quiet for a while. "I messed up," Drifter said, keeping his voice low. He told himself it was not to wake Mary; he always told himself the best lies. "I only put us in danger taking that fight at the Drum. I got baited and we almost died for it. We got lucky. That's all it was — dumb luck. A stroke of dumb luck."

"If we wasn't there, Toby might've not been here right now. That little boy is safe 'cause of you, Luke." Moses rewrapped him with new bandages. "You said the same thing when we were flying here to C'dar. Stroke of good luck here and there. It piles up. There's an old saying I heard a while back: *once's chance, twice's coincidence, and third's a pattern.* You ain't dumb luck. Never have been."

"Tell 'im again, Monty."

Seeing his beautiful wife in the morning light brought a tingling to his face; they'd been together for decades, but that hadn't changed. Maybe he was a sap, a hopeless romantic caught in an endless loop of affection. Waking up to her happened to be one of his favorite times of the day, now and forever. He took her by the hand and gently pulled her up and into his arms by the small of her back. For his troubles, she kissed him on his cheek.

A stupid level of warmth hit his cheeks like a young man on his first date. He doubted there was a luckier bastard in the whole world. They left the comfort of their bed together, Moses bowing out gracefully to give him some time to get ready. They took their time after he was gone.

When they were ready, Drifter escorted his wife – or she escorted him – out of the bedroom and into the living room. To his surprise, all his brothers were here. Pit played with his dog, Sprinkles – a massive black-furred beast with three heads, almost the size of her master and drooling pink silva. Doc tinkered with Thunder's new cobbled-together prosthetic arm on the floor, going through routine maintenance and referencing his several dozens of red and orange screens. Moses began on breakfast in the kitchen not too far away, the mess of the cooking meat stirring excitement in all three of Sprinkles's heads. It was nice to see his mishmash group of brothers sitting around. *At least our pa did one thing right. He didn't give us a mom but gave me a family.*

"Look who finally decided join us," Pit muttered. He always tried to be tough. Can't be too tough when petting a goofy three-headed dog named Sprinkles. "Thought we lost you."

"I didn't," Doc said, unamused. "He's tougher than that."

"Dang right. So…" Drifter looked around, peering from person to person. "What's going on here? Why're y'all in my house?"

"Woody asked us to come," Big Thunder said. "Ow. Ow. Ow. Too tight. My stump's still healin'."

"Stop bein' a baby, Bobby," Doc growled.

"Well I'm the –"

"You're well in your fifties, you can't use that baby brother excuse anymore. Man up." Doc pulled a lever on the prosthetic limb for good measure. Big Thunder slapped his knee with his other hand, blinking tears from his eyes. "Alright, it should be working. Evan did a good job with it. I don't know how it works, but it does. Your boy's a genius."

Drifter frowned. "Evan did that?"

"Your kids been really stepping up to the plate, Luke." Pit reclined on the couch, petting his dog (or dogs?). "Jo and Evan's kept tabs on the Coats while Woody handled gettin' us all on one page. Y'know, I'm sorry for ever doubting your kids. Without 'em, I think we would've done somethin' real stupid… again. We're lucky that the Bluecoats ain't acting yet. Probably doing like us, trying to get their acts together for a final push. Woody wanted to talk 'bout the plan in small groups. He should be back in a few."

Drifter stole a look at Mary, who didn't seem at all surprised by the prospect of Appetite taking the lead. Leadership hadn't appealed to him before. *Always the follower; never the leader,* a common trap for brilliant fellas like Woody. That had changed. Seeing his pa touching death must've lit a dormant spark in the young man's noggin.

Pride as thick as mud ran through Drifter at the thought of his oldest boy taking the helm. The worry of any parent boiled down to a single thing: how will they manage when you're gone? To see that in his absence their world wouldn't fall apart brought a tear to the old eye.

Among all the pride, there was a small feeling that he was stupid to try to ignore; he felt a little worthless. *They don't need you anymore. Nobody does.* He swallowed and choked the thought down like warm, cheap beer. Didn't bring nothin' to the table. The next generation needed to step up at some point. He pushed the thought deeper inside and outta his head. *You haffta step aside some time, Luke. It's how it is.*

He took his seat beside Pit and his excitable dog, Mary Lu right beside him.

Not even a minute later, the door swung open.

There was a certain grace in the way Appetite came in. He didn't burst through the door with the weight of his entire body but was instead smooth and effortless like a massive predatory cat. Drifter noticed that for the first time in a while, he kept Ham Bone on him, the massive shotgun in its holster on his hip. He also couldn't help but notice that the boy was big. Standing upright with his head a little higher, he dwarfed everyone.

Sprinkles jumped from his owner's lap and towards Appetite, barking and jumping from excitement. He petted her with a grin.

Vermin, Shepherd, Eleen the Silk Spider, and Scott "Tiger" Caldwell shuffled in behind him. The second generation of Caldwells was a diverse group, like their fathers. Drifter hadn't seen them together in a long time. Though not nearly as close as the first generation among themselves, the oldest kids had their own bond. It wasn't easy. The cousins didn't like each other much, at first, touching dangerously close to hating each other at points. Drifter always thought that was his own shortcoming. With everyone already against you, you didn't need your family added to that list.

"Looks like everybody's here," Appetite said, closing the door. He took the seat closest to the door.

"Looks like you brought the gang too." Moses smiled, giving his smaller and well-built son Tiger a big hug. Tiger gave a small smile on his soft face with a dark beard, his one good eye gleaming with pride. The father rustled his fingers through his boy's hair. "I didn't know you were back on planet."

"Came back this mornin'." Tiger took a deep breath and shook his head. "I leave for a while and everythin' goes to the crapper. C'mon, guys, didn't I teach you better than that?" He grinned. "Y'all supported me during my tough times, the least I can do is come back and give these guys what's coming to 'em."

"You're lookin' good, Scott," Drifter said.

"Feel much better too, Uncle Luke. Feeling much more like myself these days. Been spendin' every credit I can trying to pay for the dang thing. Hadn't even had the chance to buy myself some new clothes on my way back. I have a box of my old clothes for Kindle if she wants it. She should be about my size now." He laughed.

Moses gave his son another hug. "We'll fix you up, don't you worry about that."

Dusk Mountain Blues

They exchanged a few talks back and forth through the family, catching up on everything that'd happened. All the while, Appetite waited in the patient way only he could, petting the happily yapping three-headed dog on his lap. They went through their greetings and pleasantries, their news and gossip, before reeling back around to the elephant in the room. Drifter found himself about to speak when Appetite shook his head. They needed to get away from it for a little while. *He's right, gotta let 'em be people first. That's why we're in this mess in the first place.* Maybe he could learn a little patience.

Drifter stirred in his chair, trying to keep himself from fidgeting. Mary Lu slapped his thigh to keep him still. When they finished their chatter, Appetite took the center stage. Eleen quieted everyone down with a sharp hand.

"Thanks Elly." Appetite took a deep breath. "Y'all know why we're here. I've already made this talk a couple of times before. I'll cut to the chance. I think I know why they Coats are here." Drifter felt his stomach drop. "'Course, they want to get rid of us for their colony. But they got me thinkin'. Uncle Bobby collected things and put them at the Drum. It only makes sense they found somethin' special here. Then I got thinking, why would they come all the way back to a backwater planet to kill a few mutants? Why would they come all this way and send a Major and Captain? Don't make no sense unless we had a thing. Then I got thinkin' again, what is something every colony needs?"

The old boys — Drifter included — blinked at the thought. Doc might've figured it out if he wasn't too busy tinkering.

"A good place to live. This planet isn't like the others around; it's almost perfect. I hadn't thought about it before. Wouldn't have if Scott didn't turn up. They're lookin' for a terraforming core. It's the only thing that makes sense. The rest of the Dusk Orbit planets aren't nearly as good as this one. "

It made sense. Drifter knew vaguely about terraforming cores. They weren't a thing they could recreate without having one intact, which they hadn't had any luck with so far. When the first Civilization fell apart, they left a whole lotta things behind; so much that they had plenty to live on for decades. It only made sense that the dead shell of what they once were would try to recollect an arm or a leg of itself occasionally. A discovery like that might turbo charge them into all types of developments for the shareholders and catch the interest their higher-ups.

Drifter stroked his beard. "It's the reason why they're takin' it slow with us and not blasting us away."

"It makes sense." Doc nodded. "Terraforming technology ain't easy to make on such a large scale."

"Putting it like that." Pit sat up, interested. "It would jump start their technology by years, decades even. You can't say that it ain't a good idea to swipe it before they do. Maybe even get rid of it all together."

Drifter shook his head. "We'll cross that road when we get there. We haffta find it first. Got any ideas?"

"I was hoping that y'all would know," Appetite asked.

Every child took a look at their father; Eleen's calm and sure, Vermin's anxious, Shepherd's impatient, Tiger's interested. Drifter locked eyes with his son, and the cool, patient expression on his face softened.

Drifter rolled his shoulders and exchanged a look with his wife. She shrugged back. Drifter pinched his nose, looking out into the living room but letting his mind relax. He knew a lot about C'dar, being he'd lived here since he was younger lad. Over fifty years wasn't nearly enough time to search the entire planet, not even with all the extra eyes and hands around. There were bound to be places they hadn't gone. *Ain't enough time in the world.* Drifter dove into his thoughts, trying to find a place where a goody like that would be.

Then it hit him; one place was big enough for that. One that he had been to, but…

There were nasty things in the Old City, the one they cut through to get to Coyote's place. They had tried to explore it before. Wild mutants, malfunctioning Old World 'roids, and strange, dangerous animals roamed that place. Drifter always thought it was a bit big for a colony city, perhaps a haphazard start to fancy capital city or some sort. Big people liked their big buildings. What they liked more was messing with things they should'nt've. *We're a good example of that,* Drifter thought.

"I think I might have a good place to look," Drifter said finally. "Old City. Only place I can think of that we ain't searched. Too dangerous before."

Appetite smirked. A sinister thing, one that Drifter caught himself doing from time to time.

Appetite paced around the room, heavy thuds of his boots pounding into the floor. "Sounds like a good place to start. Whether it's there or not ain't important; what's important comes down to how greedy the Coats are." He scanned the crowd, looking for the spark of inspiration. "We know about greed. We can get a good jump on them there, and best-case scenario is that they take the bait. They can't sit on us like they did at the Drum. Out there, we can give 'em what they paid for – a fight." Black grit caked those last words in a certainty he hadn't heard before.

A fight; and not a fair one. Drifter realized that. They weren't gonna drive them off with power and anger. No, that hadn't been how he was taught. Did a fish have a chance to complain at the end of a hook? Nah. *Play dirty or don't play at all.*

"So, how 'bout it," Drifter said, taking in a deep breath. "Let's hammer out details to give 'em hell."

Chapter 14

Vanilla and Cloves
Kindle

"You don't understand what's going on here. A little lamb lost in a field, waiting for a wolf to snap your neck with its teeth. Let me enlighten you." –Ignace Breaux

Kindle thought all of this was stupid. She didn't think of herself as somebody with a temper until this very moment, dealing with an uncle she hadn't even known until now. The dark-skinned man with a spiderwebbed scar on his face always watched her. His people were everywhere, as plentiful and annoying as a swarm of mosquitoes. Their gazes weren't too different from a bug bite, either; a minor annoyance that she scratched more than advised.

Today, he joined her at one of the market stalls and soured her meal with his company. Elijah, a friend of her pa's who owned the stand, gritted his teeth and rolled his eyes. "Meal's on him, Cass," the gruff stall owner muttered, pushing over another bowl of stewed beef before shuffling away. She took it happily. Ignace didn't need to know that it was already on the house.

"What, you can't even say hi to your uncle?" Ignace leaned in. "The Caldwells are all 'bout family, right?"

"I don't know you."

"How's that my fault?" Ignace managed a smile. It didn't look quite right on his face. The scar dug deep into his skin, leaving half of his face unresponsive, like a poorly-made action figure. The dent in the right side of his shaved scalp only cultivated that crazed look. Like every Breaux and member of this village, when she stared at him for too long something 'bout him changed, as though he came out of focus. She often wondered if the mysterious natives did it on purpose. "All this time and you hadn't met any of us. Yet, the very moment something bad happens up on that mountain, y'all come runnin'. I'm not sure why I'm surprised. In this galaxy, when someone wants to know something, they come to us –"

He said something else, but Kindle promptly ignored him. She stuffed some of the stew in her mouth and focused on that instead. The man rambled on and on about one thing or another, trying to goad her, get a reaction of some sort. She wasn't gonna play this game with him. *Not today.* Or…at least that was what she thought until the she heard her mom's name leave his lips. Kindle snapped her attention at him, frowning, face warm. She swallowed hard, almost choking on the beef she was savoring only seconds before.

"'Scuse me, but what?"

Ignace laughed, leaning back. He pulled a long ornate pipe from his pocket, lit it, and began smoking it. An odd light blue smoke danced from his lips, smelling of fresh vanilla and ground cloves. They called it the White Noise, a highly addictive depressant cultivated from one of the Early Lights planets. One of her cousins had tried it once; messed him up bad, so bad that even to this day the taste of vanilla sent him into a cold sweat. Kindle tried it once…and it didn't do much of anything for her.

Ignace gave another puff, making no effort to change the direction of the smoke. A minor annoyance atop a mountain of them.

"What did you say about my mom?" Kindle asked.

"Oh, now you're listening?"

"'Cause you have something I actually want to hear."

"Rude. Where's your manners?"

"Where's yours?" Kindle snapped, slamming her fork on the counter. "Gettin' your thrills picking on a fifteen-year-old girl. I don't have time for this, Uncle Ig."

He frowned, annoyance a fire in his eyes. "You look like her, but you sound like him." The venom in his voice made it sound like it was forged as an insult in his head. When that didn't work, he dug deeper with a nail into the heart. "Ina didn't want to leave, you do know that right? It wasn't a choice *she* made. It hurt her to leave. The very last thing she wanted was to go, to leave your dearest pa and her newly born daughter. But she left. She left to make sure that you stayed alive." Another puff from that sweet smoke. Another half-smile. "You weren't sick when you were born. The Flame's selfish. It only wanted one."

"What do you get out of this?" Kindle stood up, heart slamming against her ribs. What *did* he get out of this? Telling her this only served to hurt her. An anger like no other swept through – hot, wild, and terrible like a desert storm. She clawed at the stall counter, wood peeling underneath her nails. She wanted to shout louder than that, shout so loud that her throat felt raw and pained, but she knew that would only give him more of that gross satisfaction he craved. Try as she might, she couldn't bring her anger down. It continued to boil underneath every word and every thought. "Didya hate my mom as much as you hate my dad? Do I happen to be everyone you hate wrapped up in a single person? If so, must be *real* satisfying for you right now, I reckon. I'm glad I can make you feel better."

"You're wrong."

"What?"

"You're wrong. I care 'bout Ina. And yes, I hate your dad with every fiber of my being; but there's one person that I hate more." Ignace blew out a ring of smoke, face relaxing. Whether it was from the weed or the thought, Kindle couldn't tell. "And you have been playing into his hand since you got here. When will you wake up and see that I've never been your enemy, and I don't care either way if you like me more or not? What bothers me is seeing a sheep sitting by the wolf, not knowing it's there. You're much too smart for that, little sheep. Wake up."

Elijah stomped in from around the stall, sleeves rolled to his veiny forearms. "Alright, that's enough, Ignace. Go bother someone else, will ya. The girl's trying to eat."

Kindle took a glance at her plate, long forgotten and growing cold on the table. Ignace tapped his pipe dry, noticing the food for the first time, the used leaves' ashes sprinkling on the ground. He tossed some credits their way, the small chips clattering onto the table, and thankfully left without another word.

The rage he left her with remained and festered in her chest. She managed to keep the tears in, lower lip trembling from the effort. All she could imagine was her mother holding her in her arms, knowing she had to leave her daughter and her father without a word. There was a bliss in not knowing her mother's pain, the choice she made. She hated that she knew and her father, abandoned and forever heartbroken, didn't. *How's Pa gonna react? Is this even true? Was he lying? Why would he lie?* She watched him, hated him, and wished she could learn more.

"Don't worry about it, kid. He's trying to get in your head," Elijah said, giving her an awkward reassuring tap on the shoulder. "He's like that with everyone…"

"Is it true that he had a good relationship with my mom?"

Elijah cocked his head. "No one disliked Ina. She was a nice kid that grew into a good woman. She wasn't perfect, but ain't nobody. We all thought she was a wild girl who fell in love with an outsider and got cold feet. That was what it looked like..but…" He took a deep breath. "It's worth looking into, champ. He could be lying, he could be telling the truth; there could be something in between we can't see. The best you can do is find out what you can while you're here."

"Thanks, Elijah."

The man grunted and grinned, much like what her pa would've done after a good piece of advice. Kindle saw in that instant how they became friends. After an awkward one-armed hug, he sent her on her way with a canteen of the unfinished stew. His kind words and hospitality eased the anger and confusion swelling all over body. She had to find out what was going on here, and answers didn't find themselves – well…not usually.

Kindle waved a final goodbye to Elijah, stuffing the canteen in her bag and heading off through the market and back towards the grand manor. As she walked, she thought she caught another whiff of that sickly-sweet vanilla and found herself hating her uncle all over again.

Ø

Remy wasn't home and Kindle wasn't surprised in the slightest.

The manor was empty except from the quiet servants in pale white masks scurrying from floor to floor. Living here for a little over a week now, she had learned it was easy to forget the servants existed or if they were even human. Staring at them she realized they might've not been at all. Their bodies moved stiffly, like their bones were made of wood and their skin of stones. She also hadn't realized they hadn't spoken to her much either. Her imagination stole away pieces of her confidence. What were they? Did he make him? Were they 'roids or some other sorta sentient life? How loyal were they to Remy? Second by second, new questions flooding in every moment. She wished her dad was here, or at least her grandpa.

Or mom?

That rabbit hole had no bottom; if she started to think of her mother, she wouldn't be able to dig herself out. She didn't know whether the servants or the thoughts scared her more – probably equally, if she was gonna be honest with herself.

Kindle squirmed in the small chair set out for her outside the study. She felt for Coal at her side, the weapon a comfort in all this madness she felt. She thought of happier times with the pistol instead of the mess she found herself in. Odd that some of her favorite memories were tied to a weapon.

The Caldwells always gave a weapon to the young kids when they got old enough, not a second before. The women and men brought into the family through marriage didn't quite get it at first. Kindle couldn't even remember who started it, but she was grateful for them. Shooting gave her comfort, some control. She almost wished she'd left to find something to shoot rather than wait and wrestle with her own thoughts.

Over an hour passed. She had called over one of the servants, asked for a bowl, and finished the rest of her stew cold. The flavor remained the same; a sign of a good stew, as her pa would say. She placed the bowl to her side. Within seconds, the servants swept in and took it, even washed the returned the canteen. Kindle tried to speak with one of them and heard nothing but a humming sound similar to that of a bee. She didn't try again. She waited some more.

By the second hour, Kindle had lost her patience. As much as she would have loved to channel her father's unwavering self-restraint, she felt the inner workings of her anger flare again. *Funny that you aren't home when I need ya. Funny how you're makin' me wait.* Somehow, she knew that he was watching. Remy knew that she was here, waiting on his return. This was how Kindle figured a starved dog must've felt having a slab of meat dangled outside of their reach. She was ready to bite his throat out by the time he strode into his manor, twirling his cane and smiling with all pearly white teeth. The name the Crocodile made a lot more sense now.

He handed off his long wooden cane, his black tall hat, and plush violet coat – each taken with an artistic flare. Their eyes met from the across the room. Kindle already felt her brow furrowing hard on her face. He knew. She saw it in his eyes, the way he strode through every small detail before sauntering her way. She saw it in the way he smiled, the almost bored expression knowing what this conversation was going to be about.

Ignace's words ran deep into her head: *"There's only one person that I hate more."* The smell of vanilla and cloves tingled in her nose.

"I honestly expected you to talk with Ignace sooner," Remy said, voice mildly disappointed, like she stole a cookie before dinner. "What did he tell you?'

"Don't ya know?"

"Fair enough." Remy smiled. "Mind if we take this inside my office? If we're gonna have a messy argument, we might as well not disturb the servants."

Kindle stood up sharply from her chair, prepared to ask him her questions in front of the whole dang place if she had too. He ignored her and entered his office. She stomped in after him, slamming the door behind them.

The door rattling remained the only sound for a very long time. He didn't turn to stare at her, didn't go to sit. Instead, he kept walking towards the large window on the other side of the room and flung it open. The *barj* rolled over every chair, desk, bookshelf, and lamp in the room like drops of ink moving through pools of water. He stood in front of the door, palms on the pane of the window, standing tall. On another day, she would've found him intimidating, or even cool. Today she was too fed up to care.

"I will do anything to protect C'dar," he began. "It's my job as the Shadow. No matter how you react, the truth remains the same. You came here on your own to protect your family. I asked you to come for my own reasons. But if it helps you focus, I'll give you two truths: one you know, and one that you don't. Where do you want me to start so we can get this over with? Which one would you rather hear first?"

"Did my mom have to leave?"

"The truth you already know then," he sighed. "Yes. The Shaman can live without the Flame to an extent; never for long periods of time, but it is possible. However, two Shamans can't coexist in the same space. She had no choice but to leave. The Flame had chosen you. She felt it the moment that she gave birth to you. Given that she still held a lot of power within...she had no choice but to leave. It's not easy to give the complete power over to one so young; it would've killed you. It tried to kill you."

"Then why couldn't she come and visit... talk to me at least?"

"Think about it. If she connected with you, she would've grown attached and stayed. For the betterment of your life and your development, she left. Can you say that if you and your father knew the truth that you wouldn't take all your time to find a work around that doesn't exist? In the end, it would've been a waste of time. That would've been pointless when the Flame needed to be stoked for the sake of C'dar. So, I convinced her to go. Simple as that."

"As simple as that..."

"She loved you two, so left and stayed away. Perhaps you can ask her all the reasons. The fact remains she did it."

Kindle's mind swam at the thought. Knowing the truth sent her heart throbbing, her mind racing. She reached for the head of a chair and missed, crashing into the ground. There she lay for a sickening amount of time. Her stomach churned, vision turned and twisted. Choked breathing smashed hard against her chest. What else didn't she know? What else could he possibly be hiding from her?

Kindle forced herself up from the cold ground of the study, the *barj* cresting over her like the wave of an ocean. There was only one other truth that made sense from here. Her mind dove from coldness to heat; blissful ignorance to stark understanding. She stood, finding her shaking legs.

"You wanted to tell me somethin' else," she said, her voice foreign in her throat. Somethin' she already knew now. "Go 'head. Tell me. I'm listenin'." *I want you to say it to my face.* The truth she didn't realize before became undeniably clear when he wouldn't turn to face her. "Say it!"

Remy sighed and shrugged. "I brought the Major here and I suspect you know why I did that."

Everything made sense – the sudden appearance of the Major, their ability to find them and know where they were gonna strike, the constant communications to an unknown person. He led them here, sending everything into motion. What was the best way to get Kindle feeling helpless? Make a situation where she couldn't back down. Create a moment where she wouldn't want to feel again. Her cousin was *dead* 'cause of him. She'd watched him die, surprise on his face and empty red hole in his chest.

A fury like no other filled her. Her hand moved without thought to Coal. Her fingers didn't quake, her arm never swayed. She fired, the warmth of the gun against her skin and flash of the nozzle cutting through the dark. She wanted to see him crumple over in pain, in death, in shock.

What she got was a laugh.

Remy turned to face her, plucking the bullet from the ribbons of darkness. The inky *barj* spat out any stray metal or torn cloth from the witch doctor's clothes. The bastard had the nerve to smile.

"I knew you were going to react like this." His voice teetered on the edge of woeful disappointment and a complete expectation of the inevitable. "That might've killed me, but Old Luke's obsession to keep the Old-World guns relevant robbed you of that chance." He took a seat at his desk, fingers crossed. "I had no choice. I'm sorry that you had to see your cousin die like that, but it only served to strengthen your abilities. Abilities that the Flame needs to thrive. There are things that you must do whether you like them or not; that's the simple fact of growing up. My people have only known this planet. It's much more than how your family view it – a lucky rock that your family and later your people happened to land on. We've done our best to preserve what the original natives intended before the First Civilization. This was no different."

"It is," Kindle shouted, Coal still poised. "You could've asked. You didn't have to put me through the most stressful test you could –"

"And you wouldn't have been as strong as you are now."

"It's not about that."

"You won't say that later," he laughed. "When this is all over, you'll be thanking me for the –"

A sound of crunching wood and bone filled the air.

He stopped talking. Cold.

A smell of vanilla and cloves hit Kindle... followed close behind the coppery smell of blood.

Remy looked down. A spear poked through his chest, its tip glistening in the torch lights. He touched the tip with his fingers, coughing. The *barj* rippled as though it, too, was in pain.

The dark-skinned man craned his head, blood dribbling down the corners of his mouth.

"What are you doing?" The Shadow's voice strained against the pain that was evident in his eyes. "Why?" He coughed blood onto his chest and his nice desk. "Why, Ignace? Why now, of all times?" Remy laughed. "What do you get out of this?"

Ignace, standing on the windowpane, yanked the spear form his father's back and tossed it out of the window. The orange robes he wore fluttered inward as he stood, watching his father slowly die.

"You never did get it, did you?" he said. "I made a promise to Ina when she left. We promised not to speak of it. You didn't even know we still talked, did you? You thought forcing her to give me this," he pointed to the ugly spiderwebbed scar, "was enough. That pain might've been enough to get her spark, but it wasn't enough to break us apart. I might've not liked Woodrow, but the kid was gonna be mine to protect. Doing what you did not only put her in danger, but our entire village. I couldn't stand by and watch. To admit it even in closed company was your biggest mistake. It gave me a reason, one that I should've used a long time ago. You're a monster, even if it's for the sake of C'dar."

"The world needs both a Shadow and a Flame."

"I'll gladly take the mantle of Shadow if it means having this moment forever. Now die."

Kindle stepped back, watching the last threads of Remy Breaux's life leave him. She heard footsteps outside now. The servants pounded at the door, no doubt hearing the gunshot. She became suddenly aware that she wasn't supposed to even have Coal. Her throat tightened into a dry rope. She didn't know what to do. What would happen if everyone thought that *she* murdered the Shadow? She almost did. She would have, given the chance. *What am I doing here?* She thought, tears of panic on her face. All her anger and the energy that came with it had left her, leaving a scared girl with no plan. She almost turned but Ignace shook his head.

"You're going to be fine," he said, walking over to the body. "You stay here. You need to be here for what happens next."

Emotions duller than an overused knife, Kindle stood there as the door swung open. Servants rushed in a river of black clothes and white masks. The huddled around the body, making that terrible buzzing sound. Some of the villagers, elders most likely, came streaming in next. Shocked faces filled this dark, cramped space. Kindle tried her hardest to melt into the background and fall into the crowd

They didn't give her that luxury. They saw the weapon in her hand and a body on the floor. The hole in his chest didn't match, but in the darkness they couldn't have known. *They're gonna blame it on me,* she couldn't help but think. It wasn't the death that bothered her. The feeling of the world falling apart at the seams was doing it for her.

"Don't worry, I killed him, not the Flame," Ignace began. He wasted no time sitting in the chair. The hole in the back of the chair or the blood on the cushions didn't deter him. "He has betrayed us. Raised his hand against the Flame and her family. He left me no choice." A lie. He hadn't touched her, hadn't harmed her physically or threatened her life outside of the trials. "This was an act of self-defense, but also justice against a betrayal to everything they stand for. Remy Breaux has broken one of the sacred laws of our world. He has told an outsider of the Terracore."

"He did what??" the villagers cried out.

The what?

"In his way, he was protecting us by forcing the hand of the new Flame – Cassandra Caldwell – to get stronger. That core must never get in the wrong hands, but he was willing to risk that for the sake of the planet. He betrayed us. And for that he died." *Another lie.* "This young lady tried to confront him, and she had no choice but to defend herself. When she couldn't, I stepped in. Simple as that."

The room went silent. A few of the servants had recovered enough to take the body away, but the room still smelled of blood. Kindle expected questions; the elders and the villagers asked none. Not all that story was true, but Kindle reckoned that it was enough. She kept quiet, mouth sour from all the lies. Given the truths she knew, she found the strength to keep quiet. Nothing was different. Given the chance she would have killed him out of the anger she felt from what she learned. Only the hand that killed him changed.

"If what you're saying is true," one of the Elders said, "where's your proof?"

Ignace pulled his pipe from his robes and sucked in the smoke from the White Noise. The *barj* followed too, slowly inhaled through his nose and mouth bit by bit. He snapped his fingers. The white screen with the weird alphabet flickered above them, raining letters vertically onto the screen. Kindle couldn't read the words. Whatever it was, it was proof enough the people needed. A few muttered what sounded like some curses. Other than those few, the room fell deathly silent.

"It's a lot to take in given the craziness of today, but as your new Shadow supported by your new Flame, we have no choice but to act." Ignace bowed. "We can't let the Bluecoats and their CEO masterminds touch one of the most sacred things we have left on this planet. We must aid the Caldwells in their fight. Won't you agree, Cassie?"

And just like that, Ignace Breaux murdered his father and received only praise for it.

Chapter 15

Gluttony Incarnate
Appetite

"Been gone so long that I forgot how crazy you bastards are." – Scott "Tiger" Caldwell

Yup. They took the bait.

Appetite watched from over one of the many hills tearing through the Old City; Tiger let him borrow his fancy binoculars from his ship, the *Hua*. Working as a smuggler and a bounty hunter in the Dusk Orbit and Early Lights planets, Tiger had picked up more than his share of odds and ends. Weapons were hard to come by, but he shared what he could. It was nice having him back. Sometimes, all it took was time away from the planet. Appetite knew this way too well. A sharp longing to do that all over again struck him hard in the chest.

First things first, we gotta get out of this mess we got ourselves in. The tank zoomed over rolling hills and through the dead and crumbling monuments of a city, ridiculously high-calorie protein bars in his free hand as he rode from the open top. Among the swirls of dust and debris, he watched the men and women of the Civilization comb through the Old City. The Bluecoats followed them like mice catching the smell of peanut butter.

Tiger, Vermin, and Jo strolled up from the bottom of the hill to meet him on the summit. Tiger wiped the sweat from his brow and swatted a bug away from his leather eye patch, gritting his teeth as he strained up the hill. Appetite heard their chatter as they ascended.

"Don't tell me that the life in the city done made ya soft. Hikin' giving the old boy trouble," Vermin teased, ignoring that he too was sweating like a pig running a marathon – maybe even more so. "Betcha have a fancy apartment somewhere, livin' it up."

"Y'know that ain't true, bud," Tiger muttered, his deeper voice still a pleasant surprise. "It ain't easy out there. Getting harder and harder to do what I do."

"Heard you're getting quite the name for yourself. I wanna meet your crew." Jo patted him on the back.

"We're making it. The crew didn't want to come home with me though. Something 'bout backwater planets givin' them the creeps. They might've heard about y'all. *Hua* can handle herself without a crew. Mulan handles most of the functions anyway."

"Mulan?" Everyone made a face at him.

"My AI on the ship."

"An AI ship?" Vermin squawked. "How'd you get one of those?"

"Eh, Mulan had a complicated relationship with her previous captain so I uh...well...removed 'em."

"You killed the captain, didn't you?" Appetite asked, finally chiming in.

Tiger rolled his one good eye. "Killed's such a *strong* word. And it's not stealing if the ship *wanted* to leave."

"It's good to have you back, Scott. I really mean that. I wish —"

Appetite swallowed his words. Kindle would've loved to hear about one of her favorite cousin's adventures. He shook off the feeling. *She's fine. She's fine,* he told himself.

Tiger must've seen the the words and worry on his face, 'cause his changed too. The chocolate-dark eye shined with a strong empathy, an inheritance from his father Moses. He sat down beside Appetite, putting a firm hand on his shoulder. Strange how that made him feel better.

"She's alright, cuz. I know she's alright. I'll tell her all 'bout it when she gets back. Right now," he said as he looked off into the horizon, "we're gonna have to do somethin' about all those people on our lawn." He emphasized his point with a slap on the back. "Eyes on the prize. She'll come back when she'll come back. Let's make sure she has somethin' to come back to."

Vermin crawled up beside them, looking a little bit like a human-shaped spider. "When are ya gonna stop worrying, big guy?"

Jo socked him in the back of the head with a closed fist. "I don't know, Beau, how 'bout when you get a lady Woody will stop worrying about his only kid?"

"That ain't called for," Vermin pouted. "I was sayin' what everyone knows."

"Y'all right, though. We got things to do."

Readjusting on the hill, Appetite watched the Bluecoats below and took another bite of his protein bar, chewing slowly. He let his mind slow down. There hadn't been contact yet. Oddly, the family listened to him, even referred to his guidance. He hadn't expected the older men to listen to him; they hadn't before when it came to the whole family. But they did as they were told – they stayed outta sight and almost outta mind. Not a single family member had taken upon themselves to take charge. They trusted him and for that, he was gonna give them the time of their lives.

He straightened his back, taking in the positions of his family, the Coats, and the shadows of the wild mutants in the area. Three factions: military, scoundrels, and scavengers. A good ol' fashioned punch up. Appetite checked his watch – a little past noon. It wouldn't be long before the wild ones got a bit restless.

Appetite had a good idea where something as important as a Terracore would be. He had done his research on the Old City in his spare time. Though information was thin, if you knew what you were looking for it wasn't a problem. Deep within the Old City was a spiraling skyscraper, a building meant for the Members of the Board of the First Civilization. Whatever caused the collapse cut their plan short; people tended to forget important things when their lives were at risk. By the time the conflict finished, no one would've remembered to come back – leaving a priceless technology untouched. Given this new information and Drifter's insatiable greed, a fella might think they would've gotten it sooner. But there were places where even the Caldwells wouldn't go – not out of not wanting, but not having enough resources.

Today they were gonna make that step with the help of the Bluecoats.

When the sun glittered over the horizon, he saw the droves of wild mutants as well squads of Bluecoats. Unlike the Caldwells, the wild mutants had lost all sense of human thought. They roamed C'dar like human-shaped animals, sharing odd mutations here and there: discolored skins; open pores that leaked liquid; eyes too big for their heads; bent and twisted arms and legs; razor sharp teeth. In a way, it was like looking into a twisted mirror of themselves. One flawed gene away and they would've been like any of these monsters. Appetite groaned as the numbers swelled bigger and bigger, the monsters crawling outta every space like roaches congregating in the dark. A cold feeling of dread soaked his thoughts. Doubt came at the stupidest times.

Appetite took another breath. *Too late now, we're in it for the long haul.* He checked his watch again; 12:03. Two more minutes –

A explosion rippled through the air, tearing through one of the tall abandoned buildings and raining debris on the ground. Appetite pinched his nose. Two minutes early. At the very least, he respected his uncle's restraint until this point. The building choked up black smoke as it fell to the ground, red bursts of fire sputtering out from the weak foundation below. The wild mutants gawked in amazement for a long time, gathering like animals seeing fire for the first time. The amazement soon creeped into wild confusion as another explosion from what appeared to be an RPG opened the belly of another building to their right. Pandemonium took the city within seconds.

Appetite nodded. This was a good start. A little messy, but good. "Time to get down there," he said after one deep breath.

Appetite sprang into action, rushing to the tank as best as his big body would allow. He climbed up and into Vermin's massive beast, a personal project of his known as the *Stag Beetle*. Modified with scraps found all over the planet and parts stolen from the Coats over the years, *Stag Beetle* was Vermin's pride and joy. The inventors of the family always had somethin' up their sleeve. He wondered if they ever finished the mech too.

He held onto the ring of the manhole; Ham Bone slung over his shoulder. Vermin started the engines while everyone else piled up front. With everyone secure, they rode down the long sandy hill they were perched on and sped through the forests of glass and concrete obelisks.

"Beau," Appetite shouted over crunching debris and thick sand. "Put somethin' good on the radio and pass me somethin' to snack on. 'Member that we're here to have fun."

From the lower hatch, someone tossed up a few protein bars, vitamin-infused drinks, and a packet energy tablets. Altogether, this "snack" of rations was enough to feed two men well for two weeks. He guzzled everything down like a snake devouring a mouse, washing it all down in one unending gulp of what tasted only of water and fake orange flavor. A maddening amount of raw energy flooded him. The red fur sprouted on his chest, down his arms in thick patches. The slow, rational thoughts sped up in his head. He felt everything more in this intoxicating high of energy and power. The wind against his skin, the sand coming up his nose and down his throat, the sounds of gunshots ringing his ear, everything felt stronger. He enjoyed it.

"Where's my jams at?" Appetite shouted, hammering the top of the tank. He knew that he was getting a bit wild; it was okay. They needed a little wild.

"Hold ya horses, I'm I' it."

Then came the music – a good song, too, from the Old World. Appetite howled his excitement, knowing all too well that he sounded a fool or a madman. Were they all mad? He couldn't tell at this point. Only the itch of the battle remained. He let out another roar as they come upon the battle, tank rolling down the hill at full speed. Wild mutants and Coats alike turned, attention ripped away from their fight and onto the metal beast charging at them. Some moved too slow. Satisfying crunches and splatters hit the side in a spray of meat and bone. The rancid smell would've sickened him any other time; in this berserk-like haze, it only caused his stomach to grumble.

Appetite leveled Ham Bone on his shoulder. "Gonna make a hole, give Pops some time."

"We gotcha back!"

Appetite leapt out of the manhole of the tank. He sailed through the air and landed on a man's shoulder blades, crushing bone underfoot with his weight. *Somethin' satisfying 'bout that.* The other men gawked for a second, confused; not many men could process watching their friend get crushed by a man the size of an industrial fridge. But the surprise was gonna wear out eventually. Better milk that for all it was worth.

He let his body act without thought. Men fell to Ham Bone's blasts one by one. Every buck from the shotgun, every satisfying flash from the barrel sent chills down his back. Shells punched through men, mutants, and 'roids alike. He was an axeman in a forest of saplings, the wolf in pasture of grazing sheep. Only a few minutes passed and the bodies stacked around him. He reloaded his gun. The thirst, the hunger, didn't subside. He wanted more.

He searched the battlefield. The chaos spread, thicker than fog. The Coats' structured formation had fallen apart among the chaos, relying now on their training. The wild mutants whooped and hollered, attacking anything in sight including their own little clans within.

Then there was the Caldwells, the middle ground. Not quite feral, not quite structured. Madness following a logic that only they understood. They weren't here to wipe the Coats out, but if it happened it happened – spilled milk and all that.

Appetite charged through the battlefield, shouldering through men, blasting left and right, pushing up the main street. *BAM. BAM.* Another few slimy green-skinned mutants fell in a crumpled mess at his feet.

One had the sense enough to view him as a danger now. It sprinted at him, leaping through the air onto his back, digging at his flesh for the taste of his spine.

There wasn't any pain. Sticky blood clung to the scraps of his shirt; open wounds felt raw against the air; still no pain. The berserk in him exploded. With all the power in his arm, he ripped the mutant from his back and slammed it into the ground by its head. The asphalt of the already broken road exploded against the creature's crushed skull. Appetite pulled his blood slicked fingers from the ruined bone and gristle.

What bothered him most wasn't his raw strength or the twitching remains of the mutant. No; what bothered him most was that he wanted to taste it all. He pushed down the urge.

More Coats and ferals swarmed every inch of his sight as he gathered his breath. Those who didn't notice him fought each other tooth and nail. Lasers and bullets tore through one side; claw, acid, teeth on the other.

He needed to find him. That was his goal before this high wore off – somewhere in the madness was Captain Xan. He needed to be held up or whacked, either was fine; at least until they could get to the prize. *Once they get what they want...we're done.* Simple as that. He had to keep going. He had to find him and hope that his pops could handle the Major. He searched again, heart pounding in his chest. And –

He squinted.

There.

Deep in the fray was a flag of blue, white, and red with a horse in the center. A sizable white carrier ship floated near the ground swarmed by the the feral mutants. An elite squadron of Bluecoats, helmed and covered from head to toe in blue armor, surrounded the ship. They fired into the crowd, blue and red lasers shooting from their impressive-looking rifles.

Captain Xan stood among his men, shouting orders and mowing down swarms of me with his gatling arm – a mutant killer in a sea of targets. Again, Appetite knew on some level that he was terrifying. A fully functional 'roid – more than likely with an AI harvested from a dead soldier – wasn't anything to mess around with. He had to be careful. This high might protect him for a while, but if it ran out, he was done too.

He had no choice. Go at him or die.

"I see him," Appetite belted through the crowd to his folks. "Back me up! We need to keep him away from the building."

Appetite became a wrecking ball smashing through the crowds. He saw a few of his family holding their own; Tiger and Jo's clean shooting, Vermin's well-landed shots from his tank taking on the mechs from afar, Eleen and Loner's drones tearing through the crowd. *Madness,* he thought, *madness.* No time to think.

He pivoted, avoiding laser fire. He was a large target, strong and durable – but that didn't mean he had to take damage like an idiot. He swerved from cover to cover, alley to alley, closing the gap between the Captain and himself. *Maybe I'm crazy too.* It had to be a family thing.

Towards the middle of the cesspool of war, the soldier and the wild mutants grew more difficult. Only strongest among the men remained. The Blue Guard, the rarely seen elite among the Bluecoats, fought toe to toe with the twisted and towering abominations in the city square. Appetite moved in, slipping through the battle and saving his ammo, relying on his pure raw strength to keep him safe. One of the ten-foot beasts crashed into an already broken window of the building beside him; the creature moaned and died with hundreds of smoldering, blackened burns littering its body.

Appetite saw a little of everyone in that dying body; his dad, his daughter, everyone he had ever loved. His anger boiled over at the rim into a cold calculation. He needed an opening. Find a weak link. Exploit it. Take everything. It was how they worked – don't go for the healthy animal baring its teeth. Go for the one already bloodied.

He found that wounded target in the crowd. One of the Blue Guard stepped a bit too forward and got caught out of position. The man – a grizzled vet from his appearance and stars on his jacket – leaned heavily on what looked like an injured or mechanically busted leg. The shaded visor of his helmet was cracked, revealing a little of his war-hardened eyes. He was holding off a mass of mutants on his own in every classic story, he would've been the hero.

Appetite gave that no further thought when he blindsided him with two clean shots back to back shots from Ham Bone.

The visor shattered, leaving ruined red mess in the bowl of the helmet. A grisly scene: but ham bones are meant for soups. He rushed over, reloading and then shooting a few surrounding stranglers before letting Ham Bone drop to its holster to pick up his prize – a Civilization Rifle, a 402-CV.

The 402-CV was a fully developed laser rifle with very little need to recharge, meant for the best of the best of the Civilization's defenders. For it to be in some backwater bumpkin's hands must've been mighty disrespectful – but neither respect nor disrespect mattered much on the battlefield. They couldn't be used long outside of the Bluecoat's themselves due to security measures. Didn't matter. A few seconds was all he needed.

Appetite unloaded on the fools around him, blue lasers tearing into their ranks. A sick satisfaction rose in his chest as they croaked their surprise. Captain Xan, though a little late, reacted to save the rest of platoon, flinging a wide hexagonal hard-light shield up from his arm, its surface absorbing the blows. His expressive face and gritted teeth were betrayed by his cold, distant eyes.

"That doesn't belong to you," the Captain said from behind his shield. "Smart using the environment against us, but time's running out."

He was right. The Bluecoats were the one on the clock. They could run it down.

Captain Xan widened the shield, stepping forward. The glint of red in his pupils spread to the rest of his eyes, removing all human from them. "You all are mistakes. The only reason you're alive goes down to one simple reason: you have something that we want." The Captain's voice lost all emotion now as well, leaving a hollow, reverberating robotic shell. "You have a key on your chain to a lock you didn't know you had. That's why your worthless family hasn't been wiped off the map. And you're the perfect person to bring that key out."

Kindle.

It was the only way.

The Flame was connected to the planet, and so was the Terracore. He hadn't made the connection before and felt all the dumber for it. Only through pure luck had they sent Kindle away to her grandfather's.

Or was it? Were they all playing some sort of game? Piece after piece fell perfectly in his head, and with it an anger beyond anything he ever felt.

Anger drove him to dig deeper than he had ever before. They wanted Kindle for something. He didn't know what, he didn't care. The very thought of his baby girl in their hands brought out a new kinda crazy in him. *No one messes with my kid.*

Against better judgment, against all logic, he charged at them, dropping his new weapon to the ground.

Whether it was the rage, the high, or the madness so common in his family, he punched at the blue hard-light shield. Lightning sputtered in all directions, forking around him. He felt his skin fry with every thunderous punch. Raw and bloodied fists slammed into the shield, each louder the next. Pain shot up his knuckles until he didn't feel the surface or the electricity anymore.

Crack. One crack on the shield. *Crack.* The shield splinters grew, like a pebble flung into a windshield. *Crack.* The shock on the men's face on the other side of the shield told the story. *Crack. Crack. Crack.*

SMASH.

The whole thing came tumbling down in a cascade of light.

The forked lightning erupted into storm of discharge, striking dangerously close to Captain Xan and finding its home in a Coat's chest. Appetite, at least subconsciously, knew that he was lucky as a mug; he wasted no time charging at the platoon in disarray.

The near-human android's reaction time served him well when Appetite lurched at him. He fired a few lasers that slammed into Appetite's chest. The pain registered for a brief moment and didn't slow him down in the slightest – none of that meant anything to the rage, greed, and gluttony incarnate, the very thing Uncle Monty talked about in his sermons. He slammed his blackened fist into Captain Xan's face, sending him flying into the concrete. Bad thing 'bout trying to kill a 'roid: the sight of oil ain't quite the same as blood. *Shame, that.*

"Go aid the Major," Captain Xan said, picking himself off the ground. "I'll handle this one."

His men gawked for a second, and then took the orders like good little boys and girls. There were plenty of other soldiers to help the Captain, or so they thought; no need wasting more of his elites' lives on this beast. Appetite chuckled low at their scurrying.

He only chuckled more when the Captain turned to him. Half of his sharp, angled face was a ruin of metal and wires. Torn fake flesh hung limp on nose and around his odd metallic red eyes. Captain Owen Xan grabbed another weapon from his side.

"You're tough," he huffed. Odd for a machine. "One of the zero types from Daedel. I expected the new blood to dilute your abilities in the second generation, but it seems it only made your DNA stronger. Don't matter though. If guns don't work..." He plucked two small cylinders from his side. "I'm growing tired of this. Major wanted you alive. I don't have the patience for that anymore. Time to put you down."

There were two twin flashes of blue. Appetite felt blood on his throat, on his chest, on his shoulder; the numbness was wearing off. Sluggishness clung to his every movement as he tried to dodge.

The Captain proved too fast. Appetite's eyes couldn't follow the dancing blue blades he felt cutting into him. He tried to fight, tried to scramble backwards – nothing.

Captain Xan swerved in with a clean cut towards the belly. Appetite went to knock it away, but to his dismay, Xan feinted with his left, stepped in, and sliced at the tendon on the back of his leg.

He collapsed to one knee. More pain, this time sharper and clearer than before. A small pang of fear followed. Appetite gritted his teeth, reaching for Ham Bone at his side. His fingers never made it to the trigger. Appetite looked down, seeing the bloody stumps of a once full hand. Looking down, he could still see the disconnected fingers twitching on the concrete. The pain hadn't come yet...but it would.

Captain Xan smirked. "See blood and —"

Appetite responded with a punch so strong that it sent the Captain flying into a building, barreling through the glass and the concrete to the other side of the street. The sheer power of the blow echoed over the chaos of the battle like thunder.

"S*top talkin'.*" Appetite held his stubs of his missing fingers as he wandered forward. Charred, beaten, and bloodied, he blinked through his ever-increasing agony. Thinking too long about it would lead to shock. He needed to lean on the adrenaline, focus on what needed to be done. *Kill him before he kills you. Kill him before he kills you.*

Appetite bit down on the remainder of his sleeve, ripping the fabric away with his teeth. He wrapped the mess of his right hand. Bile stung the back of his throat at the sight of two of his joint bones poking out from the poor man's tourniquet. *Don't think about it, kill him before he kills you.*

Captain Xan cracked his neck back into place, stepping from the concrete and glass. "You don't get it. I'm going to kill you by the time that you even have the chance. You're wasting your time." He flicked the two blue blades again, reforming them at his side. "You don't learn either. I suppose that's a side effect of being an uneducated pig."

Not falling for that again. Appetite smiled instead. "Ought to keep ya mouth shut sometimes, and maybe you'll get a promotion one day."

"Ah, so you do learn." He extended the blades into long blue swords the color of ice. "So maybe there will be something left for your daughter to bury."

Chapter 16

Touchlight Trigger
Drifter

"We're old. You're our future. We're giving this world to you."
– Luke "Drifter" Caldwell

They told Drifter to stay home, but he was never good at doing what he was told.

When his oldest boy hatched this plan, he wasn't included. Bless his heart, but ain't no way he was gonna stay at the Homestead and let the young folk do the heavy lifting. After a load of convincing and threatening to go anyway, he managed to convince his dear, worrying son let him at least help steal the Terracore. Taking stuff that wasn't his was what him and his boys was good at. Appetite agreed on one condition: take the Hounds, Dane and Bulldog, with them. Drifter didn't mind. It gave him the rare opportunity to show the young people that he wasn't washed up. On the other hand, he heard something else – a voice he hadn't recognized in years, haunting him.

You can't do this. You're too old for this. Pack up and leave you old man. Stop tryin' to be relevant.

Having the young people around gave him a little comfort. If he was being honest with himself, the fires at the Drum and his decisions thereafter shook his confidence somethin' mighty good. Pride had always been what drew him to make bad decisions.

The Hounds, Big Thunder, Moses, and himself had made it to the CEO building without much problem. The distraction gave them enough time to double back around to the back area and find a window on the other side to break into. A very helpful hill cut through the back of the spiraling building, half-burying the first few floors under an ocean of sand and plants. Pit and Shepherd led the charge, breaking into one of the windows with the butt of their rifles. From there, they leaped into what appeared to be the second or third floor. Felt like a heist already.

Dane, Bulldog, their father Shepherd, and their grandfather Pit took lead, sweeping the room with a scary efficiency. They pawed from place to place, relying on their animal-like senses to navigate the dark room, Pit's flashlight on the tip of his rifle the only source of light. They sniffed the air and cleared the corners almost soundlessly despite bristling with the most weapons outta all of them; hunters in every sense of the word. It was amazing how safe Drifter felt.

Safe. The word stung a little. He hadn't thought about his *safety* like that before. Drifter took a deep breath, deflating his puffed-up chest and finding solace in his revolver and extra pistol. *See. Washed up. Done let that 'roid take a little of your nerve.* Drifter groaned at the truth of his own thoughts. He felt his stomach tighten a little, the fear of what came next settling deep within his gut. *Good.* It was a good reminder to himself. There wasn't fear without courage.

Drifter followed beside Moses with Big Thunder at their rear, watching for anything outta place in this dark area. Every flash from the rifle's light gave Drifter a small tale of the world they were trying to build here. There were old cubicles tucked into every space, now covered in plumes of ivy and flowers. Old, massive computers stood around them like markers of graves long forgotten to the sands of time. The more they walked, the less clean it got. Papers lay untouched on the ground, yellowed and crumbled into almost dust. What he could read in the small chances he got talked about projects and stuff he didn't quite understand. Appetite would've been much more interested in these things. Maybe they'd come back for it.

"We're not alone," Pit whispered. "Tracks."

Drifter saw the boot treads in the dust now, heading towards the stairs to the far in of the office space. There weren't many of them from what he could tell. The

Hounds whispered among themselves, discussing; After a while, the four convened on a general guess.

"There's a few; no more than about twenty, much less than I thought," Dane said, her smooth voice echoing softly in the ruins. "One's a bit heavier than the rest. It's probably the 'borg." She stooped down for a second, checking the tracks again. "From their formation, they know what they are doing."

"Good to know. Good job." Shepherd gave his daughter a small pat on the back. It was an odd show of affection for the Hounds. *At least one good thing happened from all this.* "Stay here. I'm gonna check out the stairs. Turn off the lights."

"Don't tell me what to do –"

"Listen to 'em, Buck." Drifter cut in before his brother got all huffy. "We ain't here to boss 'em around. Let 'em do it."

Pit blinked his confusion. The dark gave his eyes a yellowish-green canine glow. He went to open his mouth to mutter something or another but stopped himself. There was the same struggle on his face that Drifter found himself dealing with lately.

Time was moving forward around them. They wouldn't have gotten this far without the younger people's

Dusk Mountain Blues

quick wit. Perhaps holding onto the metaphorical torch too long welded it to the old men's fists; young'uns need to let them take charge, sit back, let them drive.

Defeated, Pit deflated and took his position to cover his folks from afar. Shepherd and the two pups padded to the stairwell. The old men watched with bated breath. *Anything could be livin' in there.* Drifter squashed that thought before he took charge again. Old habits from old men died the hardest.

The young ones made it there and back without a problem, but their expressions had changed. Dane's already pale face lost any color that it might've had. Bulldog, poor kid, wretched on the ground.

Their father dragged in what appeared to be a corpse – or what was left of one. The massive winged creature was torn to pieces as though shredded and crushed from the waist down. Entrails leaked from the side of the open wound in its stomach and a foul smell took to the air.

"The whole stairwell is full of 'em," Shepherd explained after a few coughs. "Tried to get the jump on the Major. Didn't pan out." He tossed the corpse down into the dusty floor, green blood leaking dangerously close to their boots. *Suppose we're gonna have to get dirty one way or another if we're gonna head up there.* "They made a mess up there so ya gotta watch your step."

Everyone gave a clean nod and followed them back to the stairwell, stepping over the grotesque creature.

They didn't even make it to the door before the smell decked them; Drifter coughed and dug his nose into the folds of his shirt's collar. The smell reminded him simultaneously of rotten garbage and cooking chitterlings. Shepherd cranked up the door to the stairwell with his shoulder and it only got worse.

Moses wheezed, choking down the contents of his stomach at the sight of what surrounded them. Bodies everywhere. Drifter had a hard time processing the devastation. He took some tentative steps forward, an uncomfortable amount of squish underfoot. From wall to wall, the leathery-winged creatures painted the walls and floor with their blood and gore. *One man did this?* He pushed the thought away. Evidence proved otherwise. Only one person had the sheer force needed without a single weapon mark on the walls. The 'borg Major did this to 'em, probably without a second thought. *Just doin' his job.* Killing was no different than filling out paperwork for men like the Major. Just another day in the office.

In a sick and twisted way, Drifter respect the Major's cold demeanor towards his morbid job. It didn't seem much fun – or that interesting – but to each their own.

Big Thunder pushed through the corridor last, leaving the door open to at least let out some of the smell. With weapons drawn they ascended through the mush; Big Thunder and Drifter took turns killing any mutant that managed to survive the initial onslaught. Simple slices to the neck or stabs to the temple put them down without so much as a hush.

Thunder did his so cleanly that he never had to clean his knife. The new mechanical arm – hobbled together from rusted metals and colored wires found in the typical Loner raider style – worked well for him, but there were things that couldn't be replaced. He'd lost a bit of his confident and self-sure demeanor. In its place was a hardness that Drifter only saw in Thunder's face from time to time, the shards of a pride forcibly hammered into determination. A memory struck Drifter, seeing his brother reserved and serious. Drifter felt like the teenage kid, back in the desert planet, trying to get a smile on his brother's face. *He'll be the Bobby I know again one day. He needs some time.*

Maybe by then, he would feel more like himself, too.

They climbed and climbed up the building.

Once they got through the trudge of the first few floors, the corpses became more and more rare. Midway through the fifteenth floor and just past an enormous mutant corpse, they were in the clear. It came to them as a relief when the air returned to its standard quality of dust, mold, and staleness – anything was better than trudging through the dead. It felt mighty disrespectful if he was gonna be honest with himself.

Drifter put his knife away now, focusing only on the slick movements of their ascent. Up and up. The musk of the old building died away, leaving a freshness on his tongue that Drifter hadn't tasted before. Around about the nineteenth floor, the walls looked clean and white, the floor wiped clean of any dust. Small green lines buzzed around them, flashing and circling like hundreds of fireflies during a cold night. *Drones. Miniaturized drones.* Any manner of defense could've killed them before they had the chance to react; luckily, their only functions seemed to be cleaning and building. *Or somebody cut the defenses off.* Not a good feeling thinkin' 'bout that.

They reached the top floor and stopped at the door exiting the stairwell. Shepherd leaned against the door, pressing his cheek against the thick, green metal. He shook his head. Nothing. One hand on his rifle and the other hand free, he opened the door to the main floor with a horridly loud creak. Drifter winced. He expected gunshots, the toil of battle sweeping through them. He expected an explosion or a trap, ready to take them out the moment they stepped foot in the door. Nothing. Still nothing. The Caldwells took a few cautious steps into a world long extinct.

They were met with a white glow of the building's light mixed in with the harsh sunlight pouring in from the largest window Drifter had ever seen. There was carpet on the floor, apple red and as fresh as if it had been cleaned daily for years. There were glossy wooden bookshelves on every side, each lined with thick-spined, colored leather volumes from shelf to shelf. The walls, scrubbed as much as the upper stairwell floors, had paintings hung on them of landscapes of a now-dead world millions of light years away.

Drifter gawked, mouth open. He tried to imagine the Old World, the first one. He had tried every day of his life. Apparently, seventy-two years wasn't enough time to imagine the landscapes seen in these paintings. He took another few steps forward into the massive office, guns raised.

A form sat behind the massive wooden desk, oddly empty in all this. He sat facing the window in the swivel chair, twisting back and forth. "Expansion's always bloody. Humanity can never stand on a piece of land, sail an ocean, take to the stars without drawing lines around them and claiming it's theirs," the man said, his voice low and pensive. "It's amazing how those lines become more important than the people in them." The Bluecoat Major turned, leaning over the table. He scanned their group, frowned, and sighed. "You didn't bring her. That's a shame. It really is."

Pit fired a spray of bullets. In a flash, faster than anything physically possible, Debenham brought up a grey light shield. The bullets tore apart the desk and everything around it, slamming and shattering the window at his back. One stray bullet slipped by and for a brief second, they thought that Pit got him They couldn't have been more wrong. Debenham poked at a bullet in his palm, unamused at the prospect of being shot. He had *snatched* it from the air. The 'borg even laughed.

"You're the bastard...you're the bastard that killed my boy."

"I am," Major Debenham said, standing up with arms stretched out like he was gonna give them a hug. The bullet bounced off the ground. "I killed your boy. He attacked me – or at least tried to – and I defended myself. You would've done the same without a second thought. Already have, actually." The smaller man pressed his fingers against the bridge of his nose. "I may not look it, but I'm doing the best I can. There's people that needs this planet and they aren't gonna feel safe with y'all around. It's the truth. Tell me otherwise."

They couldn't. Or didn't care to.

On some level, he was right; they were the bane of normalcy on this world. Plenty of men and women tried to set foot on C'dar; pirates, bandits, other smugglers, vagrants of the galaxy. The Caldwells chose who they wanted on the planet and who they didn't. After a time, visitors either left or, in some cases, came to an agreement with them. They were the wolf pack in the forest, the rabid bears in the den by the road. As long as they were there, no colony here would be safe. Territorial at their best, monsters at their worst. *It's **our** planet though.* Drifter puffed up his chest, stepping forward again, ready for a fight.

"This is our land. You ain't gonna have it. You ain't gonna have nothin'. You're gonna leave here on your own or in pieces, ya bastard."

Major Debenham's laugh died. "Wouldn't be the first time I've been in pieces."

What came next sounded like a boom of thunder. One minute, he was sitting in his chair, the next he was a step away fist raised. Drifter tried to react but found himself, the Hounds, and Big Thunder yanked weightlessly into the air. Drifter felt the odd pressure for a second brief second before being pushed again, landing and crashing near the bookshelves.

Drifter blinked away tears of pain of pain. His head spun and swam in his skull. *What happened.... Oh.* Moses had moved them out of the way.

Moses pushed forward with both hands, arms bulging from the force, as thick purple tumors bubbled on his skin. He forced the Major back, step by step, the air and space around them buckling. More and more he pushed, forcing him back and to the ground. The Major's boots dug deep into the thick red carpet, tearing through it with his weight. His metal legs hissed steam and groaned from the pressure. Still he moved. Still he kept forward like a train unable to stop. Blood oozed from Moses's nose as he tried to keep Debenham back.

He couldn't keep this up. The strain would be too much at his age. He couldn't do this alone – none of them could alone.

"Let 'im go, Monty! Let 'im go now," Drifter shouted.

And just like that, he did.

Big Thunder tackled Moses out of the way of the charging 'borg. Debenham slammed into the wall behind them, bursting through it without losing any speed. They heard his body slamming through wall after wall like a pissed-off bull trying to gore a rival.If they were lucky, he would've killed himself with that dumb move. It bought them some time at least.

They huffed and puffed for a while, recovering from the sheer adrenaline that surged through them. Drifter took this time to get his bearings and helped his brothers to their feet.

"That's one crazy 'borg," Drifter said, huffing. "Notice he doesn't have a gun or a grenade or nothin'."

"The thought had struck me," Big Thunder replied. "Whatcha think we should do?"

Drifter looked around. There was a corridor to the far end of the room. The Terracore must've been over there as well as the rest of the Major's unit. "Bobby, Buck, Monty, Spencer – go get that core. Me and the Hounds can handle the 'borg."

"You sure 'bout this, Luke?" Moses wiped the blood from his now disfigured face. "I ain't seen nothing like him before."

"The best chance we got is to hold that Core over his head. Whatever's holding 'em up might not be for long. Besides, Dane and Bulldog got my back, and Shepherd got yours. Trust the young people. It's their future, let them hold it for once."

The young ones sprang into action without question; the old boys took a bit to process it. Their best chance for this to work was to split up, take the Core if they could, and run off. No one liked the idea of holding off that smiling 'borg, but somebody had to do it.

Shepherd dragged his father and his uncles out of the CEO room and to the back corridor, guns raised, leaving Drifter alone with the two young Caldwells that might've started this whole thing. Drifter couldn't blame 'em in hindsight; he only wished that it didn't cost 'em a brother. Those scars had left a hardness in Bulldog and Dane. They needed to stand off with this man or they would never forgive themselves. In the end, it was their fight as much as his.

Drifter unslung his revolver from his hip and tossed it to Dane. "Keep it safe, shoot when you can. Try not to shoot your ol' unc in the back, 'lright?"

Drifter took a step forward as he heard Major Debenham approach through the broken wall. He let in a deep breath. *This one's gonna hurt.* Resting his tense muscles as best he could, he prepared for what came next. Clothes and bandages ripped apart from his body. His bones cracked and sputtered underneath his skin, ripping open wounds and burns. He howled, roared, thrashed as he expanded. He felt himself fill the room, his body smashing through the bookcases and tearing paintings from the wall. His size alone split the room in half, creating a wall between him and the rest of his people. *He won't have another. He can't have another.*

Willing himself to move, he stepped forward, his massive lizard body only half covered by the black exoskeleton. Splatters of blood splashed onto the ground but he managed stay upright and conscious. He huffed, long lizard tongue sweeping on the ground. The taste of fabric came as a relief after all that.

"There's my monster," Debenham shouted from the wreckage. He ducked through the hole he made, white dust all over that fancy blue coat and gold leaf insignia. His sleeves and pants were ripped to the elbows and knees, revealing his massive, sleek metal limbs. "I was wondering when you would show me. My, you're a big one. Looks like Dr. Eorthorn's DNA research hasn't gone completely extinct. The scientists will have a field day with cutting you up."

"I ain't letting you go and I ain't going anywhere." Drifter slammed his massive claws into the ground.

"*Let.*" The Major gave his signature laugh, warm and fuzzy like the sound of a favorite uncle laughing at a little kid's joke. "*Let.* It makes it sound like you have a choice in the matter."

Drifter heard him coming this time and reacted; he flung up his tail. The 'borg's speeding fist slammed against him, coming to a cold stop. Drifter swiped at him with a claw, missing his now small form by an inch. He was fast. Faster than anything he had seen before. His size should've been a strength in a small area; turns out, it was another thing that the Major could use against him.

Debenham sped around, landing blow after blow with his fists. The Major didn't have a weapon 'cause he *was* a weapon. Drifter felt the punches growing in strength with every strike. All he could do was watch and learn and understand. Everything had its limit. Predators filled their bellies or went home hungry if they hadn't learned. *Watch 'im. Give them an opening. Surprise 'im.*

Major Debenham ducked into his right, jumping off the wreckage of a bookshelf with a small burst from an odd device on his calf. He came in hard, blasting him with powerful punch to the stomach. Drifter felt the pain rippling through his body, but he steeled himself to stay upward.

The Major didn't let up. He hopped up and down, bursting with small whistles as he traded blows with a beast much taller than him – but cramped into a small space. Up. Punch. Down. Jump. Over and over. Drifter watched, eyes watering from the pain.

Now.

He slashed with his claws in wide arc, swatting he man out of the air and then catching him with his tongue. He pulled the major towards his jaws.

He never had the taste for eating people. Didn't have the stomach for it. Didn't mean that he wouldn't if he had to.

The Major, for the first time, lost his smile. He squirmed and writhed in the grip of Drifter's slimy tongue. The acid from his saliva ate away at the Major's exposed legs, melting the metal with every second. Fear rose in those deceptively kind eyes; soon it was replaced by a cold rationality. Seconds before he reached Drifter's teeth, he rose up one of his arms.

His arm hissed, breaking open and folding back, revealing a massive barrel of what looked to be the barrel of a cannon. *Dang.*

It was too late for Drifter to react – all he saw was a bright light, and then a pain like nothing he'd ever felt before shot through his left eye. He howled, toppling over and losing all grip on the Major's leg. He heard the man crash to the ground. Didn't care really. The pain was far too great to find a care in the whole dang galaxy.

"And the recruits thought my arm cannon was dumb. Told them all those video games were good for ya."

Drifter growled at the man's jovial words; he focused on the man's weary footsteps instead. The acid on his leg did its work. The clunk of his walk heavily favored one side, meaning he couldn't jump or run like he had before. Effectively, he was crippled. Whether for a short time or a long time, it didn't matter. Well, it mattered a little bit; but The Major didn't need his legs to incinerate Drifter with a laser from afar.

"Time's up, old boy," he heard the Major say. He choked down the pain from his bleeding, dead eye and focused on the sounds and smells. The Major's heavy footsteps, favoring one leg. His cheerful voice. His thick breathing. A light buzzing hum.

This was gonna be the end if he didn't do something. Drifter's good eye, blurry from the pain radiating in his skull, caught the sight of the blue light again. Angry electricity snapped and crackled. This was gonna be it. This was gonna be the end if he didn't act now. *Y'think you got me, boy. Think again.*

He whipped his long tongue, spraying an entire arc of vibrant green acid. The Major yelped, having no choice but to block as best he could. He danced back and the acid ate away at his arm and shoulder, melting through his uniform and burning what skin he hadn't replaced with metal.

All offense was lost in that second. That was all they needed. The opening that they were looking for.

"Open up on 'im," Drifter roared.

Drifter flattened himself, moving a bit. The opening from him to the other half of the CEO building wasn't much, but the Hounds knew how to use cover when it was given. They shot through the small gap, bullets grazing so close he could feel their heat. No shield this time; too late for that.

Drifter watched as dozens of bullets from the rifles and pistols tore into the Major. Shot after shot, bullet after bullet, until their clips were gone. Half melted, half riddled with holes, he remained standing. One of his eyes glowed an intense blue as he cocked his head, as though confused for a second. That confusion soon dissolved into a raw, primal hate.

The bastard was still alive.

The robotic zombie craned his head and laughed. The sound was chilling, robotic and human blended together. At times, it sounded fake and clipped; other times, it sounded real and rich. Electricity buzzed and snapped around him. Blood oozed from the burns on his skin.

Drifter didn't know how, didn't want to know how, but the bastard was alive even with a bullet hole right in between his brows.

"You thought that was gonna kill me? Any of that?" He laughed harder and harder until he lost all human in his voice. "Die now."

And with that he was on them and in that moment, Drifter thought they were all dead. He remembered only the shattering of glass and a bright red light rocketing in front of them. *Ooh...you.* A smile crept on his face.

Standing in front of her family, wrapped in red flames, stood Kindle, a spear in one hand and Coal in the other. She pressed the Major back with a wide swing from her purple-tipped lance.

She didn't look the same. It only had been a few weeks, not even a month, and somehow time had changed her. She stood a bit prouder, looked a bit weathered and hard. She had seen things, knew things now. But she came. She came to save them and looked the dang part.

"You ain't takin' no one else, Major."

Chapter 17

Shadows, Fire; Separation, Love
Appetite

"I brought the pieces together. I tore down the bars between you. Praise me 'cause you owe me one." --Ignace Breaux

Appetite could safely say that he was getting his butt beaten, and there wasn't much he had to add to that.

Reinforcements for the Bluecoats came in droves over the city. A few small ships darted above, dropping off more and more of the invaders from beams of light; in the distance, a larger dreadnaught hovered on the horizon. The family were steadily getting pushed further and further back from the CEO building and surrounding areas. After a time, they might just lose the city altogether and get crushed by sheer force of numbers.

Appetite couldn't worry any of that right now. Right now, he had to worry about himself. His folk had eyes; they could see if they were outmatched.

Maybe he needed to learn that himself. Captain Xan gave him no mercy in this fight. *If he's focused on me, then he ain't goin' around killin' my folk.* That was the silver lining in all this; didn't mean that he liked it that much. He stood from the rubble he was lying in, wiping blood from the corner of his mouth. The 'roid got him good again – the skinny bastard hit him with an energy blast that knocked him almost a mile away and barreled him into an old parking garage. Without his mutation, he would've been dead to rights.

He wasn't invincible, though. He still felt the ache of his missing fingers on his one hand and the throb of a wound on his side.

In a face-to-face fight, fist to fist, he could get him without a problem. Appetite knew his own power and limits. Taking him down and ripping him apart would've been a snap; but the Captain knew that and played to his own strengths as a 'roid. *It is what it is,* was what his father would say. *Not everyone's gonna play ball on your court.* Appetite centered himself, ignoring the bloody mess of his body.

He reloaded Ham Bone and headed back out into the street. *I'm gonna get you, boy,* he thought, choking down his frustration. *Got way too much to live for.* Appetite rolled his shoulders, watching the Captain walk down the empty highway dragging his two ice-colored laser swords behind him in a small trail of fire. Intimidation. Fear. That was what he was playing on.

Appetite wasn't gonna give him that satisfaction.

Not to say that he wasn't scared. There were things, people he wanted to see, needed to see. Kindle could handle herself, live on without her ol' pa, but the thought of her alone still terrified him; he wanted to see her grow, maybe have a family of her own one day. He wanted to see her go off and find herself. Being a teenager was already confusing enough – she didn't need to do that without her pa.

She's safe with Remy, she's far away from all this craziness. Maybe it was best that she'd gone to the other side of the family. He pushed the thought from his head. Going down those roads made it sound like regrets. *I'm gonna live through this. I'm gonna see my daughter again. And maybe* her *again.*

He pushed that thought away further than the other ones. That last trail of thought was a good way to get himself killed. Appetite squared his shoulders and puffed out his chest. *Got somethin' to live for. Gotta make it.*

The Captain approached. The scraping of the laser swords ripped against the air with every step. Thin wisps of smoke spiraled into the air near his face and split around his sharp nose. There was nothing left in those eyes now; all pretenses of human emotions had dropped, leaving the cold residue of a machine executing a directive. He didn't see a living thing right now in Appetite. He saw an objective, a neat empty box waiting for a check mark.

How did a 'roid rise through the ranks of the Bluecoats? By doing the job and doing it well. Appetite would have found it impressive if he wasn't being a kill-bot at this very moment.

Captain Xan swung his two hard-light blades, slicing from impossible angles all around him. Appetite tried to keep up but going against a machine with the ability to calculate outcomes on the fly was as uphill as pushing a muddy truck up a mountain in the middle of the rain. But why the blades instead of a gun or that deadly gatling? Did he deem his other weapons unfit for his opponent?

Didn't matter. Appetite caught him in the middle of a swing with a close-ranged shot from Ham Bone – tricky without a few of his fingers. The pellets slammed against the man's wrist, knocking it back when it should've torn it off, but no matter; Appetite took the chance he got. He headbutted the Captain right between the eyes, knocking the 'roid back, and shot him square in the stomach.

Not even a flinch despite his mechanical insides flopping outside of his stomach. The Captain swiped with his uninjured hand, slashing at his neck but catching Appetite's wide chest instead.

Blood and heat. Burns and pain. He wasn't going to quit.

Appetite slammed the butt of his shotgun into the 'roid's chin with the full force of his power. His opponent's neck cracked and spun into a sick angle, turned in a direction no head should go. Didn't stop him. Captain Xan spun, ducking the next blow from the shotgun blast and slashing Appetite's legs.

Appetite jumped back, shoved his shotgun under the android's armpit, and blasted it off. The arm and the sword it carried flung into the air. The Captain's empty socket sputtered wires in all directions, slick silver oil guttering and spitting onto the ground.

Not the first time Appetite had done that to someone. Sometimes a man has to treat his opponent like dinner meat and go for the joints.

Captain Xan snapped his neck back into place and kept going, clutching his remaining sword tight within wire exposed hands.

The cold calculation of his eyes faltered into a small spark of very human fear. His swings became wilder. Panic. Appetite recognized it, hungered for it. The animal part of him, the one that had needed to travel away from C'dar for a while, awoke again. He wasn't that meek, quiet big boy.

Perhaps the Coats were right; the Caldwells were monsters. Only monsters enjoyed things like this.

Fear became a lost concept. His heart throbbed; his head pounded in his skull. He felt every vein in his body pump blood into his veins in a rush like a river underneath his skin. Xan came down with a downward slash, expecting to cut through Appetite's defense. Without thinking, Appetite flung up Ham Bone. The sword sliced through the gun with ease.

A sad loss, but better than his life. That didn't matter right now. None of it did.

He grabbed the Bluecoat by the arm, pulled him close, and ripped out the man's throat with his teeth. The taste of synthetic flesh and metal and oil filled his mouth. Not the same as blood, but the taste wasn't half bad. Much more delicious was the surprise on the 'roid's face; hundreds and hundreds of calculations didn't predict this.

Appetite, without a second of hesitation, then proceeded to pull off the man's other arm.

Every snap of a wire brought an unimaginable amount of sick joy to Appetite's mind. The bioandroid couldn't speak any more. He had to watch in silent horror as Appetite ripped his remaining arm from his body.

Appetite held it for a while, watched it thrash helplessly in his grip. He opened the fingers to take the sword.

Armless and voiceless, Xan moved his empty shoulder. A wide gatling gun shoved its way from the cavity and pointed itself in Appetite's direction.

Would you give up? Appetite wanted to shout.

Xan began shooting before Appetite could even say anything. Red lasers splashed against the surface of his hardened skin. While they did hurt and burned his red fur, they weren't enough to pierce his skin. *That explains why he didn't open up with that number.* While his father's hide was susceptible to attacks like that, Appetite's wasn't. Evolution or natural adaptation or some sort of mutation difference, he didn't know. He would be fine if he didn't change to –

Old World ammunition.

Crap.

Appetite noticed it too late. A stream of old-world bullets sprayed from Xan's gatling now at a rapid rate. Only by sheer luck, Appetite managed leap over an abandoned car nearby; he felt the familiar pain of open bullet wounds against his shoulder and right leg. He was too big of a target to avoid all of it.

Appetite growled, hunched behind a car barely bigger than him. Dozens of bullets bounced off his makeshift red-brown rusted shield of the car, punching holes here – but it stood firm all the same. The sounds soon became deafening, thick over the whole area in a sharp pitter-patter of metal rain.

This wasn't going to stand for long. Eventually, the cover was gonna give way and he was gonna be a big open target. No manner of shield or layers of mutant fat was gonna keep him alive at that rate. He swallowed his nerves and flicked the sword. Without Ham Bone, the roles were flipped. He already missed his shotgun.

Chin-chunk. Plink. A reload.

Appetite rushed out of cover, faster than a man his size should move. He felt his legs burn hot from all the motion. Bullet wounds, cuts, bruises all flared up and down his body; still he pushed. He pushed deeper than anything he'd ever felt before. He was running out of time. Without any more calories to burn, he was gonna lose the only advantage he had.

He needed to end this now.

He rushed at the Captain, the hard-light sword coming down on its former owner. He hoped to cut him in half, but sometimes you didn't get what you want.

The android pivoted at the right time, kneeing Appetite in his big belly. A burst of agony rippled in Appetite's stomach. Vomit and blood threatened to spew all over his shirt. He tumbled to the ground, clutching his stomach and trying to catch a ragged breath in his diaphragm. Tears of pain rolled down his eyes.

Chin-chunk. Reloaded. He dug deeper and didn't find a single drop of energy left. This was going be it if he didn't think of something.

I'm sorry, Cassie. I done got myself killed.

Funny how every regret and every pain came to the surface when a man touched death.

Then, nothing.

Nothing but a loud clunk and hungry snapping of wires.

Appetite opened his eyes to see a shorter woman standing over the dear Bluecoat Captain's halved body. The android whined voiceless sounds and clawed at the woman's feet with dead wires. She cleaved his halves into quarters with an axe much larger than she was. She shouldered the axe and laughed, a familiar sweet sound from years ago.

She turned to him, her warm dark skin glistening with sweat, her dark brown, curly hair rolling down the sides of her round cheeks. She extended her hand.

Appetite felt his heart twist and turn in his body. *It can't be. No. No. No. Now. Here. Why now?* Tears swelled in his eyes. The pain of seeing her made every physical pain he felt right now feel insignificant. He reached towards her with bloody fingers. It felt wrong. She shouldn't see him like this.

He should be angry.

All he felt was relief.

"Ina...?"

"You're lucky that I was in the area and couldn't watch you kill yourself, you moron."

It *was* her. Appetite gawked, blinking, expecting her to disappear. She didn't. She stayed.

"Are you gonna stop staring or what?" Her voice was smooth, soft, low. "What were you thinking trying to fight a mutant killer model alone?"

"Is that all you're gonna do after not seeing me for years? Nag?"

"I think I deserve it right after saving your life, you big idiot." She punched him in the shoulder and Appetite yelped. "Sorry," she said hastily. Whether that was for the punch or going incognito for fifteen years, he didn't know. "I'll explain after all this is done. Can you stand? We got things to do."

He, in fact, couldn't stand. Quite the opposite – he fell out before he even had the chance.

Ø

Appetite awoke in a ship flying over the city under the dancing green lights of a healing station. He'd never been in one before. It tingled and stung a bit each time it swept over his body. Smaller yellow lights worked at small wounds, picking at him and stitching his skin back into place. He looked around, eyes darting from one side of the chrome surgical room to the other, feeling like a mouse in a lab experiment. The lurching and swaying of the small vessel helped little. The faint scent of antiseptics and blood danced on the surface of the air.

He swallowed his fear. Old backwater boys often didn't like spaceships, never mind infirmaries filled with nasty-looking equipment. Putting them together made every hair on his body stand up in fear.

"Don't move."

Someone paced the paced the space around him, looking down over the city of C'dar from the window. The small ship only had a few rooms in it; the cockpit, the small infirmary, the mess room, and the sleeping quarters in the far back. The morning sunlight-colored core spun in its tall glass container, completing tasks throughout the ship, humming its familiar song.

Appetite blinked. He recognized the ship *Sundancer* now that his mind had calmed down, but he still didn't want to be here for numerous reasons; two were in the forefront.

First off, his family was still down there. Appetite rose, heart pounding. He needed to get back, he *had* to.

Hiss-clink. A needle shoved itself into his forearm and pumped green liquid into his body. Almost instantly, an odd calmness drifted through him, and he slumped in the bed.

Dang drugs, he tried to mutter. His mouth wouldn't allow him – it felt as though it was stuffed with cotton. Side effect from the medicine, more than likely, and he didn't like it. He huddled in the bed, trying to stop the shakes.

Ina smiled down at him. "Your family's fine. The Bluecoats are splitting up, and the rest are still holed up in the old Viscount Industries CEO building you guys found. Once my people came, they began breaking off. It appears that my father and the Coats had an agreement to not get into each other's business, but Ignace broke that when he launched his coup."

"What?"

"My dad's dead, Woody."

"What? How?"

"Ignace killed him."

"For what?"

"Not important."

"Hell if it ain't! What 'bout Kindle? What's going on?" More medicine. Appetite whimpered, shrinking into the comforts of his bed. His fatherly instincts roared in the back of his mind, stampeding through every thought. The sedative may have stopped his body from acting, but his mind raced through every potential outcome. He twitched and tapped in his bed. "Ina, what's happening with our daughter? What's going on?" He wanted to shout; his voice allowed only a painful creak. "What's going on?" he whined one more time.

This was all too much right now. He went to scratch where the needle pricked him and only scratched with air from his missing fingers. It didn't help his mood much.

"She's fine – or at least, I think so." She stared down at the city. "She went to save your dad from Major Steven Debenham. That's the last time Ignace saw her."

"Ignace? He's here?"

"Yes." Ina sighed. "It's complicated, Woody. Ignace, though very much a horrible person, looked out for me when our father wouldn't. I did the same for him after what I was forced to do to him in our childhood. He wanted to protect me from people like you." She shook her head. "Never mind that. The point is that Ignace caught wind of our father's agreement with the Coats and their study of the Terracore on the planet. He never told him them where it was, so they naturally assumed the resident family of bandits and smugglers stole it and kept it. My dad never confirmed or denied that. In his typical fashion, he orchestrated events to get what he wanted – another heir to the Flame. Ignace put an end to it."

"It's always 'bout that dang Flame."

"It was…" Ina whispered. "We weren't family to him. We were totems, another thing meant to protect this planet…" She sighed. "I didn't want to leave, Woody. I really didn't."

"Why did you?"

"If I didn't, Cassie would've died. The Flame would've killed her. I couldn't explain it to you then. My *father* didn't...he watched me closely even across the galaxy. I never wanted to leave you. I wish I could've explained. I –" Ina took a sharp breath. "I'm not blaming it all on him. There are mistakes that I made all on my own and there are things I don't expect you to forgive me for. I –"

"Stop."

"What?"

"Stop. That. We're gonna work on it. Don't worry about it. I'm just glad you're here, is all."

Appetite knew it was the sedatives and medicine making him blow smoke out of his butt and act all stupid. He couldn't stop it even if he tried. He sat up in his infirmary bed. The healing lights and surgical equipment reeled back and locked back into place beside him. He went to step out of the bed, ripping out his IV, but lost his footing; he crashed to the floor, taking an entire metal table of surgical tools with him.

Against the clattering of metal against metal, Ina sighed with an annoyance he knew all too well. She helped him up, wrapping his tree-trunk of an arm around her small body. "I'm not letting you back down there. You're gonna have to trust Cassie to handle this now."

"Is that how'ya slept at night without meeting your daughter?" *Crap.* He hadn't meant to say that. Apparently, he wasn't as over it as he thought.

She stared at him. In fifteen years, she hadn't changed much. Her rich brown eyes, her round cheeks, the tumble of her long curly hair, all the same. What was new was the small lines underneath her eyes and the loss of the constant smile on her lips.

"I didn't mean—"

"You did mean that...and I deserved that," she said with no hesitation. "I know how you value family and I haven't been there for her or you. No matter what...forces...kept us apart, that was inexcusable. I could've told you. I could've contacted her. But we can't change that." She helped him into a chair and put her hand in his. Despite everything, he felt warm in the face. "One thing that we can change is how we move forward. I don't expect you or her to forgive me. I never have. I hope you can. I understand if you can't. "

Appetite held her small hand in his. She ran her fingers over the uneven stumps of his fingers. He wanted to kiss her, wanted to tell her that it was going to be okay. *Was it though?* Fifteen years of baggage didn't disappear upon a reunion.

Besides, there were other things happening. His people were fighting for their lives down there. His daughter was face to face with a 'borg ready to kill her. Whatever was between them—whether pain, love, confusion, or hate—would have to wait.

He went to stand up. Ina pushed him down.

"Nope. How's 'bout this? I'll go down and check on your family. You stay here."

Ina turned and walked away from him, plucking her axe and her gun from the small weapon rack by the door. "I can't tell you everything, Woody. I've taken enough time as it is. There's something I need to stop if I can. Ignace's revenge on our father isn't done yet. There's one thing he wants to do, a nail in his coffin. Your daughter's about to make a huge mistake."

Your. That simple word left a sour taste in his mouth.

"Our. *Our* daughter. And what mistake is she 'bout to make? Make some sense, Ina."

"The Flame, the Shadow, and the Terracore are – it's a close kept secret and – " Her sentences came to a harsh, unnatural stop, as though she snapped it with her teeth. She cursed under her breath. "I can't talk about it right now." The very familiar shudder of frustration rose in her small body. "There are things I *still* can't talk about. I'm gonna fix this, all of this, Woody. You, me, the family I made and never fixed. All of it."

"Can ya promise me one thing..." Appetite clutched the arms of the chair she'd plopped him in. "That you'll come back. That no matter how hard it is, we'll talk 'bout it. I can't promise it'll all be the same, but we gotta work at it. I, at least, deserve that." Appetite bit his lip lower lip, tasting a bit of blood. It sounded stupid. Everything he said so far sounded stupid. He was that awkward kid asking her out again, except this time, they had a kid and a history between them. "I don't know. Just...go. Just go and come back."

"I never wanted to leave the first time."

Ina grabbed the last thing she needed from the small rack beside the door – a long, dusty red cloak, burnt at the edges – and wrapped it around her body. She slammed the button, flinging the hatch open. A blast of cold air rushed through the room. The pressure popped his ears, giving the open-door sirens full reign to terrorize him.

She turned and smiled, the cloak fluttering around her body. She mouthed a few words, saluted with two fingers, and fell backwards out of the ship. Appetite watched her corkscrew to the surface, waiting until her silhouette grew too small for him to see whatever she did to stop her descent.

"Show off," he muttered, readjusting in his chair.

He missed that about her. He missed a whole lotta things about her. Riding in her ship brought all those memories back. Could they get past this? Why did she come back? How? If what she said was true, what changed in the Flames? What was happening in the Viscount Building? Appetite groaned, throwing his head back into the soft headrest of the chair and glaring at the window.

He rose and instantly gained the attention of the AI Within the hard glass core.

"Hello, Master Woodrow," it said with its nervous young boy's voice, "it's a pleasure to see you again. By request of the Lady, I must not let you overwork yourself. I have been authorized to use force if necessary. I would like to not use force if at all possible. If that's okay."

"Yeah. Yeah. Don't plan on it."

"Good…" *Kaulu*'s voice stuttered for a second as though confused.

Right. It had been years since the two had talked. To an AI core with perfect memory, Appetite was still that reckless monster trying to find himself. Force would've been necessary and already used by now.

"Is there – is there anything that I can help you with?"

"You can. I got a question for you."

"Query. One moment." The young boy's voice changed into a low, mildly condescending man's voice. The sudden change in *Kaulu's* personality always rattled Appetite's nerves. It made him unsettling, as though he was ready to flip a switch to genocide at any moment. "Ready for your question."

"What's the connection between the Flame, Shadow, and the Core?"

Kaulu flickered for a second. He flashed red, then orange, and then yellow. The little buzzing sounds he made gradually changed to a low, maddened laughter. Appetite kept still, forcing himself still and waiting for the AI to finish its tirade. After a while, it blinked back into its normal swirl of colors and took a purposeful sigh.

"She figured you'd use this work around. Do you want to know?" The man's voice peaked with amusement. "You might not like the answer."

Chapter 18

Breaks, Cracks, and All Things Bad
Kindle

"I knew I was making a mistake and I made it anyway." –
Cassie "Kindle" Caldwell

"See, I told 'em," Major Steven Debenham barked as he ran off. "I told the brass that you'd come. But *noooooooo,* don't listen to the Major who managed to blow himself up in his quals and still get a promotion. He's obviously an idiot."

Kindle hadn't expected the man to have all his marbles looking the way he did. This, however, broke expectations. She thought the man would go full throttle at them, driving forward with no mercy left. What had happened was very much the opposite. The moment she stepped foot in the CEO office, barreling through the glass and leaping over the large desk with the aid of burst from a gravity dampener, the Major had lost all interest in the fight. He sprinted past her, her now-reverted grandpa, and her armed cousins, and through a narrow corridor at the very back of the room, laughing all the way.

A rage boiled inside her, rough against the scalding power of the Flame also coursing through her. Both were hard to contain; both leaked with every action she took. She started to run after the taunting squeaks of his mechanical legs and madness-soaked laughter – but her grandfather stopped her, grabbing her by the wrist.

"Wait a sec, Cass," her grandad said, holding his burnt and bleeding eye with his free hand and her wrist with the other. His transformation left him as naked as the day he was born. Scars – old pink and new, angry red ones alike – littered his body, curled up in a pool of his own blood. His face was stern, blood trickling down his side of his nose and dripping down the tip of his beard one drop at a time. "Your grand uncles and cousins are here too. See if they're okay," he said, letting go of her wrist and slapping her back with a red palm, "and give 'em hell for all of us, will ya?" He smiled the proudest smile he had ever given to her. "I'll be alright." Drifter slumped his back against the shattered bookshelf, all energy he mustered leaving. "Go get 'em, buddy."

Kindle nodded and sprinted after him. *He's gonna be okay,* she thought as she sprinted after the Major. He'd endured worse. The worry persisted, though, thick as the burning in her legs as she ran. *I gotta make it there.* She knew that if they found whatever they were looking for, nothing in time or space would keep them from killing everyone she loved.

So, she ran. Ran for her father. Ran for her grandparents. For her uncles, aunts, and cousins. For everyone. She needed to stop this now. *I helped start this, I gotta end it.* She gritted her teeth and tightened her weapons in her grip.

She followed the sounds of the Major sprinting through the long corridor. A strong smell of dust and mold filled her nose down the ancient hallway. The artificial lights – not made of anything Kindle could see that would be electric – flickered on and off throughout, flashing her shadow against the metal walls with every burst. She felt the velveteen touch of the flowers and moss blooming and growing on the tight walls beside her; and soon after an odd flexing feeling, like stepping through a pool of water.

Odd, if she gave herself time to think about it. She didn't have the time.

She kept running, the ancient smells giving way to the taste and scent of fresh water and smoke from a kindled fire. She ran for what felt like another mile before she saw the corridor opening like a river into a gulf.

When she stepped through the narrow opening, she was hit by a surge of lights and sounds, she saw that she wasn't in the building – not anymore. *A ship. Here. How?*

They would've seen it — or at the very least, the bunker that housed it. *Could it be a teleporter? To where?*

Not the time for that. She needed to look around.

Taking in her surroundings was tougher than she imagined — where she'd expected madness, she found this odd peace. Kindle stood in a circular room, tall pillars of metal and white hard light erected all around her. Green moss and flowers of every color wrapped around the supports, giving a large area of the ship the look of an old ruin. Pools of holographic water pulsed silently underneath the thin layer of translucent metal beneath her feet. Small embers floated aimlessly around them, bouncing on every surface that they could; upon closer inspection, they weren't lights, embers, or even fireflies, but some small robots radiating a familiar energy.

She touched one and felt it — raw and untamed, but reminiscent of what she felt in the Swamp. The world's memories flooded her in brief flashes, one after another; it took all her mental power to keep it at bay.

This was the source of the Flame. This was her mother's legacy. *Did she even know 'bout this?* Who did?

"Cassie? That you?"

It was her Uncle Moses' soft voice, rough and well-worn like the wool of a sweater. She rushed in his direction, following through the small creeks and webs of several metal corridors. Tucked in one of the small conclaves sat her grand-uncles and cousins.

They looked battered and bruised, torn rags and beaten eyes all around. Surrounding them were bodies of Bluecoat Elites, as well as a single quadruped mechanism that looked to be part of the ship's defenses. It was made of metal and thick black cords, molded into a massive doglike shape. The broken red eye – the color and texture of a shattered ruby – sputtered out a geyser of the same flame she used, smelling stronger than ever of smoking ash and embers.

Kindle kneeled to her family, the tsunami of drones drawing to her in a calm wave of orange at the sight of her. Uncle Moses leaned forward, shifting his uneven body weight from one side of his body to the other.

"Ain't you a sight for sore eyes," he said. "Thought we might've been a goner there."

"Whatcha do, even?" Uncle Thunder asked, frowning. "Did you press a button or somethin'?"

Kindle blinked. "What?"

"It just...stopped?" Uncle Pit frowned too; the face he made reminded her of Mastiff's, still but ready for a fight. The similarities unnerved and angered her, and the power of the Flames splashed within her. "The Major slipped past when the door opened and the thing came out." He cocked his head towards the large door, covered partly by ivy, leaves, and flowers. "Whatever you did made it stop. I ain't sure – "

The door hummed an interruption.

The nanoswarm once surrounding her spun and rushed towards it, filtering into a small device housing a translucent orb in a steady stream, until it started to beep sharply, and then settled into a sunset-color glow; the light coated the door, piecing together a long holographic face spun into a form by the 'roids.

"*NEW USER IDENTIFIED. BREAURIAN ACCESS GRANTED,*" it spoke, its long mouth opening wide with every word. The face nodded and disappeared; the door behind it opened. An abyss – an endless, ever-growing unknown – met them on the other side.

"Stay here," Kindle said, her voice odd in her own throat. "You're not allowed to enter. Head back."

Her body, stepped towards the door as though pulled by strings, with the pleas of family falling on deaf ears at her back. The door slammed shut with a load bang.

Kindle turned, returning to her senses. Nothing. She couldn't hear anything on the other side. Her heart sank.

At least they're safe, she told herself. Whether that was true or not, time would tell. She stepped more into the darkness, her sinking heart pumping blood through her body. Her footsteps echoed from wall to wall.

No. Not hers alone. Somewhere in this darkness stood the Major, having slipped through the automatic defense while his Bluecoats and her family fought; she had to find him. That, or a way out, and leave him stuck in here.

No, you have to find that Core – it's important. A wave of urgency replaced the fear and hesitation. She thought it courage or purpose for a moment – but deeper down she knew she was wrong.

The Flame or whatever it was tapped her in the right direction – gentle pushes, here or there. She felt it cool and rise within her with every decision she made. The selfish power pulled her in every direction. Old memories pushed to the forefront of her mind in flashes, but she choked them down and focused on the darkness in front of her.

One step. Two steps. Three steps. She kept moving, the whispers within her spinning tales. She didn't know what to think, what to do. She hated every second of it. *Was this how my mom lived?*

After what felt like an eternity, the darkness broke. To her left, she saw something that she hadn't expected;

through the window, she saw the world she lived in. The planet of C'dar.

She hadn't ever seen it from the outside. The vast size of it was daunting, a massive blue sphere covered in greens, reds, and small flecks of purple land here and there. She lived all her life on that planet, not knowing what it looked like on the outside. She had wished to leave the planet one day, like every young Caldwell did at least once; she hadn't expected that time to be now.

She looked around, a sudden realization striking her. She wasn't on a ship, but a satellite station within orbit. Grandpa nor any of his brothers ever mentioned anything like this before. Perhaps they hadn't known either.

What else don't we know? Knowledge – like the unknown, or space – was both terrifying and amazingly vast.

The Flame urged her forward, pushing her instincts through the winding corridors. Reminiscences of a lost civilization threaded through each room, of people both similar and foreign to the life she saw on the C'dar. Centuries of dust, ivy, and mold layered most rooms, some even inaccessible or locked off by the internal system. She turned, winding through living corners, through mess halls, through an infirmary. She hadn't the chance to look or digest any of it. The *Flame* pushed her to the edge of nausea. She was in a piece of history and she couldn't savor it.

In a trance-like march, she made it to a room labeled nothing more than the Terrarium. This door flung open without any resistance.

The power within her cooled, if only for a while.

The Terrarium was abuzz with red error screens, each blinking on the surface of glass and metal before she stepped foot into the room. At her presence, everything stopped, screens flickering off one by one until none remained. Kindle regained her composure, realizing soon after the immense size of the room she had stepped in. In every direction there were forests, lakes, cliffs, deserts, and grasslands, each sectioned off in contained areas. A large metal orb spun in the middle of the room, slowly and steadily beeping; from the center of it, a beam swept from landscape to landscape, stopping only to twist the environments here and there. Mountains rose. Rivers changed course. Dunes collapsed. All within seconds. All in a blink of an eye.

That was technological power, the legacy of dead civilization lost to time and human errors. *The Terracore.*

"You came. I thought you might've gotten lost for a second there."

Major Steven Debenham stood in the shadow of the Terracore, arms behind his back; Grandpa and the rest had done quite a number on on him. The robotic pieces of his body had been melted, while the human pieces were covered in dried blood and cracking burns. He stood tall and proud regardless, though sheer madness on his face betrayed his cool nature of his posture.

"Do you know what this is? How it can save thousands of people? No. You don't. None of you do. You're out to protect what's yours. All of you are selfish beyond compare." The Major turned to her. "But I needed you. Remy Breaux squirreled you away to activate your abilities and all I had to do was push. Make you want to save your family. But now...you're here. The Shaman has served her purpose – activating *Ogoun*. I don't need you or your family anymore. I had a good time, but it's time for me to do what I came here to do."

The Major was a wolf going for the neck or a bird swooping a fish from the pond. He came at her with bullets. She barely had time to react, to find cover. Glass shattered all around them, breaking the tranquility of creation in favor of destruction.

She ran from place to place, trying to create space between her and the Major. She fired back when she could, the satisfying sound of Coal's chamber echoing through the Terrarium; any hit she made on him, Debenham ignored as though they were inconvenient taps on the shoulder. Kindle didn't have that luxury. Shaman or not, she was still flesh and blood, and bullets didn't agree with either of those. She kept running, scrambling to the mountain area.

Don't you turn your back against a gun. Good way to get shot in the back. Funny how it wasn't the newfound powers she had that she was leaning on, but words she had heard a thousand times by her grandpa. She would've smiled at that if she wasn't running for her life.

The glass and kinetic field of the mountain area dropped at the sight of her. Lucky thing, that. She assumed it would let her in like everything else, but if she was wrong she would've ran straight into a glass wall – an embarrassing way to die.

Kindle sprinted through the artificially created land, head turned slightly to keep an eye on the rampaging 'roid. She created some space; she needed more. She darted through the cover of the land from hill to hill, from cliff to cliff within this small sample size of a world. She jumped over a lip of rocks into the cover of tall crags and cliffs.

A rock burst into pebbles from a high-caliber bullet near her head and she almost yelped. Shards scraped against her cheek and got into her eyes; small annoyances, all in all. But those minor distractions added up after a while. One second was enough to kill you.

She squatted and shuffled from cover to cover, thinking through her plans. More shards of rock fell on her shoulders, the bullet spray growing tighter and tighter; she felt the bullets graze her, a warm sting here and there among the cuts and bruises. *Block it out, block it out.* The feeling of dread mixed in with the thrill. She pushed it all down. Distractions.

Kindle spun around a rock spire; hand still wrapped around the Breaux spear she came with. She listened, waited. She heard the click she had been waiting for – a reload. She had to do it, so did he.

With all all her strength, and some borrowed from the Flame within her, she kicked off a small rock, leaping higher and higher until she hit a plateau. She saw him on the other side, the gatling in his arm spinning and spitting out shells.

He saw her a bit too late. Kindle leapt through the air, aimed, and launched the spear with all the power she had in that arm. Years of spearfishing with her father served her well. The purple crystal-tipped spear slammed clean into the Major's forearm; sparks and a small fire bloomed body, and he doubled back, both from the shock and the force. She gave him no quarter.

Landing with the grace of a cat, Kindle aimed and fired two more shots from Coal. Debenham used his dead arm and the spear itself as a shield, running behind the crags of the mountain. She would've caught him on the transition, but luck wasn't on her side; the sweeping light came. It terraformed the landscape of the rock in a sudden burst upwards and provided him a shield that wasn't there before. Her clean shot barreled into a newly formed rock.

She cursed some very improper curses that her pa would've popped her wrist for. *Stay focused.* She reloaded her own gun. *Never waste a bullet; never miss one.* She took a deep breath, wiping the sweat from her brow. This was far from over.

Kindle heard the man's soft muttering from behind the newly formed rock range. There was a sickening rip and the clattering of her broken spear to the ground. She had to have hit a human part of him. Had to. That pain was real.

"...understand. I don't get it..." She heard pieces of his muttering, distorted here and there, but couldn't see him. "Why put yourself through this effort? What's the purpose of all this struggle? Why? This technology can *help* people, change lives. A little sacrifice for the greater good." His voice was closer, soft against the AI-forged winds. "I have a daughter 'bout your age, two sons younger than that. I'm willing tear apart a thousand of you to make sure they have a life better than mine." Closer. Too close. He wanted to distract her, have her focus on his words, on his –

Whatever hit her, hit her hard. She felt herself flying and then slamming into the dunes of the next contained area yards away. Kindle rolled and rolled, millions of rough grains of sand coating the inside of her mouth, and spat blood, spit, and sand onto the ground. A sharp pain ran down the entire length of her shooting arm, forearm skin ripped and raw. Coal was tossed out of reach, steadily becoming buried among the whipping sands.

What happened? Her mind and vision spun back into focus. *Where are you?* She thought, blinking back tears of agony. She flexed her fingers. Good. She hadn't broken anything. *Where are you?* Fear rose in her chest. Was all this for nothing? There were too many questions that need to be answered. For the first time in a long while, she felt her age – lost, confused, and scared.

I can't do this.

She shook her head. No. She had to go on.

"That should've killed you," she heard his voice call out. "The Flame must be good for something."

This time she heard him coming. Kindle dodged barely, the force of his attack punching a brief hole in the sandstorm. Now she was eye to eye with the Major. His cold eyes fixated on her for a kill. He went for another punch, time slowing around her.

Was that what hit her before? A simple punch, each thundering with a force of a cannonfire. Any one of those should've killed her. Bang. Bang. Bang. Each punch was louder than the next, gradually gaining speed. He was recovering, bit by bit. Cyborgs could do that, she knew. She pulled a knife from her back with her uninjured arm between his blows, watching for an opening. Blow after blow. Each perfect. Each with the trained ability of a professional. He ducked in; feet steady against the uneven sand. Not a slip. Not a mistake in sight. She reacted out of fear, plunging her hidden knife at his neck, and only stabbed air. He pivoted at the last second, grabbed her by the wrist, and yanked her to the ground.

She crashed face first into the sand, eyes burning and head pounding. Her shoulder popped, his raw strength twisting her arm behind her back. She screamed.

No more words.

He was gonna kill her.

She clawed helplessly at the sand and roots with her free arm, his strength breaking her other. *No. I can't. I can't,*

I can't die. Sand and blood. The taste of own teeth in her mouth. She shouted again.

"Dig deeper. Break everything," a voice told her.

Another joint popped. The pain became all she knew, the only tangible thing her mind. The whispers in her mind grew stronger.

"Destroy it all. Survive."

Blood now. Blood everywhere. Breaking bones and open wound.

"Destroy it all! Survive! LIVE!"

A waft of spice and sweetness struck her nose, followed by a hard push. Whatever tenuous hold she had over the Flame slipped through her fingers. She tried to catch it, but she had a better chance catching a frying pan from the burner; she lost it, and with that loss of control came a power she didn't know she had. Pain was a mere inconvenience now.

Kindle, or what was left of her, pushed upwards with one arm and tossed the Major aside effortlessly.

White and red flames curled around Kindle as she stood. Major Debenham blinked his confusion at her. The arm that once held her wrist had been melted beyond recognition. Sirens screeched and the blinking red screens returned. Kindle didn't care to read any of it. Words didn't matter. Sound didn't matter. What mattered was that he was gone.

She raised her hand, unamused. The nanodroids of the Flame, red and angry, wrapped around her fingers.

"Goodbye, Major."

A flash of light left her hand, followed by a burst of fire. The stream hit the Major and swallowed him within seconds. He didn't scream. Not once. The pain must have been terrible, but he took it without a sound leaving his throat. She watched, her mind uncomprehendingly, wondering how he even lived through it. *You have to end this. You have to end this now.* She gave a hard swallow, adrenaline still pumping through her body.

She walked over, picking up Coal amongst the sand on her way. The Major curled within the dunes, clothes burned away and naked, not unlike how she found her granddad. A desperate scene. One she might've pitied if she felt anything. But there was a certain poetic justice in that.

She dusted off her gun and aimed it the man's head. Major Debenham turned, his eyes remarkably human.

"You don't know what you just did, do ya?" He laughed, curling within the comforts of the sand. "You broke it." His laughter grew louder. "You broke it. You *actually* broke it. Well. Great." He deflated. "All this time and I leave empty handed. Gosh darn it." Kindle touched the trigger. "Well. Guess I gotta go. I'll see you around, Cassie."

She fired her gun but found no target. A bright light swept the Major away, leaving a hole in the sand where he once was. A recall beacon. He was gone now, safe in a ship.

Kindle would've felt bitter about that, but again, she felt nothing.

The Flame cooled again within her after long minutes of sirens and screaming computer screens. All at once, all her feelings came rushing back to her – the pain in her arms, the warmth of blood on her skin, the fear and desperation. She stood, looking around the station. There was an automated voice on the intercom. She could barely hear the words over the ache in her own head. She stepped down the sandy dunes, boots digging deep through the sand. The words on the screens became clear.

STARFALL PROTOCOL INITIATED.

The words sent a panic through her. What had she done? What did she do now? Ignoring the pain, Kindle trekked down the dunes back to the middle of the Terrarium. The cold dread rose within her. *What did I do?*

The core was a red ball now, crackling arcs of lightning in all directions. She stood frozen, looking at the screens popping up all around her. There were places she recognized on the planet – familiar ones, places she'd visited. Storms brewed on the coast, snow raged on the mountains, giant waves tumbled on the seas.

C'dar was falling apart.

It struck her – the Flame was the very thing keeping this planet together. This station had terraformed C'dar like it had in this small sample size, keeping a wild planet tamed and in check from orbit. She had ruined that somehow, broken it in her own desperation. Where would she go? Where would her family go, now that she'd unknowingly broken the world? Her throat tightened. How would she –

The door behind her opened.

A woman stood in the frame, dark skin glistening with sweat. Her curly black hair was in disarray but her round eyes took in all the information in a second.

The woman locked eyes with Kindle, and her heart pounded her chest, words caught in her throat.

The woman rushed over and grabbed her by the arm. "This is not your fault," she said with a voice Kindle had only heard in dreams or visions.

Kindle knew who she was. And worse — she didn't know how to feel.

"We have to go. We have to go now!" the woman shouted over the failing systems that Kindle had somehow overloaded. Astonishingly, she didn't sound angry. There was a crack in her voice so deep that she felt it through the woman's grip. "I'll explain on the way. And... I'm sorry for what we put you through."

Chapter 19

Starlight Exodus
Appetite

"The world we knew is gone. I couldn't have predicted this. Maybe I could've if I looked hard enough." – Mary Lu Caldwell, the Augur of Owls

Appetite was watching from *Sundancer* when his daughter broke the world.

Kaulu darted from one side of his computer core, waiting for a response. The AI often flipped from being helpful, to caring, to obnoxiously amused at the dismay of humans. Showing any type of emotion that the AI wanted gave it the closest thing to satisfaction an intelligence its age could manage; Appetite struggled to keep his face devoid of emotions as he paced up and down the length of the ship. He scratched at his red-clay beard, the stubs of his missing fingers barely reaching his chin. The fear tugged at him. He knew now the burden that Ina had once carried with her, the reason why she couldn't depart the planet for any long period of time. Everything had fallen on Kindle's lap, and with it had come the worst possible outcome. Appetite hated it.

But there was nothing he could do now; what was done was done. No one had told Kindle the significance of keeping her power in check. That was the job of the Shadow to the Flame. Two sides of the same coin, pushing and pulling on a thin rope ready to snap. Ignace had let go of his end of the rope and let her fall deeper and deeper.

Appetite took a deep breath. He had to look strong, had to hope that somehow this was going to all work out. *We're alive,* he told himself. *What happens next doesn't matter. What's done is done,* he told himself again, trying to gather his words for his daughter. What could he say? His heart pounded hard in his chest.

Nothing sounded right. She was gonna always feel like the Caldwell that took C'dar away from them.

"Passenger incoming," *Kaulu* sung in his boyish voice. "Access granted. Welcome aboard."

Appetite straightened his back, preparing his words. A blinding white light threaded together, taking form bit by bit. Where he expected Ina or Kindle or both, he got Ignace.

He materialized before Appetite, his now-black robe with the look of purple shadows and starlight bellowing around him. Appetite recognized the staff that he twirled with every step; his father's staff, a trophy.

Ignace smiled at him, the side of his ruined spiderwebbed face barely twitching upwards. He strode in like he had come in from a successful hunt; he took a seat, poured himself a drink from the bar, and reclined with one foot resting on his knee, making an exaggerated *ahhh* after every sip.

Appetite didn't have the energy or the mindset to throttle him. Instead, he opened his mouth and asked a simple question: "Why?"

"Ain't it obvious?" Ignace grinned. "I was never going to be the Flame and Ina was never going to have the heart to do what was necessary. Your daughter on the other hand, she's a firecracker. She just needed a push."

"Why, Ignace?"

"C'dar was our prison, Woody," he laughed, "no different than what Daedel was to your father. My people can be one of the strongest people in the galaxy with the knowledge we know. So, I took the one thing that my father cherished most: his duty to this planet. What better revenge is there?" He shrugged, taking another long draught from his drink. "You should be happy. Even former Shaman are bounded to the Shadows that christened them, now that he's gone, you and Ina might have something again. I honestly don't know why you're upset. You and your rats can always find another planet; they're a dime a dozen. If you beg, I might even help you with the ships. So –"

"This was our home."

"As it was mine," he said matter-of-factly. "Sometimes, though, we can't stay where we are. We must move forward. That's the simple truth of the matter. The Breauxs were chained here and the Caldwells, though a softer chain, ain't that much different. You went around, lived off this land and the stole from a power stronger than you. You created a comfortable life for yourselves. Though admirable, y'all always had a thirst for something more. This world isn't the thing to quench that. How long before the Civilization comes back, this time with fleets instead of foot soldiers? You think you all would've made it that far without my father's deal, the need for your daughter, and Major Debenham's curiosity?" He sipped his drink again. "Don't make me laugh, Woody. I did you favor."

Appetite squashed the urge to lunge across the ship and strangle him. While Ignace was completely wrong on some points, there was a logic there that he couldn't ignore. They *had* been lucky; any more power from this clearly superior force, and they would have been crushed. Perhaps the Major had some sympathy for them, or maybe he wished to have the core completely under control before wiping them from the planet – Appetite didn't know. The truth of the matter was that the Bluecoats were gonna come back whether Kindle did what she did or not, and they had to be gone when they did.

That didn't excuse it. If anything, leaning that twisted logic left an even more sour taste in his mouth. The urge to strangle Ignace began to slowly evolve into imagining vivid images of each of his verberate individually breaking against his knee.

Kaulu giggled at the tension. "Sorry to interrupt," it said in its soft voice, "but the lady is about to board, and I doubt she would want violence between the two of you. So be good little boys and stay in line."

The spinning lights of the return beacon appeared, this time the color of sunlight instead of its normal white. Ina stepped through first, not losing a single stride. Kindle followed not too far behind. The difference between the two was night and day; Ina came like a storm, Kindle more like a soft rain.

Ina tossed everything she was holding to the side, then went straight to her brother and punched him in the jaw with a sharp crack. His face snapped to the side, a dribble of the brown drink streaking down his mouth. He went to say something, and she punched him again with her other fist, this time on side of his face where he had his scar. Her knuckles left a companion bruise, red and purple from swelling and blood.

"I've been wrong before," *Kaulu* muttered.

"How dare you." Her words were barely audible, language slipping into her native tongue. "How dare you put her through this?" In her anger, she looked barely human at all. She grabbed her brother by the collar. "Why would you do that?"

"Don't be silly, Ina. Both you and I knew I wasn't gonna stop at killing dad."

"But using my *daughter*."

"Funny you use that word, since you were never there for her. We both know we have no idea how parents work. No need to pretend like you're not satisfied. I did what I did for everyone."

The anger on her face rose to an uncontrollable rage. For a second, Appetite thought she was gonna draw her weapon and shoot the man in his belly. She might have if Kindle didn't push past them.

The tension in the room only grew when she stumbled forward. Appetite opened his mouth to speak, trying his best to sound strong and reassuring. All the rehearsing, all the reassurance left him all at once. Kindle walked directly into her papa's arms, her forehead resting on his abdomen.

Appetite lost all interest in what was happening between the siblings and wrapped his arms around his daughter. He pressed his forehead against the top of hers. She wasn't crying, or shaking from anger, or even muttering to herself; she remained still and emotionless in his arms. The best he could do here was to hold her, pressing his head against the crown of her head.

What could anyone say to a girl who had accidentally sent in motion the destruction of her family's planet?

Ø

The ride on the *Sundancer* back to the Dusk Mountain stretched on for what felt like millennia. Appetite looked out of the window, keeping his now catatonic daughter close. He'd hoped seeing the familiar peaks of the Homestead would've brought some sort of reaction to the young girl's eyes; it didn't. Perhaps that was a good thing. Seeing the clouds settle over the mountains, angry black and already weeping frozen flakes, left a bad feeling in his stomach.

He had expected it to bad. From what he knew from *Kaulu,* the satellite and its ultra-powerful AI was the only reason this planet remained habitable in a ring of dead or desolate planets. With its death, the planet would die too within a year or two; the entire planet would be so erratic that living on it would be impossible.

There was beauty in their home still. He saw it and ached. *No. Homes can be replaced.* The pain filled him, but for his daughter, he wouldn't let it take over.

They landed not far from the crashed ship that brought his grandfather and his brothers here in the first place. Appetite went to go for another one-armed hug, but Kindle softly pushed him away. She left the ship without a word and walked directly to their small cabin.

Appetite took a deep breath as he watched her. He couldn't even imagine the guilt that she felt. What she didn't seem to see was that she'd saved her family. Sure, some Caldwells were going to resent her, resent all of this; for those stubborn family members, there was nothing anyone could do. Whatever happened, happened. Too late to fix it. He understood her pain and let her be. *She'll recover,* he told himself, feeling as helpless as a frog without legs. She had to. If she didn't, he, too, might go mad from it all.

Hours passed in silence as they waited for the rest of the Caldwells to return; the family members left at the Homestead - those who hadn't taken part in the battle - waited with bated breath, hoping to hear news. Appetite wasn't in the mindset to give it to them.

Ina sat beside her daughter. They all watched her with hard eyes. To them, Kindle's mom had returned out of nowhere - Kindle's mom who had taken Appetite's heart and thrown it into the trash, leaving a shell of a man for years afterward. Despite any disagreement they had with Appetite, family came first and Ina had hurt him. The only reason they hadn't brought out their weapons was the fact that Ina probably could've killed any person here without a second thought. Their judging eyes and passive aggressive whispers would have to suffice for now.

Again, Appetite didn't have the energy to correct them - and worse, he didn't know whether or not he should. She had left them. She hadn't contacted them. They had a lot to push through, if only as parents. Appetite pinched the bridge of his nose. That was looking at it lightly.

One by one, the family returned. Vermin, carrying most of the younger generation, came rolling in with *Stag Beetle* and his father's 7-A mech. Both were in bad condition, but that's how Doc's boys and girls liked it. Truck after truck filtered in, each Caldwell with a tired but satisfied expression. They had won for all they knew - beat the invaders to live another day.

What they didn't know was that their hardship had only begun.

Appetite didn't want to be the one to tell them, especially the old boys trailing the rear. He hardly knew the details himself. Kindle hadn't been too thrilled about talking about it; the only detail he'd managed to get out her was a simple head shake when he asked if the Major was dead.

Appetite took a deep breath. Somewhere in the galaxy, the Major lived. *At least I got one of them.* He adjusted himself in his seat, gathering the loose threads of his courage. What he wanted to do was have dinner and go to bed. Both would have to wait.

Pa and Moses came in on the last truck. Drifter stumbled out; his pale body covered in a long blanket. It bothered Appetite how frequent this scene was. What made it worse this time was an eyepatch on his father's eye, that entire side of his face burned to a cracking charcoal black. It was pure luck he even survived that, let alone able to walk and remain conscious. The Caldwell mutations saved him, no doubt - the mistake the Civilization wanted to erase was the very thing that saved their hides from time to time. Soon their luck was gonna run out, but not today, it seemed. They lived, this time as a shame upon the Bluecoats' perfect record.

Too bad I'm gonna haffta ruin our parade. Appetite coughed and stood, puffing out his chest and squaring his shoulders. *They have to know before it gets bad.* "Hey," he cried out, "gonna steal a moment from ya for a second."

Everyone looked up in surprise but didn't interrupt. They had taken to listening to when he spoke now. His voice boomed loud enough, and he looked dang intimidating with his scars and missing fingers. "Settle in, I got something to say." His heart thumped so hard he felt it through his body. Would they believe him? They had to, right? Crazier things had happened. Thick-tongued, he pushed his thoughts and words forward through his mouth. "Something happened."

Drifter's good eye grew wide. Everyone's did. "Where's Cassie?" Pa asked, his voice frantic. The wind howled, carrying with it thick flakes and spears of ice. Already, the snow coated the tips of his father's white beard. His lips trembled, but not from the cold. "Where's Cassie?"

"She's okay," Appetite said hurriedly, "but we aren't safe here. Not anymore."

Pit opened his mouth to speak, but Drifter quieted him with a hand before sniffing the air. The snowflakes tumbled from the sky a bit harder and the wind whistled sharper. Thunder boomed in the distance. Lighting streaked on the surface of the sky.

Drifter licked the air, flakes dissolving on his tongue. The rest of the old boys followed with equally odd inspections of the world around them. They split up for a second and whispered among themselves. C'dar had been their home for fifty odd years; looking closely, they felt that something was wrong. Heck, Appetite knew it. Their slow reaction dug deep within them slowly going from confusion to a soft panic. There was no way to say that your world was dying.

"We have to leave C'dar," Appetite said, trying to keep his voice strong.

Never before had the Homestead been so quiet. Long seconds stretched on into long minutes. After a time, Appetite tried his best to explain the situation involving *Ogoun,* its terraforming satellite, *the* Flame, and the Shadow. The more he tried, the angrier the mob seemed to grow. Who they were angry at didn't matter; Ina, the Breauxs, himself, and of course, Kindle. The mob wanted to be angry, they wanted something to blame. This was their planet and somehow one situation screwed over the whole thing. The silence soon broken into a million pieces. They spoke over one another until no voice was clear.

Appetite lost control of them for a brief second, looking for his father in the crowd for help. He didn't find it; Drifter, too, was too shocked to take in the information.

Dang it, stay calm. Appetite clenched his fists. Ina gave him a bit of a tap on the shoulder, her eyes hard.

"Everyone shuddup," he shouted, louder than he ever had before - even thunder booming behind him sounded soft in comparison. "Are we gonna just sit here and scream at each other or are we gonna do what we always have, and survive? We're Caldwells. We can either sit here moaning and complaining, or we can do somethin' 'bout it. We can make it off this planet. We can find another one and give the Bluecoats hell on our way. There's an entire galaxy out there that only a few Caldwells have experienced. 'Bout time we leave our little corner." His eyes swept the crowd. This wasn't going to be easy. "Change ain't so bad. We're alive, ain't we? Time to act like it." Blank stares. Appetite shook his head. "We've taken a crap worth of things from these Coats. 'Bout time we put them to use. We'll make it up as we go."

Make it up as we go. The words stuck to him. It was reckless and dumb. There was an expanse of galaxy out there with dangers and obstacles. Given the time left they had on this dying planet, they at the very least could cobble together some ships. Tiger was here; he knew the workings of large ships and could maybe bring in some help from his crew. They had enough fuel and supplies to make it a couple of months, and more than enough food to work with. The next months might be rough, but they'd be manageable.

Appetite squared his shoulders, aware how towering of a man he was in this crowd. "We gotta move forward, never back."

Appetite half expected to be torn apart or, at the very least, laughed off the mountain. But the stony eyes of the Caldwells, young and old, slowly turned to resignation. They knew he wouldn't lie about something like this. He wasn't the prankster type. It had to be the truth; the truth, cold and relentless, never moved.

The whispers returned one by one. He could hear the gist of what was happening, only bit and pieces here and there. Some were excited about the prospect of leaving, mostly the young men and women. Others were resilient and dead set on staying. This wasn't over, only postponed.

For now, the family splintered into pieces, each recovering from their quarrel with Bluecoats and the wild mutants of the Old City. Appetite exhaled, deflating and slumping his shoulders. His nerves frayed.

He turned to Ina; she sat in an uncharacteristic stoniness, frowning, eyes distant. He expected her to say something, anything. She never did.

Jo, Loner, and Drifter strolled up. Drifter was leaning on his daughter's shoulder, his good eye staring Appetite down. "What ain't you tellin' us?" Drifter asked. "I ain't blind, only halfway there. Cassie ain't okay."

"She feels responsible for this." Jo gave her father's arm over to Appetite, who took it without pause. "We can't change that."

Drifter sighed. "Take me to her."

"Ina." Appetite turned to her. "Are you coming?"

Ina shook her head. "She needs to see some friendly faces, not more questions. The very least I can do right now is help you with those ships." She stood, dusting the snowflakes off her lap. "You'll have your ships. They might not be the best, but I'll do what I can." She looked up to the swirling storm clouds above the mountain. "I'm sorry, Woody. I'm sorry for everything."

With that, she left, heading back to her ship *Sundancer*. A part of Appetite felt a twinge of pain watching her go, feeling like he would never see her again. Another part - a dark, selfish, and cynical part of him - exhaled in relief. How they felt and where they were going needed to take a back seat for Kindle. She, at least, deserved that.

"Loner, help her if you can. If anyone can help get us on track, it's you."

Loner grinned through the green material of his gas mask. This was what he had trained for; this was his shining moment. He practically jumped at the opportunity, calling his 'roid Jesse over and following Ina into the *Sundancer*. She wouldn't mind the help - at least, Appetite hoped so. Loner, in his mechanical prowess, wasn't the best at communicating what he wanted to anyone around him; he hadn't gotten the nickname for nothing. They would figure that out.

Let 'em be, Woody. They'll get us outta here. Focus on what you have to do now.

Appetite led Drifter and Jo into his cabin, braving the cold winds and earning a warm embrace of the fireplace on the other side. They took the time to shake off the cold, take off their weak and dingy jackets, and enjoy the comforts of home.

After they got their act together, they made their way to the back bedrooms. To his surprise, Tiger sat with Appetite's mother, Mary Lu, chatting in chairs outside of Kindle's room. In his mother's lap was a bundle of fresh clothes for Drifter, who took them with a welcoming and loving smile. Appetite lowered his father from his arms, allowing him to change while they waited outside of his daughter's door.

"How is she?" Appetite found himself asking, knowing all too well the answer.

Tiger shook his head.

"That bad, huh?" A piece of wood snapped in the fire in the living room. "Has she said anything? Done anything?"

Another head shake. The dread in Appetite's chest tightened. He rapped on the door with his knuckles.

"Hey, can I come in?" No response. He tapped the door again. "I'm coming in."

He hadn't expected to see what he saw.

The smell of smoke choked the air from the room. Blackened charcoals littered the floor. Small fires burned softly in the corners, eating away at the already blackened remains of her knick knacks and her vid-tapes. Clothes lay scattered on the floor from the smashed drawers and nightstand. Every picture was torn from the walls, leaving paper scraps and empty frames. Appetite tip-toed over the glass from a shattered lamp, braving through minor cuts here and there to make it to the other side of the room to the bed.

"Cassie, are you -" he touched the lump in the bed and felt nothing. He tossed the sheets aside. Nothing. A cold wind hit him on the side of the face. *The window's open.*

A fear like no other lanced through him. He looked over the edge of the window and found nothing. He looked through the mess on the floor.

Coal was nowhere to be found, as was she.

Confusion dove to anger, anger to panic, panic to distress. There was no way he would catch her; with her craftiness and skills, she could be anywhere by now. Appetite felt his mind fall deeper and deeper into an animalistic panic. Was it destiny for everyone he brought into the family to leave him without a word? He fell to his knees, nails scratching against the floor of the wood. He remembered making this house for them, all of them. Tears rolled down his face, blood oozing from his bitten lips.

Kindle was gone. She was gone and she didn't even say goodbye. He wept. He screamed. He shouted. He roared. Everything felt as black as the charcoals in this room. People flooded into the room, but he didn't hear them, not even when they spoke to him. The sick feeling in his stomach didn't go away. He thought he was gonna vomit.

"Woody," he heard his father say. "It's okay. It's okay. We'll find her." Drifter put his head on his. "We'll find her."

Epilogue

Freedom of the Stars
Ina

"You don't know what you want until you have it. You don't know what you got until it's gone." -- Ina Breaux

Ina never thought that she would consider killing her brother in the same way she'd thought about it with her father. The temptation ran through her as she watched the smile slithering on the man's face. How could he be so satisfied?

The darker side of her knew that answer. It didn't matter who was in his way; Ignace wanted a complete and dominant win. She should've known better. Today happened to be the day that she was on the other end of that pain.

No, not only me. Her daughter felt the brunt of it. Not for the first time today, her fingers danced on the hostler of her gun.

"How does it feel," Ignace asked her, kicking back the chair where he murdered their father, "to be free from it all? From the Caldwells, from your responsibilities, from this backwater dump of a planet? I did that. I did that for you. I did that for our people. Tell me that it doesn't feel a little bit good. That you aren't just a teensy bit relieved. C'mon."

Times like this, it was better to stay quiet around Ignace. He had this way of twisting words that even a sibling couldn't work their way out of. Instead, she sat there, boring a hole into his eyes with an unflinching stare. *I'm not gonna play this game with you,* she thought, keeping a straight face. "I came back 'cause you said that you fixed it. I should've asked how."

"You've never been good at fixing things on your own, sis."

"And you've never been a good person, Ig, but everyone has their faults."

"Like running away?"

"Don't you dare -"

"Y'know Kindle came to me right, not even an hour before you came here asking for a ship. As her uncle, I couldn't turn her down; even gave her a few of my men to at least get her started. She said she wanted to get away from it all, start anew." Ignace paused, tapping his chin. "*That* sounds very familiar. Running away from her problems and asking me for help, I wonder where she got that move from." He laughed. "I don't mean to poke fun at you, Ina, I really don't. But there's a bit of comedy in all this. Up until now you didn't want to be involved in anything, but the moment Pops is six-feet under, you came running. No one wants to lie in the grave they dug, but sometimes you gotta. That's how it goes."

Ina didn't have anything to say. At the core and through the muck of his mocking, he was right. She hadn't been there for Woody or Cassie. They'd lived their lives and she'd lived hers. She'd told herself that they'd move on. She had almost hoped that Woody had found another by now and raised Kindle with that woman instead.

Coming here and saving their lives was a selfish attempt to make things right, or at least start to. But that wasn't gonna happen. What was left was a fire she had no clue how to put out. It was all hopes and fanciful thinking by an impulsive woman that didn't learn her lesson.

I wonder where she got that move from. Those words dug deep within her.

"I can't forgive this, Ignace. You knew what was gonna happen. I hope you're happy." She spat the words at him. "I'm gonna check on the ships." It was the least she could do, and it kept her busy.

She tried her best not to storm out of the study or show any sign of weakness; her knuckles twitched, her fists shook, and she forced her mouth into a hard line. *Don't give him the satisfaction.* Rising from her seat, she made a beeline to the door and closed it behind her.

A sorta familiar feeling swept over her, nights leaving her father's presence with heated words on her tongue. Amazing she'd never noticed how similar her brother was to her father, picking at her with immeasurably harsh words.

Ina cursed under her breath and bit her lip. That would've hurt him. That would've hurt him bad. She thought for a moment to turn around and say it. The only way she convinced herself not to was to focus on the task at hand. There were more important things. She quickened her pace.

They had some time to get out of here. Ina hadn't told them, but the weather was gonna be the least of their worries.

Kindle had triggered a protocol known as the *Starfall*. In short, it was a doomsday clock triggered by the current Shaman, the heir to the bloodline of the C'dar's natives and the survivors of the Civilization civil war. Ina was taught that the pact was struck to save both societies, which ultimately melded into one. *Starfall* was an extreme failsafe in case anything got into the wrong hands. The satellite would fall into the atmosphere, nearly destroying everything on the surface of the planet, scrubbing everything clean.

A year was the timer. A year before C'dar was nothing more than ash. Pushing Kindle to the point where she accidentally tripped it was a terrible move, one Kindle herself would have to live with.

If you'd kept in contact with them, you could have warned them. Instead, you were gallivanting across the galaxy. Regret did nothing. She had to look forward.

Ina continued down the twisting paths of the manor that was once her home, down to the cellar, further down into the catacombs. She nodded toward the heavily cloaked servant Exocurios, who buzzed their greetings back.

One stood at the gulf of the black abyss of the cellar, its six arms tucked within the folds of his oversized robes. Zech had worked here longer than she could remember. His short body hopped at the sight of her, and she earned a song from his vibrating throat. Immediately, he began turning on the lights; Exocurios preferred to work in the dark but suffered the light for her sake. White light bathed the catacombs from the creaking wooden stairs she'd come from to the endless winding stone caves.

Zech bowed and led her through the caves. The smell of dank water, grassy moss, and eventually a sharp tang of meta filled her nostrils as the natural caves gave way to metal corridors, each wall buffed to a chrome-like shine. She knew the way like the back of her hand but she enjoyed the little creature's company. He was the only thing she missed in this swamp.

Zech bowed once they reached the massive steel hangar doors. "Thanks, buddy," Ina said, patting him on the head.

He sung a brief song of odd and beautiful chords. *"You're welcome"* was the best translation, but it went deeper than that; the song of gratitude wasn't given to just anyone. Zech reserved it for her and her alone. For that, she'd taken the time - even away from the swamp - to learn more and more about them.

She added a whistling sound, the best a person could do to imitate their language. Zech hopped in excitement and went to go. "No, please stay," she added quickly. The Exocurio nodded. She needed the company.

Ina opened the small hatch on the side of the door and punched in a keycode. The green numbers flashed for a second and then turned red. Incorrect. She frowned. She tried it again. Again, incorrect. Her heart sank. Did Ignace or the Elders lock her out? A terrible burning wrath coursed through her. She pulled the gun from her side and went to shoot, but stopped at Zech's insistent poking at her leg.

He sang another song, the chords of determination hard in his voice, and hopped from the ground to the keypad, pressing a button with every fluttering winged leap. With the last button, he corkscrewed in midair and landed on his feet with an impressive ease. He gave a small bow with his three right arms, the numbers a stable green. The door clicked open.

"You clever bastard," she told him. He chortled. Exocurios weren't *supposed* to know the password to the hangars, but that didn't stop them from figuring it out, apparently.

She flung the hangar door open. This time she stormed in. Zech hopped behind her.

On the other side of the door, she was met with the Elders and the once-dormant fleet. Ships of all sizes filled the halls, a collection of the Old-World ships that once carried people from Earth to here.

Some were in better shape than others. The retrofitted ones - the cruisers and the warships - were in top shape and claimed by the Elders of the villages. The masked and robed Elders stood around the largest of the warships, known formerly as the *White Falcon*. They muttered and whispered under their voices, all turning at once when they saw her storming in. The leader nodded towards her, a lazy half gesture of respect.

"My, what a surprise. The former Shaman graces us with her presence. I could have sworn that we changed the locks." The man's voice was one she didn't recognize, no doubt one of Ignace's groupies. "Any particular reason you've come?"

"I've come to make sure you all honor your promises to the Caldwells."

"We've given them some of the ships and already carted them to the mountain."

"Working ones?"

"You didn't specify." The leader of the Elders laughed; of course, the rest followed suit. "Perhaps if they can't figure out how to get one working, they deserve to die on this planet. Just a thought. You've *always* had this weak spot for those... hill folks, Ina. We've never truly understood your attachment to them. They are greedy, selfish, and a downright plague to anyone on this planet. But you would go head over heels for him, especially that *big* one." The rest of the Elders nodded in approval. "Remy's death was a shock to us, yes, but Ignace ultimately is right in this matter. Why should we have to sit here and guard knowledge of things that even this current Civilization cannot recreate? Why do we have to sit by and waste away, hoarding these unspeakable secrets, when we could be living a better life among the stars? Isn't that why you left, to be free?"

Ina balled her fists and clenched her teeth. She'd left Ignace to get away from the mocking, not to find it coming from a different mouth.

"The truth is, we're in a different time. The Bluecoats and the Civilization are going to want their revenge on us now that we've betrayed them. It's better that we're prepared when that time comes, don't you agree?"

"I don't care."

"Of course, you don't," the Elder said, tilting his head. "You never *have* cared about your people. So how about this? You go help those savages get on their feet and leave us alone. That's what you want, right? Maybe you can find that daughter of yours somewhere in the stars. Last time I heard, she was headed to the Dawn Orbit planets, directly into the heart of the Civilization. Maybe trying to find Major Debenham. To kill him, maybe? I don't know. Honestly, we don't care."

"Why are y'all being like this?"

"You. *Left*. Us. Ina." The Elder's back straightened, stepping a bit too close for Ina's liking. "Who would have thought that it would be your brother that would take us into this new age? So, go. We've honored our end of the bargain. Ten red falcon freighters are more than enough for your once-lover and his--"

Bang. She didn't stop herself this time. In the blink of an eye, she drew her pistol and fired. The man howled in pain, falling over and clutching the blood pooling through the black fabric of his robe at his knee. The other members of the council exchanged panicked looks back and forth, taking cautious steps backwards.

"I'm done," she shouted. "I'm done with y'all. If you want to go out into the galaxy so bad, then do it. You don't have the Flame or the Shadow binding you here anymore. The pact is done, but I guarantee that wide galaxy is gonna eat y'all alive. When that happens, I'm gonna laugh. I'm gonna laugh so hard 'cause you didn't know what you had here. You never know what you have until you miss it." She spat out the words, forced them through her lips. "I'm taking one more ship for them. A good one too." She peered around and pointed to the assault carrier. "I'm taking that one for them and if anyone has something to say about it, I won't aim for knees next time. C'mon, Zech. Get your friends and family, we're leaving."

Zech sang the sharp sound of surprise but followed her all the same.

Ina was done with these politics, done with the whole tiptoeing on eggshells. They wanted her to leave? *Fine.* She stormed down through the docks, the sounds of the metal mesh clunking underfoot. She stood in front of the ship she claimed. It was a massive beast, not as big as a destroyer or a warship, but well-equipped with blasters and missiles for a ship of its size. Rusted, battered, and dented here and there, it wasn't gonna win any beauty contests; more importantly, it was a manageable size for a new crew and a new pilot.

Would this gift fix all the trouble she and her brother caused? No.

But it was a good start.

ABOUT THE AUTHOR

Deston "D.J" Munden is a fantasy and science fiction author with a Bachelor's in Game Art and Design. Deston loves video games, anime, comic books, old samurai films and fantasy/scifi novels. He lives in the woods of North Carolina near the Outer Banks. Also, the author of the fantasy series Dargath Chronicles novels under the same name.

Tavern (Book 1 of the Dargath Chronicles)
Duke's Brand (Book 2 of the Dargath Chronicles)
(Winter 2020)
Dusk Ocean Blues (Book 2 of the Dusk Orbit Blues)
(Early 2021

Printed in Great Britain
by Amazon